Praise for Mothers and Sons

'It may not be going too far to suggest that Irish fiction
has found its first Master of the new century'
Scotland on Sunday

'Colm Tóibín is a writer of extraordinary emotional clarity
. . . These are beautiful stories, beautifully crafted'
Literary Review

'Measured and humane . . . a set of stories with precise,
assured and lasting significance'
New Statesman

'A wonderful read. The characters are well drawn, considered,
rounded individuals, each with a complex history that is
teasingly revealed'
Independent on Sunday

'Compelling . . . Tóibín is a master of the
blind alleys of desire'
The Times

'Tóibín is tender and shocking: women and men are
finely drawn in a prose style that pierces the heart in its
silences as much as in its sounds'
Saga

'A rich but subtle prose style seals each story's – and thus
the collection's – absolute success'
Booklist

Mothers and Sons

COLM TÓIBÍN was born in Ireland in 1955 and lives
in Dublin. He is the author of five novels including the
Booker-shortlisted *The Blackwater Lightship* and *The Master*.
His non-fiction includes *The Sign of the Cross* and
Love in a Dark Time.

COLM TÓIBÍN

Mothers and Sons

PICADOR

First published 2006 by Picador

First published in paperback 2007 by Picador
an imprint of Pan Macmillan Ltd
Pan Macmillan, 20 New Wharf Road, London N1 9RR
Basingstoke and Oxford
Associated companies throughout the world
www.panmacmillan.com

ISBN 978-0-330-45372-1

1 3 5 7 9 8 6 4 2

A CIP catalogue record for this book is available from
the British Library.

Typeset by SetSystems Ltd, Saffron Walden, Essex
Printed and bound in Great Britain by
Mackays of Chatham plc, Chatham, Kent

For

Michael Loughlin

and

Veronica Rapalino

ACKNOWLEDGEMENTS

I wish to acknowledge the following publications where some of these stories, often in earlier versions, first appeared: the *Guardian* ('A Song' and 'Famous Blue Raincoat'); the *London Review of Books* ('A Priest in the Family'); *Finbar's Hotel* ('The Use of Reason'); the *Dublin Review* ('The Name of the Game'); *In Dublin* ('A Journey'); *The Faber Book of Best New Irish Short Stories* ('Three Friends'). 'A Long Winter' was first published in a limited edition by the Tuskar Rock Press.

The title of the story 'A Priest in the Family' comes from a definition of Irish respectability: 'A well in the yard; a bull in the field; and a priest in the family.'

I am grateful to Angela Rohan for her careful work on the manuscript; to my agent Peter Straus; to my editors Andrew Kidd at Picador in London and Nan Graham at Scribner in New York; to Catriona Crowe, John S. Doyle, Jordi Casellas and Edward Mulhall.

Some of this book was written at the Santa Maddalena Foundation outside Florence in Italy. I wish to thank Beatrice Monti for her kind hospitality there.

Contents

The Use of Reason

THE CITY WAS a great emptiness. He looked out from the balcony of one of the top flats on Charlemont Street. The wide waste ground below him was empty. He closed his eyes and thought about the other flats on this floor, most of them empty now in the afternoon, just as the little bare bathrooms were empty and the open stairwells were empty. He imagined the houses on the long stretches of suburb going out from the city: Fairview, Clontarf, Malahide, to the north; Ranelagh, Rathmines, Rathgar, to the south. He thought about the confidence of those roads, their strength and their solidity, and then he allowed his mind to wander into the rooms of suburban houses, bedrooms empty all day, the downstairs rooms empty all night, the long back gardens, neat, trimmed, empty too for all of the winter and most of the summer. The sad attics empty as well. Defenceless. No one would notice an intruder scaling a wall, flitting across a garden to scale the next wall, a nondescript man checking the back of the house for a sign of life, for alarm systems or a guard dog, and then silently prising a window open, sliding in, carefully crossing a room, watching for an easy exit. He would open a door without making a sound, so alert as to be almost invisible.

He thought of the emptiness of Clanbrassil Street as his mother made her way to the Dock. It was as though the very air around her, the pavement too and the bricks on the buildings, were aware of the danger she posed and got out of her way. Her blonde hair untidy, her house slippers dragging as she slouched towards the public house. A fake gold ring, and fake bangles, and loud gold earrings hitting against the redness of her lipstick, the green of her mascara, the blue of her eyes. His mother turned now to see whether a car was coming so she could cross the road and found, he imagined, the road completely empty, no traffic at all, the world made empty for her deepest pleasure.

His mother, as she neared the public house, knew that the neighbours were afraid of her sudden kindnesses as much as her tantrums and her drunken rages. Thus a smile from her could be as unwelcome as a scowl. Mainly, she managed a look of indifference. In the street as much as the pub, she did not need to threaten, it was known who her son was, and it was believed that his loyalty to her was fierce. He did not know how she had managed to make everyone believe that he would extract revenge for the slightest insult to her. Her threats too were empty, he thought, emptier than anything.

He stood at the balcony and did not move when his visitor, who had approached the building by the hidden side door of the complex, appeared. He allowed, as he did each week, Detective Inspector Frank Cassidy to pass him and enter the small flat, which was owned by his sister-in-law, and used by him only once a week. Cassidy was in his day clothes, his ruddy face displaying a mixture of furtive guilt and businesslike self-confidence. He paid Cassidy every week, a sum either too much or too little, the amount wrong enough to make him feel that Cassidy was fooling him rather than betraying his own side. In return for the money, Cassidy gave him information he mostly knew already. Nonetheless, he always felt that if the forces of law and order were coming close to him Cassidy would somehow make this clear. Cassidy would let him know, he believed, either as a favour, or as a way of making him panic. Or perhaps both. He himself told Cassidy nothing, but he could never be sure that some day his reaction to a piece of information might not be as much as Cassidy would need.

'They're watching the Wicklow mountains,' Cassidy said by way of greeting.

'Tell them to watch away. The sheep are eating grass. It's against the law.'

'They're watching the Wicklow mountains,' he said again.

'From a cosy armchair in Harcourt Street,' he said.

'Do you want to hear it a third time?'

'They're watching the Wicklow mountains,' he imitated Cassidy's midland drawl.

'And they've put a young fellow on to your case. Mansfield is his name and you'll be seeing a bit of him, I'd say.'

'You told me that last week.'

'Yeah, but he's busy already. He doesn't look like a Guard. He's looking for jewellery.'

'Tell me something new next week.'

When Cassidy left he went back to the balcony and surveyed the grimy world once more. As he turned away, something came to him, a sharp memory from Bennett's jewel robbery. They had ordered five of the staff, all men, up against the wall when one of them asked if he could use his handkerchief.

He was alone guarding them with a pistol, waiting for the others to round up the rest of the staff. He had told the guy in a fake lazy American accent that if he wanted to blow his nose then he had better take out his handkerchief all right, but if he took out one other thing, he would be dust. He had sounded casual, trying to suggest that he was not afraid to address such a stupid question. But when the guy removed the handkerchief, all the loose change in his pocket had come too, coins rattling all over the floor. The men looked around until he shouted at them to face the wall again quickly. One coin kept rolling; his eyes followed it and, as he bent to pick the other coins up, he moved to pick that up too. Then he walked over and handed the coins to the man who had needed to use his handkerchief. This made him feel calm, relieved, almost happy. He would rob more than two million pounds' worth of jewellery, but he would give a man back his loose change.

He smiled at that thought as he came back into the flat and took off his shoes and lay on the sofa; he would wait for an hour or two now that Cassidy had gone. He remembered too that in the heat of that robbery one of the women workers had refused to be hustled into the men's toilet.

'You can shoot me if you like,' she had said, 'but I'm not going in there.'

His three companions, Joe O'Brien with his balaclava

on, and Sandy and that other fellow, suddenly not knowing what to do, had turned to him as though he might give orders that they should in fact shoot her.

'Take her and her friends to the ladies',' he had said quietly.

He picked up the newspaper and looked again at the photograph in the *Evening Herald* of Rembrandt's *Portrait of an Old Woman*, asking himself whether it was the painting which had reminded him of that story, or the story which reminded him to look again at the photograph. There was an article beside it saying that the cops were working on a number of leads which could result in the recovery of the painting. The woman in the painting looked stubborn too, like the woman in the factory, but older. The woman who refused to go into the men's toilet was the sort you would see coming back from bingo with a group of her friends on a Sunday night. She did not look like the woman in the painting at all. He wondered what the connection between them was until he realized that, except for the stubbornness, there was none. The world, he thought, was playing tricks with his mind.

Your mind is like a haunted house. He did not know where the phrase came from, if someone had said it to him, if he had read it somewhere, or if it was a line from a song. The house from which he had stolen the paintings had all the look of a haunted house. Maybe that was how the phrase had occurred to him. Stealing the paintings had seemed like a good idea at the time, but it no longer seemed so. He had stolen the Rembrandt picture which now appeared two months after the robbery on the front page of the *Evening Herald*, plus a Gainsborough and two Guardis and a painting by a Dutchman whose name he could not pronounce. The robbery had made headlines for days in the newspapers. He remembered laughing out loud when he read about a gang of international art robbers, experts in the field. The robbery had been linked to others which had taken place in recent years on the European mainland.

Three of these paintings were now buried in the Dublin mountains; no one would ever find them. Two others were in the attic of Joe O'Brien's neighbour's house in Crumlin. Between them, they were worth ten million pounds or more. The Rembrandt alone was worth five million. He studied the photograph of it in the *Herald*, but could not see the point of it. Most of it was done in some dark colour, black he supposed it was, but it looked like nothing. The woman in the painting appeared as though she needed cheering up, like some sour old nun.

Five million. And if he dug the painting up and burned it, it would be worth nothing. He shook his head and smiled.

He had been told about Landsborough House and how much the paintings were worth and how easy the job would be. He had spent a long time thinking about alarm systems and even had an alarm system installed in his own house so that he could think more precisely about how they worked. Then one day it had come to him: what would happen if you cut an alarm system in the middle of the night? The alarm would still go off. But what would happen then? No one would repair the system, especially if they thought that the ringing was a false alarm. All you had to do was withdraw when the alarm went off, and wait.

Then an hour later when the fuss had died down you could return.

He drove to Landsborough House one Sunday afternoon. It was only a year since the house had been opened to the public; the signposting was clear. He needed to check the alarm system and to look at the position of the paintings and get a feel for the place. He had known that most visitors on a Sunday afternoon would be family groups, but he hadn't brought his family with him, he did not think that they would enjoy a trip to a big house or tramping around looking at paintings. He liked getting away on his own in any case, never telling them where he was going or when he would be back. He often noticed men on a Sunday driving out of the city with an entire family in the car. He wondered what that felt like. He would hate it.

The house was all shadows and echoes. Only a section – a wing, he supposed the word was – was open to the public. He presumed that the owners lived in the rest of the house, and smiled to himself at the thought that as soon as he could make proper plans they were in for a shock. They were old, he thought, and it would be easy to tie them up. Old people, in his experience, had a tendency to make a lot of noise; their howls were somehow louder or at least more irritating than those of their younger counterparts. He must remember, he thought, to bring strong and effective gags.

At the end of a corridor there was an enormous gallery, and this was where the paintings were hung. He had the names of the most valuable ones written down, and he was surprised at how small they were. If there were no one looking, he thought, he would be able to take one of them and put it under his jacket. He imagined, however, that there was an alarm behind each painting and that the guards, who seemed sleepy, would, if alerted, be able to move very fast. He walked back down the corridor into the small shop, where he bought postcards of the paintings he planned to steal and posters of the Rembrandt, which would be the jewel in his haul. His brother-in-law later framed two identical posters for him.

He relished the idea that no one – no one at all, not the guards or the other visitors or the woman who had taken his money and wrapped the cards and posters for him – had noticed him or would ever remember him.

THE COPS knew he had the paintings. A few weeks after the robbery, a front-page article in the *Irish Independent* announced that he was the Irish Connection. He presumed that by now they realized there was no international gang with whom he was associated, that he had acted alone, with merely three helpers. These three helpers had now become the problem, as each one believed he was going to get at least a few hundred grand in cash. All three had instant plans for the money, they continued to ask him about it. He had no clear idea how to make these paintings into cash.

Later that evening, two Dutchmen were going to book into a hotel on the north side. They had made contact with him through a man called Mousey Furlong, who used to be a scrap dealer with a horse and cart and now sold heroin to children and teenagers. He shook his head when he thought about Mousey Furlong. He did not like the heroin business, it was too risky, there were too many people in on each deal, and he hated the idea of having strung-out kids arriving at his door, skinny, pale-faced kids with huge eyes. Heroin also turned the world upside down, it meant that men like Mousey Furlong had contact with Dutchmen, and this, he thought, was an unnatural state of affairs.

Mousey spoke of the Rembrandt as though it were a new and lucrative narcotic on the Dublin scene. The Dutchmen were interested in the Rembrandt, Mousey said, but would need to verify it. They had the money available to them in cash and could come up with it once they had seen the painting. They could talk about the rest of the hoard later, Mousey added.

The Dutchmen had to be careful too, he supposed; if they had the money with them it would be easy from a distance to show them the poster, see their money, and then tie them up and walk away with the loot, leaving them to go back to Holland with a lovely framed poster. He did not plan to show the Dutchmen the Rembrandt until he had taken the measure of them; instead, he would show them a Guardi and the Gainsborough first to prove to them that he had the paintings.

A robbery was mostly simple. You stole money and it was instantly yours; you kept it somewhere safe. Or you stole jewellery or electrical goods or cigarettes in bulk, and you knew how to offload them. There were people you could trust, a whole world out there that knew how to organize such an operation. But these paintings were different. This involved trusting people you did not know. What if the two Dutchmen were cops? The best thing to do was wait, then move cautiously, and wait again.

He stood up from the sofa and went to the small window

which looked onto the balcony. Then he walked out onto the balcony itself. He half expected to notice a figure lurking in the grim spaces below, a lone man beside a motorbike, but there was no one, that emptiness again, as though the world had been poured out for his amusement, or as a way of frightening him. He supposed that Cassidy told his colleagues about this flat, and maybe they needed no one to watch him since they had Cassidy who, he thought now, gave the money each week to the Garda Benevolent Fund. It was enough to make him sick. He asked himself if it was time to do something about Cassidy, but he would wait until the paintings had been successfully sold. He had learned over the years that it was always wise to tackle one matter at a time.

He went back and lay on the sofa. He stared at the ceiling and thought about nothing. He slept well at night and was never tired at this time of the day, but he felt tired now. He lay on his side, putting a cushion under his head, and, knowing that it would be a few hours before his sister-in-law returned, he slowly faded into sleep.

When he woke he was nervous and uneasy; it was the loss of concentration and control which disturbed him and made him sit up and look at his watch. He had only been asleep for half an hour, but he realized that he had dreamed again about Lanfad, and he wondered if he would ever stop dreaming about it. It was twenty-four years since he had left it.

He had dreamed that he was back there again, being brought in for the first time, between two Guards, arriving, being shown along corridors. But it was not himself as a thirteen-year-old boy, it was him now, after all the years of doing what he liked, being married, waking in the morning to the sound of children, watching television in the evenings, robbing, making plans and deals. And what unsettled him in the dream was the feeling that he was happy to be locked up, to have order in his life, to keep rules, to be watched all the time, not to have to think too much. As he was led through those corridors in the dream, he had felt resigned to it, almost pleased.

He had felt like this for much of the time when he served his only adult sentence in Mountjoy Jail. He had missed his wife and their first child, and missed going where he liked, but he had not minded being locked up every night, he enjoyed having all that time to himself. Nothing unpredictable occurred and that made him content; the other prisoners knew not to come too close to him. He hated the food, but he paid no attention to it, and he hated the screws, but they knew to be careful of him as well. He made sure when his wife came on visits once a week that he gave nothing away, no emotion, no sense of how lonely and isolated he sometimes was. Instead they spoke about what would happen when he would get out, as she slowly put her finger into his mouth, a finger she had just wriggled around inside herself, so that he could take in the smell of her, and hold it, letting her talk about the neighbours and her family while she made it fresh again for him. He touched her hand so that the smell might stay with him for the rest of the day.

His first days in Lanfad were the ones which lingered most in his mind. Perhaps because it was in the midlands and he had never been outside the city before. He was stunned by the place, by how cold and unfriendly it was and how he would have to stay there for three or four years. He had allowed himself to feel nothing. He never cried and when he felt sad he made himself think about nothing for a while; he pretended that he was nowhere. That was how he dealt with his years at Lanfad.

In the time he was there he was beaten only once and that was when the entire dormitory was taken out one by one and beaten on the hands with a strap. Usually, however, he was left alone; he kept the rules when he knew there was a danger of being caught. He realized that it was easy to slip out on a summer's night as long as you waited until everything was quiet and you chose the right companion and you did not go too far. He learned how to raid the kitchen and made sure not to do it too often in case they set a trap for him. As he thought about it now, lying back on the sofa, he realized that he had liked being on his own, standing apart from the others, never the one caught jumping from bed to bed, or locked in a fight, when the brother in charge entered the room.

On one of his first nights there, there was a fight in the dormitory. He heard it starting, and then something like: 'Say that again and I'll burst you.' This was followed by cries of encouragement. So there had to be a fight; there was too much energy in the dormitory for something not to happen. Although it was dark, you could make out shapes and movements. And he could hear the gasping and the pushing back of beds and then the shouting from all around. He did not stir. Soon, it would become his style not to move, but at this early stage he had not developed a style. He was too uncertain to do anything. Thus when the light was turned on and one of the older brothers, Brother

Walsh, arrived, he did not have to scramble back into his bed like the rest of them, but still he felt afraid as the brother loped menacingly about the dormitory. There was now an absolute silence. Brother Walsh spoke to no one but walked around the beds looking at each boy as though he would pounce on him. When the brother looked at him, he did not know what to do. He met his gaze and then looked away and then back again.

Eventually, the brother spoke.

'Who started it? Stand out who started it.'

No one replied. No one stood out.

'I'll pick two boys at random and they'll tell me who started it, they'll tell me all right, and it'll be worse for you now, whoever started it, if you don't stand out.'

The accent was strange. He could not think what to do except pretend fiercely that this was not happening at all. If he were picked on, he would not know what to say. He did not know anyone's name, and had not seen whoever it was who had started the fight enough to identify him now. Also, he did not know what the rules were, if it were agreed among the boys never to tell on anyone else, no matter what. He was puzzled as to how all the rest of them had learned each other's names. It seemed impossible. As he thought about this, he looked up and saw that two boys were now standing beside their beds, their eyes cast down. One of them had the top of his pyjamas torn.

'Right,' Brother Walsh said. 'The two of you will come with me.'

The brother went back to the door and turned the lights out, leaving pure silence behind. No one even whispered. He lay there and listened. The first sounds were faint, but soon he heard a shout and a cry and then the unmistakable sound of a strap, and then nothing and then a howl of pain. He wondered where it was happening, he thought it must be in the corridor outside the dormitory, or the stairwell. Then the beating became regular with constant crying out and yelping. And soon the sound of voices shouting 'No!' over and over.

Everyone in the dormitory remained still; no one made a sound. It did not stop. Finally, when the two boys opened the door and tried to make their way to their beds in the darkness, the silence became even more intense. As they lay in bed crying and sobbing, the other boys did not make a sound. He wished he knew the names of the boys who had been punished and he wondered if he would know them in the morning, if they would look different because of what had happened.

In the months which followed it seemed to him unbelievable that the boys around him could lose any sense of caution and forget what had happened that night. Fights would regularly break out in the dark dormitory and boys would shout and get out of bed and leave themselves wide open to being caught when the lights came on and Brother Walsh or some other brother, or sometimes two brothers together, stood there watching as everyone scampered back to bed. And each time the main culprits would be made to own up and then taken outside and punished.

Slowly, the brothers noticed him; they realized that he was not like the others and gradually they began to trust him. But he never trusted them, or allowed any of them to become too friendly with him. He learned instead how to look busy and seem respectful. In his time there he never had a friend, never let anyone come close to him. At the beginning, when he had trouble with Markey Woods, a bloke older than him and bigger, he had to put thought into how to deal with him.

It was always easy to get a companion, someone who would work for you if you offered them protection and attention. He found a wiry fellow called Webster, but he did not tell Webster what he had in mind. He told him to let Markey know that there were cigarettes hidden in the bog, a good distance from the school but within its grounds. He let Markey threaten Webster that if he did not lead him to the hidden cache, he would beat him up. Thus he found himself walking with Markey and Webster towards the outer and remote limits of the Lanfad estate. He had primed Webster to run at Markey at an agreed signal, simply knock him to the ground. He had been experimenting with knots and ropes, having stolen a length of rope from the workshop, so he knew how to tie Markey's legs quickly and then extend the rope to his hands and tie them too. This would be the difficult part, but with his legs tied, Markey could struggle all he liked, he would not have a chance.

All this took more time than he had imagined as Markey struck blow after blow at Webster, causing him to become afraid, almost useless. Eventually he pinned Markey down and got the knot around one wrist, jerking it so that it almost broke his arm and then turning him face down so he could tie his wrists together. He had worked out that there was no point in trying to beat Markey up. It would mean nothing to him. Which was why he had brought a blindfold, and a small pair of pliers he had also found in the workshop. Once the blindfold was on, he turned Markey on his back and told Webster to start kicking him in the ribs, and as Webster was doing this with relish Markey had his mouth wide open roaring threats at him.

He studied Markey's mouth for a second as he continued to roar, and then he moved in quickly with the pliers gripping hard on one of Markey's upper back teeth on the left-hand side. Even though Markey instantly clamped his mouth shut in shock, the pliers held fast.

He began to loosen and pull at the tooth, worried now about the noise, the hysterical set of screams coming from Markey. He knew that the pliers had precisely a single tooth in their grip, but he could not understand the length of time it was taking to loosen and extract the tooth. In his own single visit to a dentist, when he had realized how simple and effective this would be, the tooth had come out very quickly.

Suddenly, instead of putting pressure on the pliers and trying to loosen the tooth, he yanked the tooth back and forward and then he pulled the pliers hard. Markey let out a howl. It was finished. The tooth was out. Webster, when he came to examine it, seemed almost as pale as Markey.

He took off Markey's blindfold and showed him the tooth. He knew that it was important now not to let Markey go in a hurry, to keep him tied up, to let him bleed a bit as he talked to him quietly, letting him know that if anyone in the school ever touched him or Webster again, he would take out another tooth until Markey would only have gums left. But, he explained to Markey, if one of the brothers ever got word of what had happened, he would not take out teeth, he would go for Markey's mickey. Did he understand? He moved the pliers down between Markey's legs and tightened them around his penis. He spoke gently as Markey sobbed. Did he understand, he asked him. Markey nodded. I can't hear you, he said. Yes, Markey said, yes, I understand. He released the pliers and untied Markey, forcing him to walk back to the school with them as though they were friends.

From then on, the other boys in Lanfad were very afraid of him. Soon he felt unthreatened. He could, if he wanted, stop fights, or take the side of someone who was being bullied, or let a boy depend on him for a while. But it was always clear that this meant nothing to him, that he would always be ready to walk away, to drop someone, including Webster, whom he had to threaten in order to stop him from being his friend.

The brothers allowed him to work out on the bog and he loved that, the silence, the slow work, the long stretch of flatness to the horizon. And walking home tired at the end of the day. Then in his last year they allowed him to work in the furnace, and it was when he was working there – it must have been in the winter of his last year – that he realized something he had not known before.

There were no walls around Lanfad, but it was understood that anyone moving beyond a certain point would be punished. In the spring of each year, as the evenings became longer, boys would try to escape, making for the main road, but they would always be caught and brought back. All the cottages in the area seemed to have figures posted at the windows ready to report escaping boys to the brothers. Once, in his first year, two such boys were punished with the whole school watching, but that did not appear to deter others who wished to escape as well. If anything, it egged them on. He found it hard to understand how people would escape without a plan, a definite way of getting unnoticed to Dublin, and maybe then to England.

That last winter two boys who were a year or two older than he was had had enough. They were in trouble almost every day and seemed afraid of nothing. He remembered them because he had spoken to them once about escaping, what he would do and where he would go. He became interested in the conversation because they said they knew where to get bicycles, and he believed that this was the only way to escape, to start cycling at midnight or one in the morning and go straight to the boat. He added, without thinking, that before he left he would like to stuff one or two of the brothers into the full blazing furnace. It would be easy enough to do, he said, if you had two other guys with you and you gagged the brother and moved fast. The blaze was strong enough, he said, that there would not be a trace of them. They would go up in smoke. If you were lucky, you could stuff four or five of them where the fuel normally went. No one would know a thing about it. You could start with one of the doddery old fellows. He said this in the same distant, deliberate way he said everything. He noticed the two boys looking at him uneasily as it struck him that he had said too much. As he stood up abruptly and walked away, it struck him that he should not have done this either. He was sorry that he had spoken to them at all.

In the end the two boys escaped without bicycles and without a plan and they were brought back. He heard about it as he was bringing a bucket of turf up to the brothers' refectory. Brother Lawrence stopped him and told him. He nodded and went on. At supper he saw that the two boys were still not there. He supposed that they were being kept somewhere. After supper, as usual, he went down to the furnace.

It was a while later, close to lights-out time, when he was crossing the path to get more turf, that he heard a sound. He knew instantly what it was, it was the sound of someone being hit and crying. He could not make out at first where it was coming from, but then he understood that it was happening in the games room. He saw the lights were on, but the windows were too high for him. He walked back stealthily to the furnace to fetch a stool; he put it down under the window. When he looked in he saw that the boys who had tried to escape were face down on an old table with their trousers around their ankles and they were being beaten across the buttocks by Brother Fogarty with a strap. Brother Walsh was standing beside the table holding down with his two hands the one who was being beaten.

Suddenly, as he watched this scene, he noticed something else. There was an old light-box at the back of the games room. It was used to store junk. Now there were two brothers standing in it, and the door was open so they had a clear view of the two boys being punished. He could see them from the window – Brother Lawrence and Brother Murphy – realizing that the two brothers administering the punishment must have been aware of their presence too but perhaps could not see what they were doing.

They were both masturbating. They had their eyes fixed on the scene in front of them – the boy being punished, crying out each time he was hit with the strap. He could not remember how long he watched them for. Before this, he had hated it when boys around him were punished. He had hated his own powerlessness amid the silence and the fear. But he had almost come to believe that these punishments were necessary, part of a natural system of discipline in which the brothers were in charge. Now he knew that there was something else involved, something which he could not understand, which he could not bring himself to think about. The image had stayed in his head as though he had taken a photograph of it: the two brothers in the light-box did not look like men in charge, they looked more like old dogs panting.

HE LAY BACK on the sofa knowing that he was going over all this again as a way of not thinking about the paintings. He stood up and stretched and scratched himself and then walked out onto the balcony again. Something beyond him, he felt, was beckoning; he wanted to leave his mind blank, but he was afraid. He knew that if he had done the robbery alone he would dump the paintings, burn them, leave them on the side of the road. When he was finally let out of Lanfad, he brought with him the feeling that behind everything lay something else, a hidden motive perhaps, or something unimaginable and dark, that the person on display was merely a disguise for another person, that something said was merely a code for something else. There were always layers and beyond them even more secret layers which you could chance upon or which would become more apparent the closer you looked.

Somewhere in the city, or in some other city, there was someone who knew how to offload these paintings, get the money and divide it up. If he thought about it enough, if he sat back on the sofa and concentrated, would he know too? Every time he considered it, however, he came to a dead end. There had to be a way. He asked himself if he could go to the others who took part in the robbery – and they were so proud of themselves that night, everything had gone perfectly – and explain the problem. But he had never explained anything to anyone before. Word would get around that he was weakening. And also, if he could not work this out, then they certainly could not. They were only good at doing what they were told.

He studied the waste ground in front of the flats. There was still nobody. He wondered if the cops had decided that they did not need to watch him, that he would make mistakes now without any encouragement from them. Yet that was not how their minds worked, he thought. When he saw a cop, or a barrister, or a judge, he saw the brothers in Lanfad, somebody loving their authority, using it, displaying their power in a way which only barely disguised hidden and shameful elements. He walked back into the flat and over to the sink in the kitchen, turned on the cold tap and splashed his face with water.

Maybe, he thought, it was all simpler than he imagined. These Dutchmen would come, he would take them to see the paintings, they would agree to pay him, he would drive them to where they had left the money. And then? Why not just take the money from them and forget about the paintings? But the Dutchmen must have thought of that too. Perhaps they would threaten him and make clear that, if he broke any agreement, they would have him shot. Nonetheless, he was not afraid of them.

He could not decide if the Dutchmen were a trap or not. He sat down and found that he would do anything now to avoid thinking that led to no conclusion. He trusted no one. That thought gave him strength, and he went on to feel almost proud that he felt love for no one – maybe love was not the word – but he felt no need to protect anyone. Except, he thought, his daughter Lorraine, she was two now. Everything about her was beautiful and he looked forward to waking in the morning and finding that she was awake too and waiting for him to come and pick her up. He liked it when she was asleep upstairs. He wanted her to be happy and secure. He did not feel this about his other children. He had felt the same, however, about his younger brother Billy, but Billy was killed in a robbery, stabbed with a knife and left to bleed to death. So he supposed that he did not really feel much about Billy anymore, he knew how to stop his mind thinking about him.

If he could get rid of these paintings he would be fine, he thought. He could go back to normal. Maybe he should take a risk with these Dutchmen, try to work out a way to get the money from them in exchange for the paintings without any further complications. But, he thought, he mustn't do that. He must be very careful.

HE DID NOT drink and did not like bars, but the hotel he had told Mousey to put the Dutchmen into had a quiet bar and a good side entrance close to the car park. Nonetheless, he felt unsafe, watching a loudly dressed American woman at the bar ordering a drink and wondering for a moment if she were a cop. He caught her eye and glanced away as quickly as he could. From the cops' point of view, he thought, it made sense to send a woman dressed like an American into the bar. It would also make sense for Mousey Furlong to make a deal with the cops, set this up as a first step towards rehabilitation. Soon, he thought, Mousey's wife would open a crèche or a posh off-licence with all his heroin money and they would raise funds for charity when Christmas came round. On the other hand, the American woman might just be a tourist and Mousey might not have changed very much.

When the two Dutchmen came, he recognized them instantly. He had never been out of Ireland in his life and he had never, to his knowledge, met anyone Dutch before. But these were Dutch, he thought, they just looked Dutch. They could not have been anything else. He nodded at them. They would recognize him, too, he supposed.

He wrote on a piece of paper 'Stay here' and handed it to the skinnier one as soon as he sat down. He put his finger to his lips. Then he walked out into the car park and sat into his car. That would give them something to think about, he imagined, Dutch or not. The car park was empty. He watched out for the slightest movement, but no one appeared, no car came to park. He would wait here for a while more, having decided to resist the temptation to go and check out the front of the hotel and the lobby. It was important, he knew, to remain calm, to stay hidden, to make the minimum number of moves necessary. He did not play chess, but he had watched someone once playing the game on television and he had liked how slow and careful and calculating they were.

They were both drinking coffee when he returned. He waited until the barman was out of sight and wrote on a piece of paper: 'Is the money in Ireland?' One of them nodded. 'So?' he wrote. 'We need to see,' came the reply. Then, having checked again that the barman was not within hearing distance, he said in an audible voice: 'You need to check the paintings, I need to check the money.'

He tried to look controlling and menacing and wondered if the Dutch had a different way of doing this. Maybe, he thought, wearing glasses and being skinny and drinking coffee meant tough in Holland. They looked, in any case, professional. He motioned them to follow him out to the car park. He drove first to the North Circular Road and then down through Prussia Street to the quays. He crossed the river and made his way to Crumlin. No one in the car spoke. He hoped that his two companions did not know what part of the city they were in.

He drove down a side street and then a lane, turning into a garage whose door had been left open. He got out of the car and pulled down the sliding door of the garage. They were now in darkness. When he found a light and turned it on, he signalled to the Dutchmen to stay in the car. He went out of a door into a small yard and tapped on the kitchen window. Inside, three or four children sat around a table, a woman stood at a sink; the man standing beside her turned and said something. It was Joe O'Brien. The children rose at once and took their plates and cups and left the room without looking at the window. Joe, he realized, had them well trained. The woman soon gathered up her things as well and left the kitchen.

Joe O'Brien opened the door and walked out into the yard without speaking. They crossed to the garage and took a look at the Dutchmen through a small, dirty window. Both men were sitting motionless on the bonnet of the car.

He nodded to Joe O'Brien, who went into the garage and motioned to the two Dutchmen to follow him. They went into the lane and through a door further along to the yard of the neighbouring house. There was an old man at the kitchen table reading the *Evening Herald* who stood up to let them in when Joe tapped at the window. He went back to reading the paper straight away. They closed the door and walked past him and went upstairs into the back bedroom.

He did not know whether the uncomfortable look they wore was a fundamental part of the Dutchmen, or if they looked uncomfortable just now, and it was unusual. They peered into the upstairs bedroom as though they had been allowed one glimpse of outer space. He was tempted to ask them if they had never seen a bedroom before as Joe put a ladder against the small opening in the ceiling which led to the attic, climbed up and came down with two paintings – the Gainsborough and one of the Guardis. The two Dutchmen looked intensely at the paintings. No one spoke.

One of them took out a notebook and wrote: 'Where is the Rembrandt?'

He took the notebook brusquely and wrote: 'Pay for these two. If there are no hitches, we get you the Rembrandt tomorrow.' The Dutchman took the notebook back and wrote: 'We are here for the Rembrandt.' Instantly, while the Dutchman still held the notebook, he wrote: 'Are you deaf?' Both Dutchmen read this carefully as though it had some deep and hidden meaning, knitting their brows in unison, their expressions hurt and puzzled.

He took the notebook again and wrote: 'The money?' When he handed the notebook back to the Dutchman, he noticed that the next remark was written in much clearer handwriting: 'We need to see the Rembrandt.' He snatched the notebook and wrote quickly, almost illegibly: 'Buy these paintings first.' The other Dutchman now took the notebook: 'We came here to see the Rembrandt,' he wrote in writing like a child's. 'Since there is no Rembrandt, we have to get instructions. We will get in touch again soon, via Mousey.'

Suddenly, he realized that these two men were serious about the rules which had been established. He had agreed to show them the Rembrandt and now he had broken the rules. It was done for the sake of caution. He would not weaken or adjust his tactics, but move slowly, taking as few risks as possible. They knew now that he was in possession of the other paintings from the heist, and he presumed that they were not being followed by the cops, although he could never be totally sure about that. Even though, by their sullenness, they suggested that the deal was in danger, he was sure that he had done the right thing, aware all of the time that Joe O'Brien was watching him. He felt an urge to grab one of the guys and tie him up and tell the other guy to go and get the money or they would kill his companion, but he had a sense that these two Dutchmen had that eventuality and many other such possibilities covered. They did not themselves act on impulse, but he felt that they would know what to do should he go down that road. It was, he thought, a mistake dealing with foreigners, but there was no one in Ireland with either the money or the inclination to pay ten million for a few paintings.

They both, as they walked out through the house, passing its owner in the kitchen, remained calm. It was their calmness which disturbed him, held him back, made him think. And then it made him unable to think. He could not tell anything about these two men. It was hard to imagine they had ever spent time in jail, unless Dutch jails taught skin care and inscrutable manners. Whoever sent them, he thought, chose them not only for their calmness, which must, he believed, mask a toughness, but also for their skill in knowing the difference between a real Rembrandt and a fake. Maybe that is all they knew, he thought, and they were going to leave the rest to real criminals. Maybe they were art professors, indeed they had the same look as some of the men who came on television to discuss the value to humanity of the paintings he had stolen.

He did not want the Dutchmen to go without some further promise or enticement. He signalled that Joe O'Brien would take them back to their hotel and then he asked for the notebook and he wrote: 'This day next week, I will have the painting here.' One of the men wrote in reply: 'We will have to get instructions.' He nodded to Joe O'Brien and threw him the keys of the car.

He wondered now if it might be a good idea to get Joe to frighten the two other accomplices in the robbery, let them know they were not being cheated or anything like that, but let them know also that they had best lower their expectations for quick money, and make clear to them that any demands or even requests from them for cash would be dealt with briskly.

Joe O'Brien was the only man he had ever worked with who would always do precisely what he was told, who would never ask questions, never express doubts, never turn up late. He also understood things, such as wiring and locks, explosives, and the engines of cars. When he had wanted to blow up Kevin McMahon the barrister, send him flying into kingdom come, Joe O'Brien had been the only man he approached and told about it.

That was when his brother Billy was up on robbery charges. He had sat in the court watching McMahon strut and prance for the prosecution and win a conviction on the basis of trumped-up evidence. And then when Billy was up for murder, McMahon became very personal about Billy's entire family, saying things in court which were none of anyone's business and must have come from Billy himself or from his mother or from someone who knew them all, knew too much about them all. McMahon seemed to be not just doing his job, but relishing it.

He paid good money to have two members of the jury frightened enough to do their duty and have Billy let off, but he decided, as he watched McMahon sum up, that he would get him, as a warning to other barristers of his kind and maybe a few judges as well. It would have been easy to shoot him, or have him beaten up, or burn his house down, but instead he decided to blow McMahon sky-high when he was in his car, to remind everyone that more people than the IRA could put bombs in cars. It happened in the

North all the time; the aftermath, he thought, always looked good on television. It would give the rest of the legal profession something to think about.

Even now, he smiled when he thought about it. How foolish these people were! The more they were paid, the more they were careless. McMahon left his car every night in the driveway of his house. And, once more, the emptiness helped. Between three and four in the morning on weekdays nothing moved in those streets. It was as though the dead were sleeping. There was silence and you could do anything. It had taken Joe O'Brien five minutes to put the device under the car and attach it to the engine.

'It'll blow up the minute he starts the ignition,' Joe O'Brien had told him. He had never asked why McMahon was being blown up. He never displayed any form of curiosity. He would do anything. He wondered if Joe were like that at home. If his wife asked him to do the washing-up, or stay in babysitting while she sat in the pub, or let her stick her finger up his arse, would he just say yes.

In the end the bomb had not gone off when McMahon started the car, but about fifteen minutes later when the barrister had reached a busy roundabout. It had not killed McMahon, merely blown his legs off, and this, he thought, was a better result as McMahon hopping around the Four Courts on wooden legs was a daily reminder to his kind what could so easily happen to them too. McMahon dead could be quickly forgotten.

He remembered meeting Joe O'Brien a few days later and neither of them mentioning the car or McMahon for a while, and then him saying to Joe that the entire affair, denounced by the Taoiseach as a threat to democracy, gave the phrase 'getting legless' a whole new meaning. O'Brien had just grinned for a moment, but said nothing.

THE DAY AFTER the Dutchmen had seen the first two paintings, Mousey Furlong came to visit him. Mousey wore a sad look, like a priest disappointed by the amount of sin in the world.

'The Dutch,' he said, 'are different. They listen to what you say and they think that you'll do what you say, down to the letter. That's the Dutch. They have no imagination.'

'When are they coming back?' he asked Mousey.

'It will take a lot to get them back,' Mousey said.

'What will it take?'

'And don't underestimate them either,' Mousey said. 'One of those gentlemen yesterday could kill you in one second with his bare hands. He's the best in the business.'

'Which of them?' he asked Mousey.

'That's the problem,' Mousey said. 'I don't know.'

'And who's the other?'

'He's the art expert and he wasn't too impressed with the art you showed him. It was worth fuck-all.'

'How do you know these guys are straight?'

'Because they're Dutch,' Mousey said. 'If a Dutch guy is going to stick a knife in your back, he'll let you know a few weeks in advance, and there's nothing you can do because on the day his knife will meet your back. That's the Dutch. If they say Monday they mean Monday, if they say they'll pay then they'll pay and if they want to see the

Rembrandt, then there's no need for me to spell it out, is there?'

'Who wants the painting?'

'One of the top men in the drugs trade wants to be the only person in the world, barring a few close friends, who will ever lay eyes on it,' Mousey said. 'That's the Dutch. They are not like us. They want this painting the way one of us might want a week in the Canaries or a great big ride or a hacienda in Baldoyle.'

TWO DAYS before he was due to present the Rembrandt to the Dutchmen, he had his weekly meeting with Detective Inspector Frank Cassidy. He noticed, as he watched him approach, that Cassidy had more bounce in his step than usual. He was carrying a briefcase.

'Have you been promoted?' he asked. 'Are you going to drive the Taoiseach around his constituency?'

'Are you sure we're safe here?' Cassidy asked.

'You're the cop,' he said. 'I'm just a poor criminal.'

Cassidy walked into the flat.

'You're in trouble,' he said.

'They found Shergar?'

'I mean trouble,' Cassidy said. 'There's a tout in your camp.'

'I don't have a camp,' he said.

'You do,' Cassidy said and took a small cassette player from his briefcase. He looked around for somewhere to plug it in.

'You remember Mansfield?' Cassidy asked as he plugged out the television and plugged in the cassette player.

'The fellow who thinks he doesn't look like a cop? The chap who looks like a cop trying to look like a North Side hippie?'

'Yeah,' Cassidy said. 'Him.'

'What about him? He's been fiddling his expenses again?'

'No, he has a new friend, a drinking companion.'

Cassidy fiddled with the tape.

'What's that got to do with me?'

'He's been drinking a lot with his new friend,' Cassidy said.

'Malcolm MacArthur?'

'No.' Cassidy stood up and looked at him evenly. 'Mansfield has been drinking with your mother.'

Immediately, his mind fixed on some point in the distance, something both remote and precise. He smiled for a moment.

'I hope he's paying, because I'm broke.'

'Yeah, he's paying,' Cassidy said.

He had shot a few guys and, once, stabbed a man who later died, but he had never strangled anyone. He wished now he had learned that skill.

'Do you want to hear it?' Cassidy asked.

'That's what I pay you for.'

'Sit down so.'

At first there was nothing, the sound of static and something hitting against the microphone and then complete silence broken by the waves of the cassette going around in the cheap machine.

'Turn it up,' he said.

Cassidy put his hand out signalling to him to be quiet. Slowly, a voice could be heard, a woman's voice, but he could not make out any words. Then it was clear that someone was fumbling with the machine, moving it, bringing it closer until his mother's voice could be heard and each word understood. She had been drinking.

'I don't see him all the time. He does be busy, oh he's busy, I'll say that much for him now, he's never idle like some are idle. And this is a rough area, it's rough and it's tough, and I'd like to say that I have lovely neighbours but I don't. The rats live all around. They shouldn't be talking to the Housing Department of the Corpo, but the rodent department, because they are rats. And they all know that if one of them even let their dogs do a poo in front of my house, my son would deal with them. And it would be hard and heavy. If they looked at me sideways, they'd know what would be coming. So I feel very safe here.'

The sound then became muffled again. Somebody was moving. He could hear drink being poured into a glass, her large gin he supposed, and then the clink of ice cubes and then a more generous pouring of tonic. And then the noise of a can of beer being opened. And her voice again unclear as she moved away from the hidden microphone and, after a while, easy to understand when she sat back in her chair. She was in mid-sentence.

'. . . that's where things are safe and there's no Guard knows his way around there. Sure, he's been going there all his life. He'd know his way around it in the dark. Oh, the things that are buried down there! You could run the country on it. Sure they can look away. They could look every day of the year and they'd find nothing. He's a quiet fellow, you know. No smoking. Never took a drink in his life. And you'd never notice him. He's a bit like a fox. And that's his nature and there's nothing anyone can do. All the same I don't know where I'd be without him. His other brother was no good. Oh no good! Billy was no good for anything.'

He could imagine her now taking a gulp of her drink and staring into the false gas fire as though life had made her sad. In the silence that followed the tape came to an end.

'That's it,' Cassidy said. 'I can't leave the tape with you. I'll have to bring it back before it's missed.'

'Did they tell you to play it for me?' he asked.

'Who?'

'The bosses.'

'I'm doing you a favour,' Cassidy said. 'Your ma is a squealer.'

'Thanks,' he said, and handed Cassidy the money in an envelope. Cassidy plugged out the cassette player and put it back into his briefcase.

HE ALWAYS parked the three cars he used in unlikely places not associated with him or his like. Early that evening he checked he was not being followed. He walked into a city centre car park and then waited, out of the sight of the CCTV cameras, on the top floor, which was open to the sky and often empty, to see if anyone would appear. When, after ten minutes, he had not been disturbed he walked down the stairs and out into the street, and caught a taxi to where one of his cars was parked. That night he drove out to the mountains, stopping regularly and pulling into a siding to see that no one was coming behind him. It was only nine thirty. He wanted to be back early enough in the city not to be noticed. Once off the main road there was no traffic; any car on the lookout would see him now, he would have to be vigilant, ready to turn back if there was the slightest suspicion that he was being followed. When he finally stopped the car and turned off the ignition, there was absolute silence, a silence that came to him like power. If anyone approached or moved, he would hear them. Until then, he was alone.

He could work in peace. He had a shovel and a large torch hidden under the back seat of the car. He knew where he was, everything was carefully marked. As long as he was alive these paintings could easily be brought back to the city. Were anything to happen to him, they would never be found, they would remain unseen for ever. Joe O'Brien knew the general area where they were buried but not the exact spot. He walked up a small clearing until the ground to his left began to slope away. Then he counted seven trees and then turned right and counted five more, and just beyond that there was a rough space overhung by trees.

Even though the ground was soft, the digging was not easy. He stopped after each heave and listened for sounds, but he heard only stillness and a mild wind in the trees. Soon, he was out of breath from digging. But he enjoyed working like this when he did not have to think and let anyone else bother him. He wished he could do this all night so that his mother's voice could be erased from his memory. It was not the voice on the tape that seemed to seep through the great guard he had placed around himself. It was an earlier voice, more shrill and more insistent, a voice that he had managed most of his life never to think about or allow into his conscious day.

There were strange gaps when he tried to remember that morning in the court, the time the judge sentenced him to complete his education at Lanfad. For example, he had no idea how he got to the court. He thought that he must have been collected by a Garda car, but he had no memory at all of that. He did not think that he went there by himself, and he had no memory either of a summons, or how he knew that he must go to court that day and not any other. His life at home in the short period before Lanfad was a blank to him now as well. He had no memory whatsoever of his mother mentioning the court or the trouble he was in.

What he remembered came after the sentence as the Guards got ready to lead him away. No other defendant had yet appeared in the dock, the social workers and the probation officers and the solicitors were busy with files and papers. The judge was waiting. All of this was clear in his mind. There was maybe a minute of this and then the Guards motioned him to follow them. There were no handcuffs or anything like that.

As he moved away from the bench with the Guards, his mother appeared from nowhere. She was, he saw, in a bad mood. Her hair was untidy and her coat was open. She began to shout. He stepped back until he realized that she was not shouting at him, but at the judge.

'Oh, God Almighty, O Lord, what am I going to do?' she screamed.

There were too many people around her for the Guards

to get to her quickly. She was pushing her way towards the bench.

'He's the best son, the best boy, oh don't take him, don't take him from me, don't take him from me.'

That became her cry as the Guards grabbed her and tried to prevent her moving closer to the bench. Her arms flailed about her. When they seemed to have caught her, she got free of them by letting them have her coat. Then she became even wilder.

'Give him a second chance, your honour.'

One of the Guards held him to the side as the other Guards gathered to stop his mother moving any closer to the judge. They had her now by the arms and they turned her and marched her through the crowd as she shouted at them to leave her alone. When she saw him as she passed, she tried to free herself so she could touch him, but he moved away from her. She was shouting all the time. When they put him into the van, she banged on the windows, but he was careful not to look at her. He did not want to see her as they drove away.

During his years at Lanfad, she visited him every few months. She was belligerent with the brothers when she arrived, and she always had to be dragged away from him at the end. In the middle part, where they were facing each other across a table, she said nothing much, but sighed and tried to hold his hand until he pulled it away. She sometimes asked him questions but he never told her anything. When the brothers instructed him to write to her to tell her when he was getting out, he gave her the wrong date in the letter. He came home on his own, and soon he drifted away. He did not see much of her until Billy got into trouble. The only way he could see Billy was by seeing her. He had begun then to give her money.

He was still digging, working quickly and mechanically, stopping for a second so that he could concentrate harder, and keep other thoughts at bay, when every so often the spade hit the hard frame of one of the paintings. It was tough work then to pull them out. They were protected by masses of plastic sheeting. He laid them all out, filling in the hole again. Then he left the shovel down and walked back to the car. He remained still for as long as he could, checking that there was no one else around.

It struck him for a moment that he would be happy if everything were dark and empty like this, if there were no sound at all in the world and no one living to make any sound, just this stillness and almost perfect silence. He would be happy at the thought that it might go on for ever like this.

He carried the paintings to the car. He would leave them with the others in the attic of Joe O'Brien's neighbour's house. Still, he felt depressed about them, and sorry he had ever stolen them. The idea that he had no power over them or the Dutchmen or Mousey made him feel in danger, but it also gave him a strange fearlessness, a sense that he could do anything now if he got the opportunity. He felt an extraordinary surge of energy as he drove back into the city.

Once the paintings had been stored safely, he walked down through the south city to his house and let himself in quietly. He took his shoes off and left them in the hall. The others had all gone to bed. Silently now, he made his way up the stairs, glad this was a new house where the stairs did not creak.

He opened the door to the room which Lorraine shared with her sister and went in. She was still in a cot and he could see from the landing light that she was fast asleep. He knew not to touch her, not to stroke her face, because he did not want to wake her or disturb her in any way. Looking at her like this was enough. He got down on his knees so he could be closer to her and he stayed there for as long as he could watching his daughter. Then he tiptoed away and closed the door to the room without making a sound.

IN THE morning he went to see his mother. She was usually wrecked in the morning, half-dressed, smoking one cigarette after another, drinking cups of cold tea. When she opened the door to him she walked back into the sitting room without greeting him.

'I brought you money,' he said.

'Sit down.'

'I won't stay.'

'That's all right.'

She began to cough and once she had finished, she suddenly seemed better, more relaxed.

'I'd make you tea, only—'

'I don't want tea,' he said.

'I'd say you're very busy.'

'Ma, I have to say something to you.'

'Oh, say away.'

'You're not to be talking about me to people. You could get us all into a lot of trouble.'

'I know that well. I hate idle talk myself. There's too much of it.'

'You're not to be talking about me,' he said, his voice quieter and his tone more direct than before.

She sipped her tea.

'You might be better to quit that drinking altogether,' he said. 'I'll have to tell them in the Dock to keep an eye on you.'

'They're afraid of their lives of you. You should keep a mile away from them.'

'Yeah, good, well, I'm going to tell them to serve you one or two, and that's it.'

'They wouldn't go against me.'

'You should stop drinking.'

'Oh, we all should stop doing something.'

'And, Ma, you should never say anything bad about Billy to anyone.'

'About Billy? What would I say about him? My own son. Lord have mercy on him.'

'Nothing, that's what you would say about him, Ma. Nothing. Do you get that?'

'Something bad? Are you saying I said something bad?'

'Yeah, you said something bad about him and I heard it back.'

'Don't believe—'

'I believe it all right. Are you listening to me? I'll take action against you if I hear another word. Do you get me?'

'You should stop blaming yourself for Billy.'

She looked at him and shook her head.

'You have yourself eaten alive about it. It wasn't your fault,' she said.

'You keep quiet now. I don't want to hear another word against him.'

'Give over. It wasn't your fault, son. No one blames you.'

'Anyway, I've said what I had to say.'

He stood up and left a wad of money on the table.

'I'll go now. But I don't want to hear any more yapping from you.'

'You are very good to look after me the way you do.'

ONCE HE HAD left her house, he knew that he could not do business again with Mousey Furlong. It was as though he had gone to his mother's house to be washed in the use of reason. As he walked away, he felt that he was thinking clearly for the first time in months. He also, as he moved towards the city centre, had that lovely feeling that he had become oddly invisible. No one, he believed, saw him or noticed him; no one would remember him. He was, he felt, at his most powerful.

He would burn the paintings, all of them. He was sure that was the right thing to do. With Joe O'Brien, he could manage a spectacular robbery, and they could pay off their two accomplices then, having warned them not to ask for the money before they got it, but having explained to them too that the paintings could not be sold, the risk was too high. If they did not see this as wisdom, then Joe O'Brien could help them to do so.

He would take the paintings some night in his car,

working alone, explaining nothing to anyone. He would find a special place for them, the emptiest place. He might even go out west towards the big stretches of bog, but he did not think so. He would stick to his mountains, to the great barren emptiness which lay south of Dublin. He would bring fire-lighters rather than petrol so that he could burn each one slowly, letting the canvases shrivel up in the flame, leaving Rembrandt's sour old woman until last until it was a heap of ash. It would make a vivid emptiness in the space where it had once hung. The people who had come to look at it could look at nothing now. It hardly mattered. What mattered was the small flickering flame he would start in the night, a hissing sound as something old and dry was set alight, and then slowly, as he stood over it, the painting would disappear and then the frame would also begin to burn. He would go back to the city renewed, unafraid, smiling to himself at what he had done. He had the solution now. He was sure he was right.

A Song

Noel was the driver that weekend in Clare, the only musician among his friends who did not drink. They were going to need a driver; the town was, they believed, too full of eager students and eager tourists; the pubs were impossible. For two or three nights they would aim for empty country pubs or private houses. Noel played the tin whistle with more skill than flair, better always accompanying a large group than playing alone. His singing voice, however, was special, even though it had nothing of the strength and individuality of his mother's voice, known to all of them from one recording made in the early seventies. He could do perfect harmony with anybody, moving a fraction above or below, roaming freely around the other voice, no matter what sort of voice it was. He did not have an actual singing voice, he used to joke, he had an ear, and in that small world it was agreed that his ear was flawless.

On the Sunday night the town had grown unbearable. Most visitors were, his friend George said, the sort of people who would blissfully spill pints over your uillean pipes. And even some of the better-known country pubs were too full of outsiders for comfort. Word had spread, for example, of the afternoon session at Kielty's in Millish, and now that the evening was coming in, it was his job to rescue two of his friends and take them from there to a private house on the other side of Ennis where they would have peace to play.

As soon as he entered the pub, he saw in the recess by the window one of them playing the melodion, the other the fiddle, both acknowledging him with the tiniest flick of the eyes and a sharp knitting of the brow. A crowd had gathered around them, two other fiddlers and a young woman playing the flute. The table in front of them was laden down with full and half-full pint glasses.

Noel stood back and looked around him before going up to the bar to get a soda water and lime; the music had brightened the atmosphere of the pub so that even the visitors, including those who knew nothing about the music, had a strange glow of contentment and ease.

He saw one of his other friends at the bar waiting for a drink and nodded calmly to him before moving towards him to tell him that they would soon be moving on. His friend agreed to come with them.

'Don't tell anyone where we're going,' Noel said.

As soon as they could decently leave, he thought, and it might be an hour or more, he would drive them across the countryside, as though in flight from danger.

His friend, once he had been served, edged nearer to him, a full pint of lager in his hand.

'I see you are on the lemonade,' he said with a sour grin. 'Would you like another?'

'It's soda water and lime,' Noel said. 'You couldn't afford it.'

'I had to stop playing,' his friend said. 'It got too much. We should move when we can. Is there much drink in the other place?'

'You're asking the wrong man,' Noel said, guessing that his friend had been drinking all afternoon.

'We can get drink on the way,' his friend said.

'I'm ready to go when the boys are,' Noel said, nodding his head in the direction of the music.

His friend frowned and sipped his drink, and then looked up, searching Noel's face for a moment, then glancing around before moving closer to him to him so that he could not be heard by anyone else.

'I'm glad you're on the soda water. I suppose you know that your mother is here.'

'I do all right,' Noel said, smiling. 'There'll be no beer tonight.'

His friend turned away.

As he stood alone near the bar, Noel calculated that, as he was twenty-eight, this meant he had not seen his mother for nineteen years. He had not even known she was in Ireland and, as he looked around carefully, he did not think that he would recognize her. His friends knew that his parents had separated but none of them knew the bitterness of the split and the years of silence which had ensued.

Recently, Noel had learned from his father that she had written to Noel in the early years and that his father had returned each letter to her unopened. He had deeply regretted saying in response that he wished his father had abandoned him rather than his mother. He and his father had barely spoken since then and Noel resolved as he listened to the music rising and growing faster that he would go and see him when he got back to Dublin.

He found that he had finished his drink quickly without noticing; he turned back to the bar, which was busy, and tried to capture the attention of John Kielty the owner, or his son, young John, as a way of keeping himself occupied while he worked out what he should do. He knew that he could not leave the bar and drive away; his friends were depending on him, and he did not, in any case, want to be alone now. He would have to stay here, he knew, but move into the background, remain in the shadows so that he would not meet her. A few people in the bar would know who he was, he supposed, since he had been coming here in the summer for almost ten years. He hoped that they had not noticed him, or, even if they had, would not have occasion to tell his mother that her son, two hundred miles away from home, was among the company, that he had wandered by accident into the same bar.

Over the years he had heard her voice on the radio, the same few songs always from her old album, now released on CD, two of them in Irish, all of them slow and haunting, her voice possessing a depth and sweetness, a great confidence and fluency. He knew her face from the cover of the album and from memory, of course, but also from an interview done in London maybe ten years earlier for the *Sunday Press*. He had watched his father burn that week's edition but had surreptitiously bought another copy himself and cut out the interview and the large photograph which had been printed alongside it. What had struck him hardest was the news that his grandmother in Galway was still alive. His father, he later learned, had banned her visits as well, and visits to her, once his wife had fled to England with another man. His mother told the interviewer that she often returned to Ireland and travelled to Galway to see her mother and her aunts, from whom she had learned all the songs. She did not mention that she had a son.

Over the months that followed he often studied the photograph, noting her witty smile, her ease with the camera, the dazzling life in her eyes.

When he had begun to sing in his late teens, and the quality of his voice was recognized, he was used on a number of albums as harmony and backing vocals. His name was printed with the names of the other musicians. He always looked at the CD covers as though he were his mother, wondering if she would ever buy these recordings, and imagining her idly glancing at the names listed on the back, and finding his name, and stopping for a second, and remembering what age he must be, and asking herself about him.

He bought another soda water and lime and turned from the bar and faced the company, trying to work out where he should stand. Suddenly, he found that his mother was staring directly at him. In the dim light, she seemed not much older than her photograph in the *Sunday Press* had made her appear. She was in her early fifties now, he knew, but with her long fringe and her auburn hair she could have been ten or fifteen years younger. He took her in calmly, evenly, not smiling or offering any hint of recognition. Her gaze was almost too open and curious.

He glanced towards the door and the dwindling summer light; when he looked back at her she was still watching him. She was with a group of men; some of them, by their dress, he judged to be local, but at least two of them were outsiders, probably English, he thought. And then there was also an older woman whom he could not place, sitting in their company.

Suddenly, he noticed that the music had stopped. He looked over in case his friends were packing up their instruments, but saw that they were facing him as though waiting for something. He was surprised to see that the owner's wife Statia Kielty had appeared in the bar. It was a rule she explained to all comers that she never stood behind the bar after six in the evening. She smiled at him, but he was not sure that she knew him by name. He was, for her, he thought, one of the boys who came down from Dublin a few times each summer. Yet you could never tell with her; she had a sharp eye and missed nothing.

She motioned him to move aside so she could get a better view of the company. As he did so, she called across to his mother, seeking her attention.

'Eileen! Eileen!'

'I'm here, Statia,' his mother replied. There was a faint English edge to her accent.

'We're all ready, Eileen,' Statia said. 'Will you do it now before it gets too crowded?'

His mother lowered her head and lifted it again, her expression serious. She shook her head gravely at Statia Kielty as if to say that she did not think she could do it, even if she was ready to try. John Kielty and young John, by now, had stopped serving, and all the men at the bar were facing towards Noel's mother. She offered them a girlish smile, pushed her fringe back and lowered her head once more.

'Silence now!' John Kielty shouted.

Her voice when it rose seemed to come from nowhere. It was more powerful, even on the low notes, than the voice on the recording. Most people in the bar would know, Noel thought, one or two versions of the song she sang which were plainer, and some might also know his mother's version. Now, however, this rendition was wilder, all grace notes and flourishes and sudden shifts of tone. As she moved into the second verse, she lifted her head, her eyes wide open, and she smiled at Statia, who stood behind the bar with her arms folded.

Noel believed that she had started too intensely, that it would be impossible to get through the eight or nine verses without losing something, without being forced to bring the voltage down. As she carried on, however, he knew he was wrong. Her control of her breathing for the high grace notes was astonishing, but it was also her naturalness with the language which made the difference; it was her first language, as it must have been his, but his Irish was half-forgotten now. Her style was the old style, with electricity added, almost declamatory at times, with hardly any interest in the sweetness of the tune.

He had not intended to shift from where he stood, but he found that he had come closer to her and stood alone between her group and the bar. The song, like many of the old songs, was about unrequited love, but it was different from most of them in its increasing bitterness. Soon, it became a song about treachery.

She had her eyes closed as she worked on trills and long notes. At times she left half a second between lines, not to catch her breath but to take the measure of the bar and its inhabitants, let them hear their own stillness as the song began its slow and despairing conclusion.

As she started these stanzas of pure lament, his mother was now staring straight at him once more. Her voice became even wilder than before, but never too dramatic or striving too much for effect. She did not take her eyes from Noel as she came to the famous last verse. He, in turn, had worked out in his head a way of singing above her. He imagined fiercely how it could be done, how her voice would evade such accompaniment, and perhaps deliberately wrong-foot it, but he believed if he was ready to move a fraction more up or down as she did that it could be managed. However, he knew to remain silent and watch her quietly as she looked into his eyes; he was aware that everyone was watching her as she sang of her love who took north from her and south from her, east from her and west from her, and now – she lowered her head again and almost spoke the last words – her love had taken God from her.

When she finished, she nodded at John Kielty and Statia and turned modestly to her friends, not acknowledging the applause. When Noel noticed Statia Kielty looking at him, and smiling warmly and familiarly, he believed that she knew who he was. And he realized then that he could not stay. He would have to summon the others, try to exude a natural impatience; he would have to make it look normal that his mother would remain with her friends and that he would leave with his.

'God, that was powerful,' one of them said when he approached the recess at the window.

'She's a fine voice all right,' Noel replied.

'Are we going to stay or what?' his friend asked.

'I told the others that I'd transport you to Cusshane as soon as I could. They'll be waiting for you.'

'We'll drink up so,' his friend said.

As they slowly prepared themselves for departure he kept an eye on Statia Kielty. She had moved from behind the bar, and was accosted by a few drinkers for polite banter, but she was clearly on her way to speak to his mother. It could take Statia a while to mention that Noel was in the bar. Indeed, she might not mention it at all. It could, on the other hand, be the first thing that she mentioned. And it might be enough to make his mother stand up and search for him or she might smile softly, half indifferently, and not move from her seat or change the expression on her face. He did not want either of these things to happen.

He turned and noticed that his friends still had not finished their drinks; they had barely put away their instruments.

'I'm going out to the car,' he said. 'You'll find me out there. Make sure you grab Jimmy up at the bar. I'm taking him too.'

When one of them looked at him puzzled, he knew that he had spoken falsely and too fast. He shrugged and made his way past the drinkers at the front door of the pub, making sure not to look at anybody. Outside, as the first car of the evening with its full headlights on approached, he was shaking. He knew he would have to be careful to say nothing more, to pretend that it had been an ordinary evening. It would all be forgotten; they would play and sing until the small hours. He sat in the car and waited in the darkness for the others to come.

The Name of the Game

As SHE CAME DOWN the stairs, Nancy glanced at the photograph; she wondered when it would be right to take it down. The wallpaper had been there for years, and she knew the space behind the frame would stand out. It reminded her even more sharply than the traces all around – the few pieces of heavy dark furniture, the plasterwork in the hall, the two or three oil paintings – that these floors over the old spirit grocer's in the Monument Square had once housed George's family in what had passed for splendour. The hallway was full of boxes now, and the plasterwork had not been painted and the old furniture had been left in rooms over the storehouse next door, and George was dead, and his mother, sitting nobly in a large chair in the old photograph, was long gone to her grave. There was no need any more, Nancy thought, for a photograph of a teenage George, overdressed, standing behind his mother. Some day, she thought, she would take it down and put it in the storehouse.

That morning, alone at the cash register, while Catherine who worked with her was on her break, she had caught a woman stealing. She had noticed the woman standing in the centre aisle with no wire basket, merely a dishevelled shopping bag; she had begun to look through a catalogue of frozen food but had kept an eye all the time on her. And as the woman made a dart for the door, Nancy moved quickly and stood in front of her blocking the way.

'Leave it down here.' Nancy pointed at the ledge beside the cash register.

The woman stood motionless as Nancy turned and locked the door.

'Quickly, now, quickly.'

The woman took two packets of shortbread biscuits from her bag. She dropped them on the floor.

'In future,' Nancy said, 'you can do your stealing up in Dunne's Stores. They have plenty of biscuits up there. Open your bag to make sure you've nothing else.'

'You think you're great,' the woman said, opening out her bag for inspection. 'With your little feck of a supermarket. You've nothing at all in it.'

'Go on,' Nancy said, unlocking the door.

'Sure, you're only a huckster, the same as your oul' mother.'

'If you don't leave this instant,' Nancy said, 'I'll call the Guards.'

'Oh, do you hear her? She got all posh in the Square.'

'Go home now,' Nancy said.

'Are you still selling the Woodbines in ones and twos?' the woman asked. She was ready to go. Her face was red with rage.

There was one other customer, a woman, moving quietly in the centre aisle of the supermarket, pretending not to listen.

'Not one of you wiped your arse up there. I don't know how the Sheridans ever put up with you,' the woman shouted.

Nancy moved towards her and pushed her out into the Monument Square.

'Go on now,' she said. 'Go on up to the Hill with you where you belong.'

Nancy closed the door and went back quietly to the cash register as though she had an urgent task in hand. She noticed the packets of shortbread biscuits on the ground and walked over to pick them up; some of the biscuits were broken and the packets could not be sold. She put them aside and picked up the catalogue of frozen food again and studied it with fierce concentration. No one in the town was interested in frozen food, she thought, except for fish fingers. Still, she flicked through the pages of the catalogue, waiting for her lone customer to come to the cash register. When the woman finally put her basket down on the ledge, her posture suggested that something deeply offensive had been said to her. Nancy hoped that she was not from the Hill, or had not heard her closing remarks to the shoplifter. She had not seen this woman in the shop before. There seemed no point in trying to humour her. Silently, Nancy keyed in the price of each object as her customer emptied the wire supermarket basket and filled her own shopping bag with slow gestures. The woman was wearing a green knitted cap. As Nancy gave her the change, the woman kept her eyes down and her mouth tightly closed. When she had gone, Nancy stood at the window and watched her walking briskly across the square.

Gerard, when he arrived from school, wanted to drop his school-bag by the side of the cash register and leave immediately without speaking.

'You can't leave your bag down here,' she said. 'Go upstairs with it.'

'They're all waiting,' he pointed to a group of boys standing by the monument.

'Go upstairs with it,' she repeated.

'Where are the girls?' he asked.

'Music.'

He made a face and then went out of the shop door and opened the door into the hall. She could hear him running up the stairs and then thumping back down again. When she heard the hall door bang, she went to the window to see which direction he was going in; she noticed a young woman with a pram who was standing staring at her as though she were a dummy or a model wearing the latest fashions. The young woman was chewing gum, and slowly her stare became cheeky, almost malicious. Nancy turned away from her, whoever she was, and walked to the back of the shop.

THE SCENE at the bank had remained with her, like a rash, or the side effect of some strong medicine. She knew that George had left no money because just a month before the accident when she had mentioned that they might change the station wagon he had told her bluntly – 'bluntly' was one of his words – that they had no money. Whatever tone he had used, it did not leave her free to suggest that he go to the bank and ask for a loan. He would not, she knew now, have been offered a loan at the bank, because he had mortgaged the shop and the living quarters above it, and the store beside it, and the payments equalled or sometimes exceeded the income from the shop.

Mr Roderick Wallace, the manager, having written to her, had agreed to see her. She liked his neat moustache and his easy smile. She had never spoken to him before, merely been greeted by him warmly as he walked a Pekinese dog around the square when the bank had finished its business. He apologized several times as she came into his office for keeping her waiting. When she sat down he apologized again.

'No, no,' she protested. 'I've just arrived this second. I wasn't waiting.'

He looked at her with sudden interest and then stared away towards the high windows which gave onto the square.

'Whoever made time did not make enough of it,' he said.

'Oh, that's true all right,' she said.

He continued to look towards the window, closely examining its upper reaches, as though about to come to a conclusion about something. Nancy saw that his desk was completely bare except for a blotting pad and a pen. There was no paper or file, and there was no telephone to be seen.

He began by mumbling words that she was so used to hearing.

'I'm so sorry now for your trouble. It must have been a dreadful shock. I could not believe it when I heard it. And so sudden, so sudden. That is a dreadful bend in the road.

I've observed it myself. But I never thought . . . Oh I never thought . . . Anyway, I'm very sorry for your trouble.'

'Thank you,' she said and looked down at her handbag and her high-heeled shoes.

Mr Wallace studied the wall behind her for a few moments before he spoke again.

'I suppose you are busy now and would like to get down to business.'

'Yes,' she said and smiled.

'Now,' he said, still looking towards the wall, 'I received the cheque from the car dealers, Messrs Rowe. You seem to have bought a second-hand car.'

He said the words with an emphasis which she thought strange. He pursed his lips. His eyebrows, she felt, were too bushy.

'Well, we're going to honour that cheque. I should let you know that.'

She tried to think if she had written any other cheques recently. Two or three, she thought, in the past few days. Mr Wallace puckered up his face and knitted his brow as though a difficult thought had occurred to him. She watched him, waiting to see what he was going to say, but he turned his face towards the window again and said nothing. Later, she wished she had spoken to him about what was needed or what she was going to do, and a few times over the days that followed she wished she had stealthily tiptoed out of his office at this point of their interview and closed the door behind her, leaving him to his thoughts.

He straightened himself in his chair.

'The problem we have is that the repayments are not

coming in. Instead, we are getting cheques, written on the account, and there's no money in the account, there's less than no money.'

He stopped and smiled as if the thought of less than no money amused him.

'And if we were a charity,' he went on, 'of course, it would be a lovely situation, because then we'd dole out the money to our hearts' content.'

He took her in, watching her response as he covered his mouth with his hand.

'That's right about the cheques,' she said. 'You see, I have to keep the business going.'

'Oh, it's going all right,' Mr Wallace said drily.

She made an effort to sound more businesslike.

'I mean if I were to sell it, it would be better to sell as a going concern.'

The longest silence was now. She reverted to something she had not done for years. She had done it when her mother had irritated her, and she had done it when she went to work first, and she had done it also to George, but not since the first year or two of their marriage. She traced the word FUCK on her skirt with her finger, quietly, unobtrusively, but deliberately. And then she did it again. And when she had finished, she traced other words, words that she had never in her life said out loud. She kept her eyes firmly on the bank manager as, unnoticed, she continued to write these words, invisibly, with her finger.

'A going concern,' he said, but he left no room for her to reply. It was neither a comment nor a question, but it was left hanging in the air above them both. He stared at it now until he said it again.

'A going concern.'

This time, there was a hint of doubt, disapproval even, in his voice.

'I mean, that it would be easier to sell it as a business,' she said.

'Have you sought advice?' he asked.

'No. I have been running the business as best I can and now, since I got a letter from you, I have come to see you.'

Speaking like this gave her courage, made her feel almost defiant.

'Running is a good word all right,' he said, pursing his lips again. 'Now if the manager of Dunne's Stores or Davis's Mills or Buttle's Barley Fed Bacon came in here and told me they were running a business then I would know exactly what they meant.'

His voice tapered off, but not before she had detected for the first time a Cork accent. She held his gaze as she wrote another word, the rudest she had ever attempted, beginning at her knee and moving upwards.

'One of my problems, and I hope you understand it,' he began again, joining his hands in front of him like a man being interviewed on television, 'is that I don't have all day. Now I have three cheques with your signature on them out there somewhere, and they might seem for small amounts to you, but those amounts are not small to us. However, we will honour them too. And that's the end, no more cheques. And instead of cheques, what I'd like to see are repayments every month on the dot without fail. That's the sort of business I run.'

He opened a drawer in his desk and found a diary or an address book, he put it in front of him and flicked through it. He became absorbed in it for several minutes before he looked up at her.

'Do you get me, Mrs Sheridan, do you get me?'

It did not occur to her to cry, but later she wondered if she had broken down at this point and become the stricken widow whether he would have stood up and comforted her and suggested a more lenient policy. Instead, she became more aggressive.

'So I go now, is that right?' she asked.

'Well, if you don't mind,' he said, his Cork accent suddenly sounding pronounced.

SHE WENT HOME and wrote down the names of all her suppliers, deciding which of them was most likely to tolerate late payment, and which of them she most needed to continue supplies. She marked them in order of priority. She thought first of opening another bank account in Bunclody or Wexford, and getting a chequebook from them and cashing her cheques there. But it occurred to her that all these bank managers would be in cahoots; they would know what she was trying to do. Instead, she took fifty pounds from the cash register the following day and, leaving Catherine in the shop, she drove to Wexford, walked into the Munster and Leinster Bank and asked for a bank draft for fifty pounds in favour of Erin Creamery, her milk supplier. The assistant made out the draft without asking any questions, charging her two pounds extra. She went home and posted the draft to the creamery. This, she thought, would keep them quiet for a while.

She waited for days to see if she would catch a glimpse

of Betty Farrell from the Croppy Inn wandering past her window. Or if she would meet her in the square. Betty had come to her several times at the cash register when there was no one in the shop and held her hand and looked into her eyes and told her that if she ever needed anything, she was just to ask. Nancy had thought of it as a kind way of expressing sympathy, but she had been struck, nonetheless, by Betty's saying the same thing each time.

In the end she phoned her and arranged that she would call into Farrells' at the end of business the following day.

She was surprised, when Betty answered the door, by her clothes, and wondered if she had specially dressed up because she knew Nancy was visiting. She was wearing a thin loose woollen suit in a sort of light purple colour that Betty had never seen before. And when Betty led her upstairs to the floor over the pub she was surprised by the largeness of the two rooms with interconnecting doors, and the newness and brightness of everything. There was a tray on a side table with china.

'You sit down there now, Nancy,' Betty said, 'and I'll go and wet the tea.'

Nancy had never been upstairs in this house before. She knew Betty from the street or the square or the cathedral or whist drives. She had known Jim, Betty's husband, all her life, but Betty was not, she knew, from the town. As Nancy looked around, she noticed that the rug on the floor was faded, yet the fading seemed to have added to the richness. The wallpaper was the same; it looked old and faded without looking shabby, and this meant, she thought, that it was new and had cost money.

'I put my foot down, Nancy,' Betty said when the tea

was poured. 'I said to Jim: "We're doing up this house, or we're building out the country where no one will know our business." But sure Jim was born here and wouldn't budge. So I brought in the decorators and I looked around a few auctions. There's a very good dealer in Kilkenny. He's the best.'

Nancy observed that Betty's nylon stockings were sheer and were a strange no-colour, neither dark nor completely see-through. When they had spoken for a while about their children, and about the problem of living in the town where you had no garden, Nancy knew it was time to tell Betty why she had wanted to see her. She began by recounting her visit to the bank manager.

'Oh, he's a so-and-so,' Betty said.

'So you don't bank with him?'

'No, Jim has always been with the Provincial.'

'Betty, I don't want to explain the ins and outs of this, but I need someone to cash cheques for me, not my own cheques, but customers' cheques, people I know.'

'Bring them up here, Nancy,' Betty said, 'or send Catherine up with them, or we'll send down for them, as often as you like, or whenever you like, and we'll cash them. That's what neighbours are for.'

'Are you sure now?'

'Well, I should ask Jim,' Betty said, 'but I know what he'll say. He'll say exactly what I just said. He was in school with George and sure he's known you since you were born. Wasn't he great with your sister in England?'

'Oh, he was,' Nancy said, 'but that was a long time ago.'

'Well, we'd like to help you, that's all,' Betty said.

'I'd be very thankful and it won't be for long.'

'You were always very capable, Nancy,' Betty said. 'Jim always told me that, since the time you were on the Cathedral Committee, that you had the makings of a real businesswoman.'

'Did he say that?' Nancy asked sharply, but Betty did not answer her, instead smiled vaguely and crossed her legs and sat back in her armchair with a warm sigh.

'I'm glad now you came,' she said.

AT NIGHT, when the children went to bed, she left them time to undress and talk amongst themselves before she came upstairs to the girls' room first and then to Gerard's room. She made it seem casual, but it was part of their ritual now, something that George's death had not interrupted nor interfered with. She asked them questions and listened to them, which she could not do when they came in first from school. She told them who had been in the shop and then they told her about school and teachers and friends. She was careful never to criticize them or offer too much advice, she tried to sound more like their sister than their mother. So when Gerard told her that he would like to beat the shit out of old Mooney, who taught him Latin and science, she merely said quietly: 'Oh, you shouldn't say that, Gerard.'

'So what should I say?' he asked.

'I don't know. God, I really don't.'

She laughed.

'Well, that's what I'd like to do,' Gerard said, putting his hands behind his head.

'It's OK to think it,' she said. 'I suppose I just wouldn't say it to too many people.'

She knew Gerard's timetable and she knew whom the girls sat beside in school and whom they liked and disliked. She told them, in turn, about clothes she might buy, a coat she had seen. But there were two things now which she never discussed with them in these short nightly talks. They never mentioned George or how he had died; and she never told them that she had stopped making payments to the bank and was paying only the suppliers she thought were essential, and that she was hoarding whatever cash she gathered in the bottom drawer of the chest in her bedroom under the good sheets. She believed that Mr Wallace would move slowly against her, even when he found out, as he surely would, that she was cashing cheques in the Croppy Inn. It would be a while before he realized that he should have foreclosed on her at the earliest opportunity. He would never see another penny from her and she would reply to none of his letters when they came. She would save the money in cash so that no other bank could hand her money over to Mr Wallace. In six months, she would have enough to move to Dublin and rent a house and live in peace while she learned typing and shorthand or some other skill which would help her to get a job.

She began to imagine herself as secretary to a businessman, taking his phone calls and announcing visitors and typing his letters and dressing beautifully, the essence of efficiency. Someone like Tony O'Reilly, or the man who ran Aer Lingus or the Sugar Company. She told no one at all about her difficulties or her dreams, even her sister and brother-in-law. She sat at the cash register in the supermarket and at the end of each day she put the cash where no one would find it.

HER MOTHER-IN-LAW had still owned the shop when George wanted to open a supermarket, the first in the town. Nancy took no part in the negotiations between mother and son, but she wished now as she drove towards Bree at eight o'clock on a Friday night that she had become involved. Her mother-in-law wanted all the old customers looked after, the ones who lived out in the country who had had accounts for years and had their groceries delivered every Friday, and the others who came into the town on a Saturday and had a drink in the little bar to the side of the shop and paid their bills when it suited them. George put his foot down about the spirit grocery. He was, he insisted, keeping the licence but making the old bar into a storehouse. People would have to go elsewhere for their drink on a Saturday night, he told his mother. And they decided that they would over time phase out accounts completely and ask their customers to pay in cash. But on the question of deliveries, George had to give in. Good customers of long standing who had no transport of their own could not be left stranded, he agreed with his mother. And now both George and his mother were dead and Nancy was left driving towards Bree alone in the second-hand station wagon loaded with boxes of groceries.

When she married George first, he spent Thursday and Friday nights making these deliveries, doing ten or fifteen a night, not arriving home until late. Slowly, over the years, however, the orders had fallen away. Some customers had moved into the town, others had bought cars. She noticed that some of these old faithful customers in recent times avoided their supermarket. Even when they met her or George on the street, they seemed sheepish and distant, anxious to get away.

Nancy was left with seven or eight customers, mostly old people who had the same order every week and had the same comments to make on each visit. Some of them, she knew, did not order enough for her to be their main supplier, and she often thought that they were continuing to deal with her for the sake of charity. It was they who felt sorry for her. Yet they were so friendly and grateful when she came to them on Friday nights that she did not have the heart to tell them it would really suit her not to have to drive along mucky lanes to them once a week as though she were the district nurse. After George died would have been the easiest time to call a halt, it would have seemed natural for no more deliveries to be made, but that was the very time when she was foolishly determined that nothing should change, that everything should be run as before. She did not know then that George had left her at the mercy of his bank manager.

As she drove, she went through all the names of the people she still had to visit: Paddy Duggan, who lived on his own in a tithe cottage which had not been cleaned since his mother died; Annie Parle and her soft sister from near the Bloody Bridge with five gates to open and close before you reached their old farmhouse; the twins Patsy and Mogue Byrne, who ate potatoes and butter for their dinner every day with boiled rice and stewed prunes for their sweet. Neither of them, she thought, ever took off his cap. The six Sutherlands, a sister, three brothers and a wife of one of the brothers, and a cousin or an aunt who was upstairs in bed, they got all their bread from her on a Friday, paid her once a month, and never ordered anything else except jars of Bovril and large pots of strawberry jam – they each had their own, they did not share. And poor smiling Mags O'Connor, alone by the fire with two dogs, in a two-storey house down a long rutted lane, she must have had money or a pension from England because hers was the biggest order of all, including duck loaves and grapefruit juice and Mikado biscuits and tins of salmon and jars of chicken and ham paste and sandwich spread.

By ten o'clock she had only Mags O'Connor and the Sutherlands to visit. She was cold and tired and wished she knew how to tell these customers that they should find another way to have their groceries delivered. As she approached Mags O'Connor's house, she noticed that there were two cars parked; one of them had an English registration. When she got out of the station wagon, a sheepdog came and wagged its tail, followed by another who nosed up against her. She took the boxes from the back seat of the car and went towards the door which was, as usual, half open.

'Well, will you look who's here?' Mags always used the same greeting.

'This woman,' she said to the three visitors who sat at her kitchen table, 'this woman is the saving of my life. I don't know where I'd be without her. How are you at all, Nancy?' she asked.

Nancy greeted her and waited.

'It's fresh and well you are looking,' Mags as usual said as the boxes were put into the corner.

'You'll have tea, Nancy,' she went on, 'because I have people here who'll make it for you.'

She was a big-framed woman who normally seemed gentle and ready to smile, but now she looked imperiously at her visitors.

'We'll all have tea,' she said, 'and wait until I introduce you now to my two nieces, Susan from Dublin and Nicole from Sheffield and then Frank there who's married to Nicole and not an Irish bone in his body and no worse for that, although you'd better not tell anyone else I said that.'

Nancy wondered if she had been drinking but realized that the company had made her talkative.

'Use the good cups and saucers now,' she said as the two nieces set about making tea, 'and sit down here, Nancy, I was telling them all about you and poor George and I was just saying that old Mrs Sheridan was the nicest woman in the whole town, there was no one as nice, and of course you're very nice too. I was saying that too, wasn't I, girls? So I suppose the gist of what I was telling them was that all the Sheridans were very nice and are still very nice. So it's a pity you weren't listening at the door, you would have heard nothing bad about yourself.'

Nancy wondered if she was imagining this. In the silence which followed she thought she saw one of the nieces with her back to them shaking with laughter.

'Oh, show me the red book before I forget,' the old woman said, 'till I see how much I owe you. I keep my money by my side, so I'd be very easy to rob. Philly Duncan up the lane does go to the post office for me every

so often. If it wasn't for you and for him and for that
wireless there and Shep and Molly, I'd be in the County
Home.'

She took a breath and then sipped her tea.

'So how are you at all, Nancy?' she asked.

'I'm very well, Miss O'Connor, very well.'

'It's always nice to see you. I wrote to the girls here and
I said it as well to Philly Duncan that Nancy won't give up.
I know the Sheridans and she won't give up, she'll be out
here, or she'll get someone to deliver. They were always
great business people, the Sheridans.'

She looked serious, her jaw set, as she poked the fire.

'And they always have the best things, sure you couldn't
beat their bread, it's the freshest, and there's nothing they
don't have, but I believe there are big changes in the town,
plenty of traffic I hear and plenty of money. And I do hear
the advertisements for Dunne's Stores on the wireless, but I
wouldn't like them at all now, they wouldn't be from the
town and they wouldn't know anyone. They'll never catch
on, Nancy, those Dunnes.'

When the tea had been finished, Mags O'Connor asked
Nancy if she would like a small glass of sherry.

'It'll help you on your way,' she said.

By the time Nancy had refused, a tray had appeared,
carried by one of the nieces, with a bottle and five small
glasses.

'And I asked the girls, and they're very good, I asked
them to get you a little token of thanks.'

Mags produced a small package wrapped in shiny red
paper and handed it to her.

'Now you'll have to remember it's just a token,' Mags

said as Nancy opened the package and found a bottle of 4711 perfume. Mags smiled and nodded her head as Nancy thanked her.

'Oh, the Sheridans were always very nice people,' she said.

It was after eleven when Nancy left the house and it had begun to rain. By the time she reached the road she knew that if she turned left she could be home in twenty-five minutes when maybe Gerard would be still awake. If she turned right, she would have three miles more and then another lane to the Sutherlands, to deliver them three large pans and four batch loaves, six pots of jam and six jars of Bovril. She realized, as soon as the idea came into her head, that she would turn left and go home. She could still, she thought, sell the bread in the supermarket the next morning.

NANCY WAS AMAZED one night the following week when Gerard asked her if she was going to get married again. She told him it was the last thing on her mind.

'Oh now,' he said. 'That's not what I heard.'

Eventually, after much withholding and teasing, he told her how he and his sisters had seen their mother three times in the recent past in deep discussions with Birdseye, the commercial traveller.

'We were just speaking about business, Gerard,' she said. 'Don't be going on with nonsense.'

'That's what they all say,' he replied.

Over the days that followed he made a point of leaving a packet of Birdseye custard at her place at the table. He was not to be stopped so she ignored him, surprised by his confidence and his cheek and unsure how to respond to him.

She did not want him to know anything about the conversations with Birdseye, who was the most popular and talkative commercial traveller who came to the shop. He ended each sentence with 'Mrs' as though it were a Christian name. Even when George was alive he would single her out and talk to her at great length when he came to get his order, telling her the news and knowing a good deal about the plans for expansion and the inner workings of Dunne's Stores. He was small and chubby, with a large and friendly face. George had always laughed at him when he was gone, saying that he was a born salesman, that you would buy from him because he seemed so harmless.

She did not know why he was the one to whom she explained her circumstances. Maybe it was his harmlessness, and his living a distance away where no one knew her was certainly a factor, but more than anything she knew that he would listen to her, and that not a detail would be lost on him. She did not tell him about the cash mounting slowly in the bottom drawer because she could not gauge what his response to that would be. But she told him the rest, and he stared at her as he concentrated on each word, waiting for the next piece of information.

'I'll come back tomorrow, Mrs,' he said. 'Will you be here at four? I'll come back tomorrow and I'll have plenty to say to you then, Mrs.'

He came back the next day when Catherine was also working and he whispered to Nancy as soon he arrived, asking if he could see the store which was across the hallway. The old counter of the spirit grocery was still there and the window with the curtains drawn which gave on to the square, but the room was full of junk. He studied it silently, taking it all in.

'OK,' he said. 'I was right yesterday, Mrs, but I needed to sleep on it, and I rang a fellow I know, I didn't tell him what town it was, but he agreed with me, Mrs, so I have it now. There's only one thing you can do. Low investment, Mrs, and quick money. That's the name of the game.'

They stood in the dusty old room. He looked at her, like a small animal about to pounce, and she held his eye. She was taken aback by his seriousness and his certainty.

'Chips, bun-burgers, Mrs, quick chicken, fish in batter,' he said.

'Sure I couldn't make chips,' she said, 'the kids complain that I can hardly fry a potato.'

'There's machinery going around now that's cheap and will do everything for you, Mrs.'

'What do you want me to do? Spend all day making chips?'

'The weekend trade would be the best, I'd say,' Birdseye said.

'I couldn't stand out here selling chips,' Nancy said.

'Well, in that case you'll be standing on the side of the road, Mrs, to put it straight to you now.'

'Oh, thank you,' she said. 'That is a great help.'

'You could have the place fixed up in no time,' he said, his gaze focused on her in pure enthusiasm.

'You know,' she said, 'I would love to get out of this town and never come back.'

'You think about it now, Mrs,' he said, glancing around the room once more. 'It's a sure-fire winner.'

THE FOLLOWING Saturday was the first night of the new bar extension in Grace's Hotel, and crowds poured out into the Monument Square at half-past one. A few sat around the monument and others gathered outside the supermarket. Nancy could not sleep and worried in case the noise had reached the back rooms where the children were sleeping.

That evening she had met Mr Wallace as he walked his dog in the square. He must have known, she thought, that she had missed the repayment which was due, but nonetheless he smiled at her even more warmly and politely than usual. For one moment, she even thought that he was going to stop to exchange pleasantries. This added to her dread of him and her determination never to sit again in his office.

She did not have a telephone number for Birdseye. She knew that he lived near Waterford and was married, with young children, and she knew that he covered Kilkenny and Carlow and Wexford and all the places in between. She would have to wait until he arrived again to ask him the questions which had been on her mind since he spoke to her. How much money could she make out of a chip shop? How quickly could she make it? And how much would it cost to set the place up? And how quickly could that be done? She could not sleep pondering these unanswered questions.

Two men were singing below her window and others joined them so that now there was a group of singers, loud and raucous and half-drunk bawling out:

'*Her eyes they shone like diamonds*
You'd think she was queen of the land
With her hair flung over her shoulders
Tied up with a black velvet band.'

She lay there waiting for them to stop, but when the song came to an end they let out a big cheer and then started another song:

'*Fare thee well, my lovely Dinah, a thousand times adieu.*
We are going away from the Holy Ground and the girls we all love true.'

One of the singers, with a louder voice than the rest, began to roar out the words, and Nancy knew as she lay in the dark what was coming at the end of the first verse, a big shout in unison of 'Fine girl you are!' before continuing with the song. She wondered if her neighbours were awake too and if there was any point in phoning the Guards.

When the singing became louder, she went to the window and opened the curtains and pulled up the bottom half of the window frame. She thought this sound would distract them, perhaps even silence them, but they kept going. She saw that there were five or six young men, with two women standing close by.

'Excuse me! Excuse me!'

At first no one heard her, but then one of the women pointed up to her and the singers moved out on to the roadway so they could see her.

'Excuse me, but we're trying to sleep and there are children here.'

'We're not stopping you,' one of them shouted.

'It's a free country,' the young man beside him added.

The others looked up at her in complete silence.

'It's very late,' she said. 'Now could you all to go home immediately?'

She knew she had sounded too posh.

'Do you hear her fucking ladyship?' one of them shouted.

'Her high and mightyness.'

She did not know whether she should stay there or withdraw. She watched as one of them detached himself from the group. He was, she thought, the loud one. She did not recognize him as he moved towards the monument and began to shout at her.

'You have your la! You have your fucking la!'

She closed the window and drew the curtains, but this seemed to infuriate the figure in the square even more.

'Your big hole,' he roared. 'Your big hole.'

'Ah, Murt, come on,' one of his friends roared at him.

But he would not stop.

'How's your fat hole? Your big fat hole.'

WHEN BIRDSEYE came the following week, she asked him if he could return at six o'clock when the supermarket had closed for the day. She had all the questions ready as he had all the answers. It was arranged that she would go to Dublin on Thursday to look at the equipment she would have to install and discuss terms with the company which would sell her what was needed. Birdseye assured her that he would make the contacts and the arrangements for her.

'Speed, Mrs, speed is of the essence,' he said to her.

As soon as he left she went upstairs and phoned Betty

Farrell and asked for the name and number of the furniture dealer in Kilkenny she had recommended. Betty gave her the number briskly and without asking any questions. When she rang, the phone was answered by the owner who agreed to come to look at what she had to sell the following evening.

He was a tall man with greying hair, mild-looking like a national teacher in a country school. She showed him into the room over the store where the old dining table was kept. He ran his finger along the surface and knelt down so he could see underneath it.

'Are you selling this?' he asked.

'And the two side tables if the price is right,' she said. 'And I have other things too.'

She brought him to the living room and showed him the painting over the mantelpiece.

'To be honest with you now,' he said, 'I wouldn't sell that. You'd never get it back again.'

'I'll sell it if I get a good price,' she said. 'I have another one upstairs.'

'It'll be hard to price them,' he said. 'I might have to wait a good while to get the right buyer.'

'Are you not a buyer?'

'I'm a dealer.'

'Well, there are books too. Do you deal in books?'

By the end of the evening, he had written out two lists. One had merely three items: a Georgian dining table with two side tables; two oil paintings of the River Slaney by Francis Danby; a full first edition of Hore's *History of County Wexford*. The other list had fifteen or sixteen items of lesser importance.

'Now come down here again,' she replied. 'The chand-elier in the hall's been there since the beginning.'

He noted it on his second list.

'So?' she asked when she had him at the hall door.

'Well,' he said, 'I'll come back to you with a price.'

'Cash,' she said.

'You sound like someone going to do a runner,' he said.

'I beg your pardon?'

'It's the first time anyone has asked me for cash for that amount of stuff.'

SHE DROVE TO Dublin on Thursday, left her car on St Stephen's Green and met her contact in the Russell Hotel. He had the same look as Birdseye, eager, friendly, positive, enthusiastic.

'Now,' he said, 'this man in Thomas Street will sell you all you need and he'll fit it for you. He's dead honest and knows his stuff. He'll need to be paid on the nail in cash.'

He stopped and studied her to ensure that she was in full agreement. She did not move.

'You're going to need a massive freezer,' he continued, 'and I know someone who has one, and you're also going to need a main supplier and that's where I come in. Everything ready and prepared, frozen, delivered once a week. Again, cash on the nail.'

Suddenly he seemed tough, almost threatening, as though offering a hint of what he might be like if the cash were not forthcoming.

'You can shop around if you like,' he said, 'but you won't get a better deal.'

She asked him the single question which had preoccupied her on the journey to Dublin.

'I want to know this,' she said. 'How much does one of your big frozen bags of chips cost and how many bags of chips would I get out of that? And how much are you changing per single frozen hamburger?'

He offered to write it out for her but she insisted that, if he had the figures in his head, he tell her instead. He gave her the details very slowly until she told him to stop because she needed to do some mental arithmetic.

'I don't need to shop around,' she said after a few moments. 'You can be my supplier.'

'Is that all you have to say about it?' he asked, flirting with her for the first time.

'That's all,' she said and smiled.

The man in the warehouse in Thomas Street was small and fat and cheerful. He already had the measurements of the store which Birdseye had asked her for. Now he showed her a drawing, his plan for her chip shop, which he would be able to install in twenty-four hours flat, he said, working day and night.

'You won't know what hit you,' he said, chuckling. 'There's only one thing more I need, besides a new leg.' He winced in mock pain as he touched his leg and then laughed. 'We need a name. We'll put you up in lights.'

'For the shop?'

'We need to make a big bright sign.'

'The Monument,' she said. 'We'll call it the Monument.'

'Right so,' he said, noting down the words. 'So we'll be ready in two weeks. I'll need half the money next week and the other half when the job's done.'

'Cash,' she said.

'You're too right,' he replied.

THE MAN FROM Kilkenny began to prevaricate on the phone.

'I can't price the paintings at all. No one knows what they're worth. They'd need to be sold at a big auction in Dublin,' he said.

'So why don't you buy them and put them into the auction?'

'That's what I mean,' he said. 'The big one especially could go for five or six times what I could give you.'

'Lucky you,' she said.

'I don't work like that. I pay a fair price,' he said coldly.

'If you make me a decent offer and pay me now and in cash, I'll take it. And there'll be no complaints from me if you become a millionaire once you pay me a fair price.'

'I'll give you a ring tomorrow.'

SHE TOLD NO ONE that she planned to open a chip shop in the storehouse beside the supermarket. Having considered telling Betty Farrell, she decided against it, presuming that Betty would react with little enthusiasm to such a venture. Nonetheless, she continued changing cheques with the Farrells and hoarding the cash. She had no further dealings with the bank. When, finally, she made an agreement with the man in Kilkenny for more money than she had expected, she drove to see him. He quietly handed her an envelope full of twenty-pound notes, enough to pay for the deep freeze and the machines and their installation as well as the sign and the decoration. But she also needed money for supplies and to pay staff and to keep the place going. Although she did not want to touch her stash of money, she knew that if she put it in the Credit Union she would be able to borrow double her savings.

Jim Farrell, she knew, was on the committee of the Credit Union. She asked Betty to enquire from Jim if the Credit Union could give her a loan in cash or a cheque which Jim and Betty could cash for her.

'Jim will arrange it in cash,' Betty told her later that same day, 'but you'll have to go to the meeting, and the other members of the committee, he says, can be very nosy, they'll want to know all your business, but he says you're not to mind them, and say nothing to them about the cash part.'

She thought once more of confiding in Betty, but realized that, if she once said out loud what she had in mind, she might lose all courage. She said nothing. Betty, she realized, must have been very curious; she admired her for not asking her straight out.

The day after she had lodged the money in the Credit Union, she waited her turn to face the committee to ask for her loan. While she had recognized no one in the waiting room, once in the office she knew four of the five men from the committee. Jim Farrell tried to be businesslike, making clear that they all knew her and wanted to welcome her to the Credit Union. She disliked the others watching her as Jim Farrell spoke, she understood they disapproved of people seeking loans the day after their first deposit. She knew that they would not be able to resist asking her questions, nor would they be able to resist telling their wives about her when they got home.

'I'd say Dunne's Stores has had a big impact on your business,' Matt Nolan, one of the committee, began.

'A certain impact, yes.' She wondered now if she had put on too much lipstick.

'I'd say you feel the pinch in the square with no parking,' he continued.

She stared at him blankly and said nothing.

'We all respected George and Nancy as business people,' Jim Farrell said, 'so if no one has any more questions . . .'

'It's funny you never came to the Credit Union before,' Matt Nolan persisted. 'And,' he raised his hand, 'if you will allow me, Jim, I'd say it might be difficult for a woman with no experience to take over a business. And so I'd be worried about you expanding. I'd like to know what advice you had, I'd like to see more figures.'

One of the other committee members, the one whom she did not know, lit a cigarette. Nancy remembered Matt Nolan as a young man coming to her mother's shop buying sweets and bags of sherbet for himself. He had the same shiny suit, she thought, and the same oily haircut for the last thirty years and the same pioneer pin.

'So if you could—' he went on, but Jim Farrell interrupted him.

'Nancy, thank you very much for coming and once again welcome to the Credit Union. We'll be in touch with you if we need any more information.'

As she stood up, Matt Nolan looked at her with resentment. She knew what he was thinking; she had married into the Sheridans and she had a nerve now to be borrowing on the strength of their name.

Late that evening, when she had come back to the living room, having spent time with the children, Betty Farrell phoned her to say that the loan had been approved. Jim, she said, would bring the money in cash the next day.

She drove to Dublin and paid half the money to the man in Thomas Street; she found the two girls whom she had previously laid off from the supermarket and offered them their jobs back, specifying that the hours would be different. They needed the work, she knew. With the help of the children, who were puzzled at her sudden need for tidiness, she removed all the boxes and other rubbish from the store and brought several loads out to the town dump. She found a man to paint the store and paid him in cash when he had finished. And she discussed each detail with Birdseye when he came to the supermarket to take her order. She phoned his friend to discuss what supplies she would need for the opening two weeks. Then there was nothing more she could do except maintain silence.

Two days later, the freezer was installed and then the supplies arrived – boxes of hamburgers, fish in batter, frozen chips. No one observed the men carrying the freezer into the store, even though it was done in full daylight; and Gerard, who liked to know everything that was happening, did not think to look into the store to see what was new. She kept the curtains in the storeroom drawn.

THE MAN FROM Thomas Street came on a Friday evening at eight o'clock. She had done the delivering a day early so she could be there to meet him. He had a van and as she stood at her door a car pulled up with five men inside.

'They're all home from England and they're hungry for overtime so I told them if they wanted overtime, I'd give them overtime,' he said. 'And I promised I'd get them home for the last pint tomorrow night. So it'll be all go.'

He chuckled.

'And when will you sleep?' she asked.

'Ah, there won't be much sleeping,' he said. 'We'll lie down on the floor, but we'll need a big feed at around midnight and another at eight in the morning. Sausages, rashers, pudding, eggs, the works.'

'When am I going to learn to use this machinery?' she asked, as the men began to walk into the store.

'There are five stages for making chips,' he replied, 'and the same goes for the fish, but it's different for the burgers. If you get paper and a pen, I'll write it out for you.'

'When will I be ready to open?'

'When we quit this place at nine tomorrow night, you just have to heat the oil and you're away.'

'You mean open tomorrow night?'

'And I have one tip for you. I have a fan here that works wonders. I'm going to put it up in the corner at the window. Heat the oil, have it as hot as you can get it, and throw in the chips. After a few minutes when they're nearly done, open the window, turn on the fan and the people of this town will smell chips and they'll come to you like a terrier who has smelt oxtail soup.'

She drove up the town and found the two girls and asked them to come to work for a few hours after nine o'clock the following night. Neither of them asked her why the supermarket would be open so late. When she came home, she made the children turn off the television and she told them what was going to happen.

'Do chips make money?' Gerard asked.

'Are you going to work there?' one of the girls enquired.

'Are we going to have the supermarket as well?' Gerard asked.

She allowed them down to view the work as it started.

'Who knows about this?' Gerard wanted to know as they stood in the hall while the men carried in heavy boxes. It struck her that he sounded like his father.

At midnight, she invited the workmen to come to the kitchen where she had the table set for them. She had made a huge fry-up, as requested, and heated up several large tins of beans. Soon, however, the food was gone and the tea was drunk and she had to begin again, frying more rashers and sausages, heating up more beans, going down to the shop to get more bread and making more tea. The men talked and laughed among themselves, noticing her only when she offered them more food. One of them had a long blue tattoo all along his forearm in the shape of an anchor.

She was woken through the night by the sound of hammering and drilling. When she dressed and went downstairs at seven o'clock, she found that Gerard was already there, sitting watching the work. He barely acknowledged her. The place was a mass of wires and sawdust, but it was now possible to make out a counter and a cooking area. She wondered how she was going to manage in the supermarket all day, what she was going to say when people asked her questions, people who had seen the work through the door of the storehouse, which would, she thought, often be open as the men came in and out to the van parked on the street.

'We'll be needing breakfast, ma'am,' the boss said.

'Have you been up all night?' she asked.

'No rest for the wicked,' he said, laughing.

'Are you really going to open tonight?' Gerard asked her.

'Yes,' she said.

'There's a queer lot of work to be done first,' he said.

After breakfast, as she contemplated the day, she found the boss.

'You know the sign?' she asked.

'The Monument. I have it here,' he said.

'Could you leave it until last? I mean don't put it up until everything else is in place.'

'Right you be,' he said.

She saw Gerard glancing at her suspiciously.

SHE OPENED the supermarket as usual at nine thirty and took in the supplies of bread. The girls left early to go and spend the day with school-friends, but Gerard haunted the storeroom and refused to go out. Catherine came at ten; both she and Nancy stationed themselves at the cash registers as though nothing strange were happening. Saturday was late opening and the busiest day. When the hammering and the drilling became intense, Catherine did not ask her any questions. She seemed too sleepy to observe that there was anything strange happening. All morning, Nancy waited for someone who came come into the shop to seek an explanation of the work next door, but no one did.

At lunchtime, she left Catherine alone in the shop and made another fry-up for the men, including the potatoes they had asked for. She waited for the boss, the man from Thomas Street, to tell her that they had forgotten to load some vital piece of machinery, or they had come across an unforeseen problem, or he had miscalculated the time it would take. But he remained smiling and confident. As the men ate, she went downstairs. Gerard was alone in the storeroom sitting on a chair. They looked at all the new machinery, and examined the ceiling which was a maze of half-connected wires; she opened the steel container where the chips would fry and they both inspected the area where they would drain, from where the chips could be scooped into the bags, which had also been provided by the supplier. Upstairs, she had the plastic salt and vinegar containers ready and red containers in the shape of tomatoes for the ketchup.

As she studied the new machinery with Gerard, she did not realize at first that the curtains in the storeroom had been pulled back and that two women were staring in at her. She stood back into the shadows until they went on their way then moved quickly to close the curtains.

'What's wrong with you?' Gerard asked.

'I'm going back upstairs. Don't talk to anyone,' she replied.

'You look like you're going to be arrested.'

'Gerard, if anybody asks you any questions, you know, anyone from the town, tell them to talk to me. But tell them nothing.'

'OK,' he said, as if he were taking control. 'You go back upstairs. And if anyone calls for me, tell them I'm not here.'

At six o'clock, as she left Catherine in charge again, her daughters arrived back and merely glanced nonchalantly into the storeroom, expressing no interest in what was going on. Gerard, on the other hand, stayed in the room staring at the work as though, were he to lift his eyes from it, it might disappear. The men now wanted ham sandwiches and tea and chocolate biscuits.

The new shop was almost ready; nothing had gone wrong. Two of the men were working on the sign, chipping at the stone over the storehouse door and window, drilling holes. Propped against the wall was the long white plastic sign with The Monument printed boldly in red.

'Wait till you see it in lights,' the boss said to her.

Nancy remained in the shadows, expecting at any moment a crowd to gather.

'Cheer up!' he said. 'It may never happen.'

'It'll happen all right,' Gerard interrupted. 'It'll happen at nine o'clock tonight.'

'Have you no homework?' she asked him, but they were suddenly both distracted by the putting up of the price list in the same brittle plastic as the sign over the door, listing what was available and how much it cost, information which Nancy had given the boss some days before.

'We'll light this too,' he said. 'And then these are the prices you told me but you can change the numbers easily. I'll leave you extra numbers. Now, before we go any further, I have two pieces of advice for you. The first is patience. Patience. The oil takes time and the chips take time and the batter takes time and the burgers take time.

The customer wants the stuff now and the smell of it cooking has his eyes watering and his tongue hanging out. Don't pay any attention to him, that's my advice to you, because he'll be the first to spread the news that the chips were raw and the batter was runny. So that's the first. And the second is this. When you put the bag of chips into the brown bag, throw in a few more chips, it'll cost you nothing but it'll look good, like value for money, and they'll all love you. Now they're two useful pieces of advice.'

'Do you charge for the ketchup?' Gerard asked.

'No,' he said. 'Salt, vinegar and ketchup are free.'

'What will we do if it breaks down?' Nancy asked.

'We're not leaving here without bringing a feast of chips with us to eat on the road. So it'll have to work. And you'd better start unfreezing the burgers. You don't want to be giving them indigestion.'

SHE CLOSED the supermarket one hour early at eight; Catherine went home, still having expressed no interest in what was happening next door. Her two daughters came downstairs just as the sign was being screwed into place over the door and the light behind it turned on. It was dark in the square now. She and Gerard and the girls and the boss crossed the street until they were standing close to the monument; she saw how bright and modern and clean her new chip shop was. As they stood there, the two girls who used to work in the supermarket arrived and they too gazed at the new chip shop.

The oil was already heating, the hamburgers and the fish

in batter were defrosting and the first plastic bag of ready-made frozen chips sat on the floor waiting until the moment when the oil was hot enough and they could be thrown in and fried. Nancy went upstairs and brought some cloths down and started to wipe every surface clean as the girls who had come to work cleaned the windows and Gerard swept the floor. They were open for business.

The boss had been right about the need for patience. He stood close to her as she threw the first bag in and watched her step back in fright as the uncooked chips hit the boiling oil in a great sizzle.

'Now,' he said, 'another golden rule. Watched chips never fry.'

'How long will they take?' Gerard asked.

'Fifteen minutes,' he said. 'No more, no less. And the fish is the same and the hamburger on the hotplate is the same.'

As the chips cooked, the men came one by one from the bathroom where they had washed themselves and shaved. Nancy had already paid the second instalment, but she had an envelope ready with a tip for each of the men.

'Well, there's one thing I've forgotten and you haven't noticed it's missing,' the boss said. 'So stop looking at the chips for a minute and think. Look around.'

They all looked around as the chips sizzled. Nancy could think of nothing.

'What if they order a lemonade or a Pepsi Cola? What will you do?'

'I have them in the fridge,' she said.

'Yes, but if you look at the list I gave you, it included a new machine for dispensing soft drinks. So where is it?'

'I don't know,' she said.

'I forgot it.' He laughed.

It was close to nine o'clock when she fished the first chips from the oil with the big new metal implement.

'You're an old hand already,' the boss said. 'It's like you were one of the Cafollas.'

She noticed that people passing began to stop and peer into the shop. As she filled the bags with chips and poured vinegar on them she saw Betty Farrell passing the window, gazing in her direction for a second and then walking away quickly. She recognized several others who paused at the window, but no one greeted her or came into the shop.

As soon as the fish and chips were ready and packaged the men made for the van and the car. She shook their hands and thanked them.

'Oh, it's a hug for me,' the boss said. He gave her a kiss on the cheek.

Nancy and Gerard and the girls waved at them as they set off for Dublin.

'You have that look on your face again,' Gerard said to her.

'What look?'

'You look like you're going to be arrested.'

THE FOLLOWING Wednesday the planning officer came and on Thursday she had a visit from the health officer. Both, she thought, behaved like greyhounds sniffing. Neither of them looked at her directly; as they spoke to her they peered at the ceiling, or the floor. The planning officer told her that she would have to close. There had been complaints, he said, but even if there hadn't been complaints, she had no permission to open a chip shop in the square. She could of course apply for permission but it would take time. In the meantime, she would have to cease trading. The health officer looked down into the freezer for a long time and smelled the oil and went on his way without saying anything.

Two days later, she received a letter from the health officer pointing out the breaches of the health regulations. That same morning, she opened a letter from the bank's solicitors initiating legal proceedings against her.

That evening she drove around the corner to the Irish Street, afraid that if she walked she would meet someone who would ask her about the chip shop, or complain about the litter. She knocked on Ned Doyle's door and, when his wife answered, she inspected Nancy slowly and cautiously.

'I don't know if he's here,' she said. 'I'll check. I think he went out.'

Nancy stared at her, stony-faced.

'I'll go and check,' she said.

Ned Doyle came out into the hallway in his stockinged feet, his shirt open a few buttons at the chest, his hair ruffled and an *Evening Press* in his hand.

'Oh, Nancy, you've caught me at a bad time now,' he said. 'But come in.'

He opened the door into a small carpeted front room whose table and sideboard were covered with boxes and papers.

'I won't keep you long, Ned,' she said.

Sweeping papers and brochures from an armchair, he motioned her to sit down. She wondered for a moment what to do, knowing that she would be able to explain to him better what she wanted while standing. Nonetheless, she sat down and he sat across the table from her on a hard chair.

'So you know why I'm here, Ned?'

'I do, Nancy. There's no point in saying I don't. There are a lot of complaints from the merchants in the Monument Square about noise and litter. And of course the regulations, there are all the regulations.'

She wished she were standing so she might be able to keep her eye fixed on him more keenly. She felt that she had no dignity sitting opposite him like this. All she could do was leave silence.

'I think it was ill advised, Nancy, opening the chip shop.'

She said nothing, but listened to the ticking of the clock on the mantelpiece. On the wall opposite there was a photograph of Ned shaking hands with de Valera.

'I would have thought,' he said, 'that George had left you comfortably off.'

'Is that right, Ned?'

'And you know a shop like that,' he looked worried for a moment and hesitated before he continued, 'a shop like that, selling chips after the pubs close, I'll put it to you this way, it wouldn't have been the sort of thing you'd associate with the Sheridans.'

'I'm not one of the Sheridans, Ned.'

'I'm not suggesting there's anything wrong with that, Nancy.'

'I know that, Ned,' she said, holding his gaze.

Again, there was silence between them, but she knew she must be the first to speak now, that she had forced him to avert his eyes. She sensed his regret at what he had said.

'So is that what Fianna Fáil does? Puts widows out of business?'

'Now, Nancy.' He put up his hand.

'Is that what it does, Ned?'

'Nancy, you opened without planning permission and you consulted nobody.'

'You'll have trouble if you try and close me down, Ned.'

'Nancy, it isn't up to us.'

'Oh, is it not? Who's the government, then? Who runs the county council and the urban district council?'

'You can't ride roughshod over the law, Nancy.'

'Can you not? What law gave the car park to Dunne's Stores? I'd say that took courage, Ned.'

She realized as soon as she said it that she had gone too far. He now had the advantage and he held it, nodding to himself silently, looking worried. The Sheridans had always supported Fine Gael; she knew that he knew that. He was aware of everyone's allegiance. But Fine Gael had no power now; all the power was in the hands of Fianna Fáil.

Quickly, she found the letters from the bank outlining the extent of her debts and the letter from the bank's solicitor threatening her. She handed them to him. He took his glasses from the breast pocket of his shirt and read the letters. Nancy, watching him, thought she was the same age as Ned; she remembered that he had left school when he was very young and wondered how he had managed to run Fianna Fáil in the town, becoming even more powerful than any of the elected politicians. For a second, she thought to ask George, who would always know these things, forgetting that he was dead.

'Oh, Nancy,' Ned said, 'how did you get yourself into this mess?'

'Look at the date of the first letter, Ned. George left only debts, and his mother was the one who signed the forms. So it was the Sheridans who left the mess. George left me with three children and huge debts.'

She had never thought of it as starkly before, but she knew now that the bluntness of her statement was more effective than tears.

'Are there no assets? No investments or savings?' Ned asked.

'Nothing, except what's in that letter.'

'You could sell.'

'The debt is more than the value of the property.'

'Yes, but since it's a debt to the bank, they would make a deal on it.'

'And what would I do then, Ned, where would I live?'

He handed her back the letters.

'So what do you want me to do?' he asked her.

'Tell them to back off.'

'Who?'

'Tell the planning man and the health man to leave me alone, and tell the merchants in the square, as you call them, the truth. Ask them if they would like to have me on the street, because that's where I'll be. Instead of the litter, it'll be me.'

'It's a lot to ask, Nancy,' he said.

She was on the point of telling him that it had been

done before, but she knew to say nothing now, play poor and humble.

'Well, I'm out on the side of the road with three children,' she said sadly.

'Give me a few days,' he said, 'but I can promise nothing. You should have consulted us before you opened.'

She could not contain herself.

'Sure I know what you would have said.'

She stood up.

When he opened the door for her, he hesitated in the hall for a moment.

'Still, despite all the troubles,' he said, 'the country's come far, haven't we, Nancy, I mean we've come a long way.'

This stayed in her mind for days as his way of saying that he would help her. The implication, she thought, was that Ned and she both had been born in houses which knew nothing about banks or solicitors or planning permissions, and now they were freely discussing these matters. This had to be progress, especially, she thought, if something could be arranged.

A WEEK LATER, he came to tell her that he could help her, but it would have to be done carefully and quietly. She was to apply for planning permission and, if it was refused, she was to appeal. It would take a long time, he said, but she would not be closed down. In return, she was to comply with all the health regulations. Again, she could move gradually, promising more each time. She must write immediately, he said, to the health officer announcing that she would comply with each and every one of his instructions. It would be a while before he came back, and bit by bit she could satisfy his demands. He was a difficult man, the health officer, Ned said.

That day she made a promise to herself that she would go and see Betty Farrell and apologize or explain. Several times Betty had passed the shop but not given her customary wave. Nancy did not need cheques cashed now, since, with the chip shop, she had plenty of cash, too much indeed for safety. She therefore made an appointment with the bank manager and, later that week, took with her in cash, when she went to see him, one month's payment on the loan, promising to pay the same each month until the debt was cleared. On the way across the square she had prepared a speech for Mr Wallace, planning to end by telling him that he could take it or leave it. Instead, his friendliness prevented her from making any speech at all, instead merely handing him the money, which included dirty and crumpled notes, watching him counting it, taking the receipt, shaking his hand and leaving.

SLOWLY, SHE LEARNED which opening hours were the most profitable, discovering that she could do business at lunchtime between twelve and two and then close until eight in the evening and stay open until the pubs shut, and later at the weekend. She wondered why no one knew how much money could be made from a chip shop, but she told no one, not even Birdseye, how high the profits were.

When she told him, instead, that the supermarket was a liability and she was going to close it, he asked her to wait.

He had another idea, he said, and he would come back to her when he had the detail worked out.

'You listened to me the last time,' he said, 'and if you have any sense you will listen to me again.'

When he came back the following week, he told her that she should close the supermarket and open a shop selling spirits, wine, beer, cigarettes and nothing else.

'I have wine here,' she said. 'No one ever looks at it, most of it is rancid it's been there so long. There's no trade in that at all.'

'That's the coming thing,' he said. 'People are going to start drinking wine and they're going to drink beer at home. You can take it from me.'

He sent her a friend of his, also from Waterford, who showed her the results of market research.

'Be the first in the town,' he said. 'Fill the window with wine and beer, with special offers, and they'll be in like flies. It'll beat selling corned beef and washing-up liquid. The profit margins are high if you get the right wholesaler. And it's a good clean business. And you don't have to open until eleven in the morning.'

Once more, she told no one except Nicole, Mags O'Connor's niece, whom she discovered was home for good. When she met her on the street, she said that she was closing the shop.

'Oh God, she's going to miss you now. She loves Friday, because that's the day you come.'

'Tell her I'll come out and see her,' she said. But she knew, as with her promise to herself to go and see Betty Farrell, that it was unlikely. By now, Betty and Jim Farrell had walked by her several times on the street without speaking to her.

Some of her suppliers had stopped delivering to her because she owed them too much money. She waited until a few days before she closed to tell the others. None of them would accept returns, so she arranged for Birdseye's friend to take the non-perishable goods for a knock-down price. And a week later, with some new shelving and brighter lights, installed by another friend of Birdseye's, she opened Sheridan's Off-Licence and filled the window with signs for special offers. Even in the first week, her turnover was higher. Catherine seemed to prefer her new merchandise. She had never tasted wine before, she said, but she liked the taste of it. The wholesaler had given her some free samples. One day when Nancy spoke to her, she almost smiled.

'Christmas,' Birdseye told them when he dropped in to see them, 'Christmas is when you'll clean up.'

BY THE END OF the summer Gerard realized how much money she was making. For most of his holidays he had run the lunchtime trade in the chip shop on his own, and he had come to understand, better than she did, what supplies were needed, how early to order them and how much they cost. While she kept all the figures in her head, and knew by the mounting cash in her chest of drawers how much money she was making, Gerard set about writing it all down, the daily income in seven neat vertical lines, and the weekly outgoings in wages, supplies and other costs. He continued this even after he went back to school.

'Do you pay tax on it all?' he asked. She told him that she did, although she had put no thought into paying tax. He frowned. The following day he came back to her and said, in the voice of his father, that he had made enquiries and she should get an accountant. He had been told, he said, that Frank Wadding was the man. He would do her taxes for her.

'Who did you make enquiries from?' she asked. 'I hope you're not telling anyone our business.'

'I asked questions, that's all. I told no one anything.'

'Who did you ask?'

'Someone who might know.'

Since he had begun to deal with the cash, he quickly noticed that when she had paid the bank and the Credit Union their monthly payments, a large amount of money was missing. That day when he came to her, his tone almost accusing, she regretted having given him so much responsibility. She had no choice now but to tell him that the building in which they lived and did business was re-mortgaged and that they were, despite the money they were making now, heavily in debt. When he asked her for precise figures, she realized that he had completely ignored the story of what she had been through, and the effort she had made. He was busy counting.

THE ACCOUNTANT'S desk was too big for him; he wrote down every figure on a notepad, and then considered it all in silence, nodding like an old man.

'Some things are clear anyway,' he said eventually. 'The loans will have to be restructured so that the interest can be offset against tax, and you'll have to set up a limited company and pay yourself a salary. And you'd better get that cash out of the house as fast as possible.'

He wrote these points down as soon as he mentioned them.

'And we'll need to keep in close touch, say once a week, for the next few months so that all your accounting procedures can be put in order. You have, on the face of it here, a very valuable business.'

THE GIRLS TOOK no interest in either the off-licence or the chip shop; Gerard's interest in both was so intense that Nancy had to ban him working in the chip shop, except on Saturdays, during term time. But since his grasp of the figures was better than hers, his weekly accounts meticulously kept, she let him prepare the figures for the accountant and deal with the bank, much to Mr Wallace's delight.

'That Gerard of yours,' he said to her one day when he met her in the square, 'will be a millionaire before he is twenty-one.'

When she asked him for a chequebook at their next meeting he immediately agreed.

Her main business was on weekend nights. When the pubs and the disco closed they were three or four deep waiting for fish and chips and burgers. She worked as hard herself as the two girls she employed, and no matter how drunk or impatient her customers were, she remained polite and friendly. She loved taking money from them, loving handling the coins and notes, and this was something she had never once felt in the supermarket, the zeal surrounding the cash register. Some of them were rowdy, and others so drunk that they were either going to abandon the fish and chips on some window ledge or vomit in the Monument Square. She took their money and smiled at them.

When the complaints persisted about the litter and the vomit, she made a point of cleaning up the Monument Square herself once the chip shop had been closed, moving around with a box for the litter and later with a bucket of soapy water and a brush for the vomit. Even though she did this quietly at three in the morning, everyone on the square got to know about it, and she learned that some of them were sorry that they had said anything.

Slowly, people in the square, those who owned shops, began to understand how well she was doing. And word got around too, with the help of Ned Doyle she believed, how much debt she had inherited. They stopped complaining about the litter. Ned Doyle called by one day and told her that she had everyone's admiration for keeping the business going for Gerard.

When she watched Gerard working in the chip shop on a Saturday, or keeping the accounts, she realized that he presumed he would be taking over the business in time, just as his own father had taken over the business from his grandmother. This explained, she thought, why his Christmas report had a complaint about him from each teacher. He believed that he did not have to bother paying attention in anyone's class.

She was sorry now that she had not told Gerard from the very beginning what her plan was, what came to the front of her mind every time she tapped the cash register in the chip shop or banked the takings from the off-licence.

All her life she had been on display like this; from the time of her mother's small shop people had been able to gawk at her as much as they liked, or look past her. She dreamed now of Dublin, the long roads with trees on the sides and house after house almost hidden. In Goatstown and Stillorgan and Booterstown, there were people who lived in houses and no one greeted them with a mixture of familiarity and curiosity every time they went outside their own door. No one knew all about them, no one felt free to waylay them to stop and talk. They were just normal people who lived in houses. And that was what she wanted, that was why she was working, to become like them. To pay off her debts and save enough money and then sell up, and go to Dublin where no one would know anything about her, where she and Gerard and the girls would be just people in a house. She dreamed of a life in the future in which no one could stand in front of her with money in their hand and command her attention.

When, after Christmas, she travelled to Dublin with the girls so they could take advantage of the sales and spend the day wandering between Switzer's and Brown Thomas, she noticed that they had both grown taller and needed bigger sizes in everything. She was surprised by the suddenness of this, as though it had happened on the way to the city in the car. As they appeared from the fitting room wearing new clothes and she complimented them and made them turn and examined the prices and the reductions, she realized that she had not looked at her daughters in six months. She wondered if, when she went home, she would find that Gerard too had grown without her noticing.

Gerard remained steadfast in his determination not to

study, despite the curfew she placed on him and the banning of him from even appearing in the chip shop. He had not grown, but had developed a walk of his own, a sloping, confident walk performed best when he had his hands in his pockets. He began to speak to people, including people three times his age, in an almost cheeky and quite familiar way. She felt a great tenderness for him as she watched him trying to become a figure about the town.

She tried to have a normal dinner ready for the children when they came home at one o'clock, leaving the girls she employed to work in the chip shop, making an appearance there only when the children had gone back to school. The problem was what to do after three o'clock. She was never needed in the off-licence, where Catherine was slowly getting to know some of the wines; she was often to be found smelling the wines and rolling a small amount around in the bottom of a glass. With the wholesalers, Catherine organized a wine-tasting course in the hotel which had become very popular. With Nancy, she only wanted to talk about a new variety of French wine which had arrived, or the inferiority, in her opinion, of Blue Nun. Nancy grew weary of her, but increased her salary as sales went up.

Thus she went to bed in the afternoon. And her sleep, she thought, must be as deep as the sleep of the dead, heavy and dreamless. When she heard the children coming in from school, she made a promise to herself that she would sleep for half an hour more, but not any longer. Even as spring came, however, she found that she was in bed until six o'clock and still found it hard to shed the sheer pleasurable heaviness of the few hours of oblivion she had just experienced. She hated opening the chip shop again at eight, and found the weekends almost unbearable. The thought of the money, however, kept her going.

Frank Wadding the accountant continued to advise her, noting a rise in profits in the off-licence and a steady income from the chip shop, enough, he said, for her to have her debts cleared in two years, enough also, he added, for both businesses to be very valuable were she ever to sell them or borrow on the strength of them. When she asked him precisely how much they were worth, he hesitated and said he could not put an exact figure on them, but when she pressed him, he gave her a rough estimate. She realized that, were she to sell the business, she would be able to pay the bank and the Credit Union off and buy a house in Dublin without having to work another day.

AT THE END OF the next summer holidays, which Gerard had spent in the off-licence when Catherine was away, and then in the chip shop when the girls who were working there took holidays, Gerard had, with Frank Wadding, worked out a more elaborate accounting system to avoid tax and a more efficient way of dealing with cash. As he was going back to school, Nancy suggested to him that he should aim towards accountancy. He shrugged and said he knew as much about accountancy as he ever wanted to.

It was strange, she thought, how little George ever entered their conversation now. Just over a year ago she knew that every single person who saw her pitied her, sometimes avoiding her so they would not have to sympathize with her one more time, or sometimes crossing the street to shake her hand and ask her meaningfully how she was. Now, she was the woman with the chip shop and the off-licence and the new car and the smart clothes. Her two daughters could have anything they wanted, and her son, even though he was only sixteen, had begun to wear suits.

But despite the money, nothing could be done about the smell of cooking oil all over the house, right up to the bedrooms. She did everything, she put in new fans, she put a new door at the bottom of the stairs, she had the whole house repainted. When she complained to Birdseye, who took a continued interest in her welfare, he told her it was a small price to pay. But when the girls began to smell their clothes before they went to school and would only wear freshly dry-cleaned clothes when going out with their friends, it became a serious matter.

It was Gerard who alerted her, almost proudly, to the news that the girls were called Chips by their colleagues in school, and by the boys in his school. When she asked them about it, the girls blushed and said nothing, blaming Gerard for telling her. They said it was hard to smell the cooking oil themselves, but everyone else could. When Nancy asked them if they minded this, they shrugged. It was clear to her that they were mortified by it.

In her mind, she had already sold both businesses and the house above them. She had paid off her debts and bought a house in Booterstown where no one knew them and where no cooking oil would ever be used. She would have a garden with roses and lavender, she thought. All she was doing now was saving money; every penny made would be put in the bank and would get them through a year or two or maybe more until she found a job.

In November, Gerard arrived home one mid-morning as Nancy was dealing with supplies on the telephone. He was wearing a suit and looked much older than his years. He put his school-bag down.

'I won't be needing that anymore. I told Mooney to fuck off and then they called Brother Delaney and I told him to fuck off. I told them all to fuck off. You can expect a visit from them, but I'm not going back, that's the end of it.'

She saw that he was close to tears.

'Gerard, you are going back to school,' she said. 'And I don't want to hear any more bad language in this house.'

'Sure, isn't that all we hear every night of the week?'

'Yes, and it's paying for your education, but I still don't want any coarse language in this house.'

'Some education!' he said.

'Well, if you want to go to boarding school, you can do that, but you're going somewhere.'

'I'm not. I'm finished with school.'

Suddenly, he had become brave.

'Well, you needn't think you are working here. This is my business and I'm not having you.'

'You can't run it without me,' he said.

'Watch me, watch me,' she said.

IN THE END Gerard apologized to the school and over the next few months an uneasy peace reigned, interrupted only by his Christmas report, almost worse than the previous year.

'Aren't you lucky to have him?' Birdseye said when he called. 'He'll make a great fist of the business. It's in the blood. I remember his grandmother here, she was a real businesswoman. And you'll be able to put your feet up, take holidays and everything.'

She imagined herself trapped, an old woman fussing in the shop where she was not wanted. Or stuck in a bungalow out the country, a little car on the tarmac drive, with nothing to do all day as Gerard, married now and with responsibilities, egged on by his wife, explained to her that he would need the business made over to him if he were going to stay there. She thought that the smell of cooking oil would follow her into the grave.

All over the town it had happened, businesses being passed on from generation to generation, the sons, as soon as they went to school, fully sure of their inheritance. They learned to stand behind a counter with no nervousness or timidity, to open their shop in the morning with ease and pride. In their late teens, they settled into the rhythms of middle age.

She noticed that Gerard had dropped most of his school-friends and this seemed to have made him more cheerful, almost hearty. What he loved more than anything was meeting one of the other shop-owners from the town and stopping to talk with them, making jokes, exchanging banter, or discussing a new development or a piece of news. She knew that the personality he displayed was brittle and invented. It would slowly harden; over a number of years he would grow into himself.

She watched him. From her bedroom window in a late spring afternoon she found herself taking him in as he moved from the shop, where he had dropped his school-bag, across the square, smiling at everyone. He was open and friendly, at home here. She noticed Dan Gifford coming out of his electrical shop; she observed Gerard spotting him too, and making a beeline over to him. As the two of them started to talk and laugh, she saw Gerard putting his hands in his pocket and sticking out his belly. The expression on his face was knowing and comfortable, mildly amused.

As she began to dress herself and prepare for the evening's work, she knew that this next battle would be the hardest, but she had no doubt about her own determination. Within a month or two, she would have a For Sale sign placed on her property in the Monument Square. She was ready, she thought, for a new beginning.

ONE SATURDAY, before things became busy in the chip shop, she told the three children that she was selling and they were moving to Dublin. She tried not to be too precise about when they would sell, or when they might go to Dublin, but she made sure to say that they would all have to go to new schools, which, she hoped, might make them understand that this was real. The girls asked various questions about where they would live and what they would do. She tried to be very direct with them so they would believe that she had everything worked out. Gerard's face grew red, but he did not speak. Later, when he came to help out in the shop, he behaved as though nothing unusual had happened.

The girls made jokes about the move, and asked further questions over the weeks that followed. They found out about schools and even wrote to one girls' school and received a brochure in the post. Gerard did not mention it, and grew grimly silent if the subject were raised in his presence. Nancy realized that he had told no one because he had no one to tell as he was no longer very friendly with any of his schoolmates and he was not close enough to any of the businessmen in the town to whom he looked up so much.

She saw Frank Wadding a few times and left him in charge of getting the right auctioneer to come to value the house. She was glad that the visit happened while Gerard was at school, but she knew also that it might have been better had she confronted Gerard with the auctioneer taking measurements of the rooms in the house. That evening, as they were eating, she found that she could not tell them that the auctioneer had been. It would be a way of torturing Gerard, she thought, who was still behaving as though the plans to move from the town to Dublin did not exist.

One Saturday a few weeks later, she knew as soon as he came into the house that someone had told him that she was definitely selling the business. He seemed on the verge of tears, he hardly ate anything. All his swagger was missing. He left the table early. When she was alone in the kitchen, the girls having gone to their bedroom, he came to the door and hovered just inside the room.

'I won't be able to work in the shop tonight,' he said in a low voice.

'That's fine, Gerard.' She turned and smiled at him. 'There'll be the two girls and myself, so it'll be enough.'

He had never before missed a night when he had arranged to work.

'They're all talking about us selling,' he said.

'Is that right?'

'I thought you were joking, just talking about selling up as a way of making us study harder, especially me,' he said. 'Making me feel that the business wouldn't be here for me to fall into. I didn't think you were serious.'

'Who is talking about us selling?' she asked.

'I met a whole load of fellows, they were after being in the pub. "Your old lady is selling up," one of them, that fellow Fonsey Nolan kept roaring. "You'll be paying for chips yourself from now on."'

'Don't mind him,' she said.

'Why would we go to Dublin? Why are we moving?' he asked.

'I think it's a better place to live where you won't get accosted like that by a group of eejits,' she said. 'And there are more opportunities there, for all of us.'

'Not for me,' he said. 'There's nothing there for me. I thought you were joking.'

'You didn't really,' she said. 'You're just saying that.'

'What are we going to do there?' he asked.

'You are going to get a good Leaving Cert, and so are the girls, and all three of you are going to go to university and I am going to get a job.'

'I haven't the slightest intention of going to university,' he said.

'It will be a great chance for you,' she said.

'Did you not hear what I said?' he asked. 'I haven't the smallest intention of going to university. I hate studying. So what about that?'

'We'll see,' she said.

'We won't see,' he replied.

'You can't work here all your life,' she said. 'It's not a business for anyone your age. You have to go to other places, see the world a bit.'

'And have nothing to come back to?'

'When you're older you'll be grateful for this,' she said.

'Well, I can tell you now that I will never be grateful. I can guarantee you that now. Grateful that I'm going to belong nowhere, have nowhere, have nothing? That's a good one, all right!'

He was still close to tears.

'Anyway,' he continued, 'it isn't yours to sell. It was left to us.'

'Oh, it's mine all right,' she said.

'My father . . .' he began.

'Don't start that,' she said. 'Don't start that, Gerard.'

'If Daddy knew what you were doing.'

'I said, don't start.'

'God, he'll be looking down on us now!' he said.

'I have to go and work,' she said.

'God, if Daddy saw you now!' he said.

She walked by him and found the two girls who worked in the chip shop already there, the first oil of the evening almost hot. She told them she would be back in a while and walked out into the square.

At first she did not know where she was going. Most of the shops were closing, and the traffic was slow. She found herself moving from window to window of every shop, at first examining what was for sale as a way to distract herself, but then, more than anything, noticing her own reflection in the windows, different each time, depending on whether the shop window was lit or dark. She looked at herself as though a stranger, someone gazing back at her, neither sympathetic nor glad to see her, almost hostile. That look calmed her down, but she still carried on from window to window, the clothes shop, the butcher's, the newsagent's, all the familiar places, her face, familiar too, growing softer, more relaxed in each reflection. She would walk around the town, she thought, as if she might never get the chance again. And on Monday she would have the sign put up saying that the business was for sale. She was safe, she thought. She could go home now and begin the night's work. It would, she imagined, be a busy night, especially later. She would need all her energy.

Famous Blue Raincoat

LISA NOTICED THAT one of the boxes of old records in the corner of the garage had been moved to the side, leaving a square of light-coloured cement. She asked Ted if he had touched the records but he shrugged and said that he had forgotten the boxes were even there.

'They're no use anyway,' he said. 'The needle on the player is blunt and I don't think it can be replaced.'

'It doesn't matter,' she said.

When Luke came home from school she thought of asking him if he knew about the box, but he was difficult sometimes if he felt that he were being criticized or accused of something, so she did not mention it. She put the box back where it had been and then was busy for days in the dark room developing old negatives for the new scanner which had been set up for her in the spare room. Soon, she thought, this liquid and this old process would be obsolete, this dark and concentrated space would no longer be her domain, and she would have to live in brightness. She hoped to postpone that day for as long as she could.

She worked now for the Employers' Union when they needed press conferences and functions photographed, but she was best known for her work from the folk boom and the early days of Dublin rock; her photographs of Geldof as a wild young star and, later, of Bono as a raw and beautiful teenager still appeared regularly in magazines all over the world.

DAYS LATER, she noticed that some records had been taken from the box and left to the side. It was then that Ted told her that Luke and a friend had begun to burn CDs so perhaps they had taken some old records for their project. She smiled to herself at the parallel currents in the house, records being put on CD, negatives on disc. The idea would horrify Luke since he did nothing at anyone else's prompting and followed no one's example, least of all that of his mother who, at more than fifty years old, must seem, she thought, like an old woman to him. Later, when she remembered the records, she went into the garage and examined the old boxes, flicking through the records which Luke had put aside, wondering for a second why he had removed so few, leaving old classics untouched. She stood up, however, when she realized what was missing from the boxes and from the pile he had put aside, what he must have been looking for. She shuddered and turned away.

When Luke had gone to bed, she told Ted that she had found the three albums in his room, the ones he had taken from the box, with her photograph and that of her sister on the first and the whole band, all four of them, on the other two. The years when she toured and sang with the band and made the three albums were seldom mentioned between them, so that even she herself had come to half-believe that she had only taken photographs during that time. It was easy, she knew, even in Dublin, to become someone else, to move to the suburbs and see no one from her life as a singer, except in a bus queue or at the airport or at a parent–teacher meeting, and it was easy to wave and smile and pretend that too much time had passed for any of the intimacies or friendships of the old days to matter or mean anything.

Ted viewed the world with tolerance and mildness. He disliked trouble as others might dislike a bad smell or a sharp pain. She knew that he would smile and nod were she to tell him that she did not want to hear her own voice or that of her sister, nor to hear the band again, if she could help it. And therefore they would have to find a way to explain to Luke that he could burn whatever songs he pleased from the boxes of LPs, except songs from the band of which his mother had been a member.

'When you explain it to him,' Ted said, 'maybe you'll explain it to me too.'

'You understand it perfectly,' she said.

'We can't just tell him to put the records back,' he replied.

WHEN ON Saturday morning Luke came to her to look for money, she spent a long time searching for her bag and fumbling with her purse. She thought of giving him more than usual as a way of making him listen to her without becoming upset, but she realized that would be a mistake. She asked him if he had listened to the albums.

'They're amazing,' he said. 'I can fit them on two CDs.'

His expression, when he spoke, was bright and innocent.

'Ian Redmond's dad has one of them, so I've heard that loads of times, but I've never heard the others.'

'You never mentioned that to me,' she said.

'Dad said you were embarrassed about them, but there's no reason to be, although the sound on the first one is pretty poxy. You know you weren't bad.'

'It's nice of you to say so.'

'I mean it. You weren't Janis Joplin or anything, but it was original. I mean, for the time.'

'Thanks, Luke.'

'I don't know why you stopped,' he said.

'To have you, Luke,' she replied.

'No, no,' he said. 'I checked the dates. You stopped long before you had me.'

She faced him for a second, holding his gaze, which had become, as he spoke, more masculine and confident. She handed him a twenty-euro note.

'Thanks,' he said, 'I'll have the CDs ready next weekend when Ian's dad lets us use his burner.'

'I don't think I want to hear them, Luke.'

'You weren't that bad. I promise. You should hear some of the other stuff Ian's dad plays, like the Irish Rovers and the Wolfe Tones.'

He smiled at her and took his coat and left the house, shouting a last farewell as he shut the door.

THE BAND HAD one great season, and there was no recording of that, she thought; there might be photographs which could show how young and happy they were, and some memories of people who had been in the audience.

The band, one reviewer had commented in the year when they arrived on the English scene, were better than Pentangle, as good as Steeleye Span and on the way to outreaching Fairport Convention. This came to be a mantra for them, something which made them laugh. Dinners, roadies and English towns all came to be graded in similar terms. They had played support for all of these groups, and Lisa remembered with fondness the time when one of their roadies had been her boyfriend. Slowly, however, they had begun to top the bill and the album they could have made at the end of that first touring season would have been their best, she thought, could have made their name. If someone had recorded them live in the spring and summer of 1973, she thought, the record would have embarrassed no one.

They began in Dublin as two sisters singing, Julie with the deep voice and deep feeling, Lisa with a thinner, reedier voice, depending always on her sister's guidance despite a larger range and flexibility, a more sparkling musical intelligence. It was strange how different they were, how Julie held herself apart, hating the flirting and easy association; she became skilled at disappearing to her room once the real energy of the night filled the rest of them with longing.

Julie was hard-headed about money; later, when the band was formed, she planned the tours and worked out the costs; she was ambitious; she held grudges. Lisa, just two years younger, took everything lightly. She did not suffer much from period pains or the monthly tensions which were capable of reducing Julie to real depression and irritability, even sudden changes in the timbre of her voice.

It was Julie who went in search of the two male singers, dragging her sister to clubs and pubs where music was played, watching the young musicians as an expert on bloodstock would watch a horse race. Julie did not know what she was looking for, but not glamour, she explained, no pretty boys allowed, no white polo necks, or guys smelling of Brut, and no smilers either, she added.

'I don't mind even if they're smelly,' she said. 'We'll deal easily with that.'

Phil, the first new member of the band, was obvious. He was from a family of musicians; at twenty-one, he seemed to know an infinite number of songs and variations of songs. His voice was not great, but his guitar-playing was agile and original. He had, they realized, a way of changing a song, moving a tempo, varying a chord, and he could work with their voices as an arranger, and he knew more about systems of recording than anyone else they had met. But it was his shoes that decided Julie. It was clear that he had owned them, and no other pair, for years, but he had never, it appeared, bothered to polish them.

Shane, the second new member, who would complete the band, was unlikely. He was Northern. His accent, Julie said, was repulsive. He hated folk music, he said, but loved jazz and blues. He only hung around the folk venues, he said, because he liked drinking. His voice was high, he could sing in Irish, he played the mandolin and the bou-zouki, although he claimed to despise both of them. He made no effort to charm the sisters, although he wanted the job, and that was almost enough for Julie. She insisted that it was his greasy hair and scruffy clothes which helped make up her mind. At their first rehearsal Shane informed the other three that he was in the band to combat their tendency to sing like Peter, Paul and Mary.

They began to work in an upstairs room off Molesworth Street. The two new members liked each other, but they talked only music, trying out introductions, choosing songs, fixing beats and tempos as though Julie and Lisa were not there, and then slowly setting things up for the sisters so that everything in the end led to their voices. All four of them drank afterwards in Kehoe's or the Lincoln, but never for long. The boys always had somewhere else to go. In those early months as they prepared for their first concert and first recording, they did not become friends.

Julie and Lisa worked out their harmonies by instinct, from trial and error. Although they both had taken piano lessons and been taught the rudiments of music theory, they used none of that in their singing. Now they watched as their two new colleagues had a name for everything as they arranged a set of songs. Shane turned out to know intimately an entire body of work he still insisted he despised – the songs of Tim Hardin, Tom Paxton, Joni Mitchell and Leonard Cohen. Sometimes he would take one of Cohen's more doleful tunes, or one of Joni Mitchell's sillier songs, and exaggerate their worst qualities to the accompaniment of a mandolin.

Then it turned out he also knew classical music.

'It was the Brits,' he said in an even more pronounced Northern accent than usual. 'They taught us everything we knew. You folks in the Free State don't know nothin'.'

They found him strumming a tune on his mandolin, making it slow and melancholy and then fast. It was a melody they did not recognize. They stopped and watched him as he sat hunched on the chair, alert to the fact that he was performing now, offering sudden variations, but coming back all the time to the slow haunting melody they had heard at the beginning.

'It's just a wee tune,' he said and put the mandolin away.

'We know that,' Julie said, 'but what is it?'

'Just a song I picked up.'

'With words?'

He glanced up at her, serious.

'You want me to sing it?'

'That's what we pay you for,' Julie said.

Lisa and Phil stood back as Shane began to strum again, this time with more uncertainty, seeming to try out a number of keys and different ways into the melody. Then he started to sing, and the song, Lisa, realized, was a classical song.

It was only in the second verse that he moved out of a classical mode, stopped sounding like an altar boy and began to riff on the melody, singing in an American accent, his tone slow and dark like a blues singer. Sometimes the mandolin failed him and he stopped playing; other times he had stretched the tune too far and he stopped singing and tried to recapture the melody on the instrument.

'Can you give me the mandolin,' Phil asked, 'and you try it on the guitar?'

Shane nodded and handed him the mandolin, crossing the room to fetch the guitar which he set to tune. By the time he was ready, Phil was playing the exact melody, but had somehow, in a way that Lisa did not understand, made it sound like an Irish tune. They began to work together, finding a key and watching each other at intervals as they strove to find a tempo. Shane, once more, started to sing, this time more simply, as if he meant the words.

'Who wrote the song?' Julie asked, when they had finished.

'Handel,' Shane said.

'As in Handel's *Messiah*?' Julie asked.

'Yeah.'

'He's dead and he has no live relatives,' Phil said, 'so he won't mind us making a pig's mickey out of his song.'

THIS WAS THE SONG they sang on *The Late Late Show*; it became their signature tune. For the first album they added new versions of Irish songs and Irish versions of modern songs, including a rendition in four-part harmony of 'Lady Madonna'. For their second album they signed with a small British record company. The sound they made was new but closer to what was happening in England than in Ireland, where their work was too hybrid to be respectable and not hip enough to be very popular. So they played the clubs in England, turning up where they were asked, travelling the motorways and staying in cheap hotels. After the first six months, Julie agreed that they could share the takings, and that future decisions could be made by all four of them, at least in theory. In practice, everything was decided by Julie and Phil.

Most of the time they sang into one microphone. They were utterly dependent on each other when they stood on the stage, and, even though the music was rehearsed, in order to have any life it had to allow for chance. They each had to concentrate fiercely, listen with care and be ready to respond. Usually, they were led by Julie's moods, because Julie's voice was the strongest, it was often what people came to hear. Lisa never minded how little she herself was noticed. When they found a solo song for her, she was uneasy about taking the limelight, always glad when it was over.

Phil was more stable than Shane, had no temper they ever saw, his moods never changed. A girlfriend appeared regularly, she was from near his home town. He never mentioned her, but paid her complete attention even in the hard hours after a concert when there was much distraction. Shane, it seemed to Lisa, fell in and out of love with girls who already had boyfriends or were married or were unavailable. One or two of them enjoyed backstage and the parties, but appeared to find the prospect of being alone with Shane less enticing. Shane's troughs in love were like Julie's periods, they were picked up by the microphone, they immediately were relayed to the other singers who had to compensate, or else they could appear as brilliant riffs or changes in register, which the others would have to follow.

Once their second, more sophisticated album was released, small success beckoned. They were almost fashionable, especially their songs in Irish which, Lisa remembered, English audiences seemed to love. They were called a contemporary band rather than a folk group. Even John Peel approved of them and played a track from their album a few Saturdays. Alan Price played a single from it on his show. They had cult status, but there was always the possibility that they could become popular. It would take the right song, some luck, and, it was suggested, a manager, but Lisa always knew that Julie would not be able to work with a manager.

The song that nearly made them stars was the one that

Shane detested above all. It was Leonard Cohen's 'Famous Blue Raincoat'. No one at that time, Lisa remembered, had noticed the song much or made cover recordings of it. Phil and Shane, despite Shane's hatred for manufactured sadness, as he called it, worked at isolating the melody, discovered that by leaving some parts bare and unadorned and filling other parts with voices, echoes, instruments and harmonies, the song could be made very powerful. For once they had a good recording studio and a sound engineer who liked their work.

Lisa was surprised the first day when Julie asked them if she could sing it alone, without any flourishes or accompaniment, and if they could record her first take. Phil and Shane were impatient, they had worked out where to put the emotion and when to pull back, they were busy making a map of the song and they did not want Julie to sing until they were ready. She still wanted to do it now.

Lisa had never, until that morning, stood back and observed her sister. But as Julie began to sing, she demanded full attention. She put no effort into the melody at all, instead she concentrated on the words, using her voice at its huskiest, the voice of a woman who has been up all night smoking and drinking. Lisa loved how she sang it, wished her sister would let her in on one of the verses to accompany her in a light harmony. She could see, however, that Shane was irritated by the unaffected display of emotion. When it was over, Phil walked across the studio and stood in front of Julie and bowed. It was, Lisa thought, the best piece of singing Julie had ever done and it was recorded that morning, even played back a couple of times over the next few days; but it was never released. Lisa wondered if, more than thirty years later, it lay in some dusty archive of out-takes and unrecorded reels made by long-forgotten singers, but she supposed it would have been thrown out as the new technology took over and the band's small fame faded to nothing.

Phil and Shane decided that only Julie and Lisa would sing on the track, working on many takes of Julie opening the song, using echo effects and laying down track over track so that at times she sang alone and unaccompanied and at other times in many layers to the accompaniment of her sister, a cello, a saxophone and a mandolin. They asked Lisa to go through the whole song singing with Julie but at the same pitch using a separate microphone. She found it almost impossible not to harmonize, she had to let Julie guide her, pull her along like a small boat. When she had finished, they told her that they had, in fact, recorded only her, and for one of the verses they were going to cut between the two singers. When she went to listen to the tape, she was amazed at how close her voice was to her sister's, almost as deep and strong in certain sections.

The track they made was seven minutes long, twice the length of a normal single. Because the band was winning the confidence of the label, and because Sandy Denny had built up a following and Fairport Convention had had a hit with 'Si Tu Dois Partir', it was agreed that it could be released with an Irish song performed by all four of them on the other side. No one expected much radio play; instead, they hoped that a new tour with Martin Carthy as support might help the sales.

Lisa remembered that they were somewhere in the north of England when they were told what John Peel had said about their new recording. He introduced them as a cutting-edge acoustic band, brave enough to release a seven-minute single, making a new sound. He made them seem almost hip and counter-culture. And then the following week 'Famous Blue Raincoat' was played just after midnight on Radio Luxembourg. A week later, their single was hovering outside the Top Fifty. It began to be played on Radio 1, mostly being faded out after the first three minutes.

On one of those nights when their single was in the Top Thirty, two men from a small independent record company and an American journalist came to a packed-out concert in Glasgow and appeared backstage later. For the rest of the tour Shane did imitations of them offering an instant contract and top billing with the Rolling Stones as support.

'You want Carnegie Hall? We get you Carnegie Hall. You wanna make an album with Jackie Kennedy? We fly her in. You wanna be more famous than Jesus Christ? You wanna meet Peter, Paul and Mary?'

He could not be stopped.

Instead of offering a contract, however, or wishing to talk business, they came backstage looking for sex, it seemed to Lisa. At least one of them did, making suggestions to her about where they might go once they had had a few drinks. She told him Phil was her boyfriend. When he asked if Julie were attached to Shane, she laughed in his face and said she did not think so.

They never saw the executives again. It was the journalist, edgy, talkative and knowledgeable about the business, who turned up in London as soon as they were back there; he wanted to attend one of their recording sessions to write a long article about them which he would sell, he said, to a magazine back home. His name was Matt Hall. He did not have a sense of humour; he was skilled at displaying resentment when he thought he was being mocked or ignored. Since Shane mocked him half the time and the others ignored him when they could, he had many opportunities to show how he felt, his face pale, his brow furrowed, his broad frame almost threatening. He would stand alone, deep in thought, his eyes fixed on a point on the ground.

In the weeks when 'Famous Blue Raincoat' failed to make the Top Twenty and then stopped receiving radio play, Matt did not disappear as they hoped he would. He waited, Lisa thought, to be sneered at by Shane and spent much of his time in their company in a sort of seething silence. Slowly, he stopped mentioning the magazine article he was meant to be writing. His presence, it seemed to Lisa, made all of them uncomfortable, yet so apparent was Matt's vulnerability that none of them had the courage to tell him to go.

Lisa remembered a concert they played in the Gaiety in Dublin during this time. It was a fund-raiser for something, with six or seven bands playing. She had her camera with her, had been photographing Planxty, and was standing in the wings watching Tríona and Maighread Ni Dhomhnaill. As she moved backwards, searching for a chair, she noticed a figure behind her on the other side of the green-room door where heavy curtains hung. As the figure stepped into the light for a moment, she saw that it was Julie, whom she had thought was in the bar, and Julie was smiling at someone in a way that Lisa had never seen before. The smile was shy and girlish and unselfconscious as Julie retreated into the shadows to embrace whoever she was with. Lisa realized that, since she herself stood in darkness, she could not be seen. Julie's smile, it appeared to her, as she had watched her, had an edge of gratitude to it, almost simpering in a way which Julie hated in other women.

It was clear to Lisa that the person Julie was with had won her affection and this brought with it not only shock and surprise but also a sharp dart of painful jealousy. Suddenly, then, a burst of applause began, and this caused Julie and Matt Hall to move into the faint light of backstage where they could both be seen.

As soon as they had returned to London to work on the new album, with Matt Hall never absent, it occurred to Lisa that Phil had known about Matt and Julie for some time. He took Matt's presence for granted, listened to him when he intervened and nodded when he made suggestions. No one, however, seemed to have told Shane; he responded to the American with blunt incomprehension and rudeness when he came into the studio with a list of songs they should record – more up-tempo material, as he put it – which were essentially, Lisa thought, three-minute pop songs which might suit Julie's voice. It was obvious to Lisa that when Julie suggested they should bring in some session musicians, including a drummer, the idea had come from Matt.

One morning Matt and Julie arrived in the studio with two new songs. They were by one of the up-and-coming new American songwriters, Matt said, who had heard the band's last album, loved it, and was ready to grant them exclusive rights to both songs. He passed the sheets around with the lyrics and the music. As Julie began to sing the lyrics Lisa realized that she knew them by heart. The tune, Lisa thought, was banal and derivative. When Julie had finished singing, Shane stood up.

'The words are cat,' he said. 'I think your friend, the American songwriter, is a bit of an eejit, Matt. What do you think?'

'I think it'll sound different when we've heard it properly arranged,' Matt said, his face already pale.

'Well, you can arrange it yourself, then,' Shane said.

'We will do just that,' Matt said.

'Let's give it a chance,' Julie said. 'We need a few contemporary songs on the album.'

Lisa noticed that Phil was sitting quietly watching Julie. Later, he told Lisa he knew at that moment that the band would break up. He did not intervene, and it was his silence as much as the determination of her sister and Matt which allowed the track to appear on the album, complete with drums and upbeat arrangement and Julie trying to sound like an American rock singer and Lisa tagging along with an equally fake accent. Luke, she thought, could be burning that too, and he would be right to feel that it might embarrass her. If he went to the album sleeve he would notice that the song was composed by Matt Hall, who had told them, when the copyright for the songs was being checked out, that he himself was, in fact, the talented young writer who admired the band and wanted it to be the first to record his songs.

One day on the tour to promote the album, as Shane became increasingly demented by Matt's gradual gaining of influence over the band, Lisa had lunch alone with Julie. They must have been waiting for the others, because Lisa remembered they had more time than usual. It was a while since they had been together for so long. Julie eventually asked her why she had never said anything about Matt.

'I take it you don't like him,' she said.

'Well, *you* like him, that's the main thing, isn't it?' Lisa said.

'Hey, I asked you.'

'I don't know,' Lisa said.

'This is serious,' Julie said. 'Tell me what you think.'

'I feel he's put you in a sort of cage.' As she watched her sister colour, Lisa instantly regretted the remark.

'I love him.'

'I hope he doesn't cause you trouble,' Lisa said.

'If he does,' Julie said, staring directly at her, 'you will be the last to find out.'

As the tour progressed, relations between the five of them were not improved by a number of reviews, both of the concerts and of the album, which suggested a turn towards commercialism, giving Shane more ammunition to fire in the direction of both Matt and Julie. On the last night of the tour, when the lights went down on the stage, Shane packed his instruments and left the venue without saying goodbye to any of them. Somewhere in her files, Lisa remembered, there was a photograph of him that night, angrier than he had ever been before. He never played with the band again. Soon, Phil announced that he wanted to take a break and go to New York. Lisa, on a trip to Dublin, read in the Irish newspapers that Julie was to begin a solo career in the United States.

Over the next year in Dublin she heard news of Julie from their father, whom Julie telephoned every Sunday with news of gigs and plane journeys and hotels. A few times when Lisa was asked to sing, she refused. Without Julie's voice, it was pointless. She preferred to take photographs. The only sign she was ever given of what was to come was a phone call from Phil from New York. It was nine in the morning Dublin time. He was drunk. He told Lisa that he had met someone who had seen Julie in a sort of folk bar in San Francisco. She was not well, he said. She was on crutches and wearing sunglasses and her face was bruised and, when she had realized that someone there knew her, she had left the bar quickly.

Julie was not on the bill that night, Phil said, but Matt was, complete with guitar, singing some of his own songs and singing also some songs associated with the band. Lisa asked Phil to find her a number for Julie, even for Matt, and he said he would find them if he could and call her back. Her father, she found, did not have a number for Julie either, but as the calls continued to come each Sunday he was not worried about her. When Lisa went to her father's house one Sunday and managed to answer the phone before he did, she found Julie friendly and distant, giving no sign that anything was wrong. Lisa wondered if Phil had not been too drunk to judge what might have been idle gossip. Phil had not seen Julie himself. Her father, when he had finished speaking to Julie and hung up, remarked at how happy she was and what a power of good America seemed to be doing her.

★

ON SATURDAY Luke told her that he had made their three albums into two CDs. Ian and himself had listened to them, he said, and she was right – some of them, especially the songs in Irish, were terrible. But some of the other songs, he added, were great and should be reissued. He was going to make a single CD of the band's greatest hits, he said. Lisa observed his confidence, his ease discussing his own musical tastes, and his utter failure to notice her at all as he spoke. She wondered how many years more his innocence would last, how long it would be before he learned to read signs that things were not always simple. She could not say to him now that she did not want to hear the CD. She would, she supposed, have to listen to it.

Luke knew, Lisa remembered, that Julie was dead. How strange that he would not ask himself if Julie's death meant that her voice, recorded on all these songs, might not carry too much sadness with it, too much regret to be listened to casually after all the years.

TWO AND A HALF years after the break-up of the band, two Guards came to her flat in the early morning and told her that Julie had been found dead in a hotel room in California. She took a taxi to her father's house and woke him and told him.

'That's the end for me now,' he said. 'That's the end.'

When she asked him if he would come with her to identify the body, he seemed puzzled and wondered if Matt would not do that.

'She died alone, the Guards told me,' Lisa said.

Her father said he did not want to go with her, and told

her he did not care where Julie was buried, or where the funeral was. It was the last thing he cared about.

'It's all over for me,' he said.

She flew to London and then to Los Angeles and then, on a small plane, to Fresno in California where Julie's body lay in a morgue. She had never been in the United States before, and perhaps, she thought, it was the hours flying and the day becoming night as much as the unfamiliarity that seemed to soften everything she saw and felt, seemed to render colours bland and voices hard to make out. The only hotel she knew was the one where Julie had been found. It did not occur to her to go anywhere else. It was a new motel at the edge of the city, and it was only when she had checked in and was lying on the bed that she realized this might not be the best place to stay. She thought of seeking out the manager and asking him to show her the room where her sister had been found, but she postponed the request. She studied the staff, wondering which of them had seen her sister dead and which of them would know if Matt had been with her on the night or day she died.

In all the years that followed, she wondered why she did not go to the police, or ask to see the police, or find the Irish consul, and she still thought that one of the men in the morgue who witnessed her signature might have been a policeman. She had phoned the number given to her in Dublin and arranged to go to the morgue the next day. She had also given them Matt's name and asked them that if he made contact, they were to tell him where she was. It sounded as though she were making a business transaction and this added to the strangeness of that time when no one recognized her, when no one spoke to her, when she could find no bar or restaurant or coffee shop where she felt comfortable. She was in a land of ghosts.

She remembered the night and morning in Fresno before she went to see her sister's body as interminable, a limbo time in which there was nothing to do, no duty to perform, no possibility of sleeping. She tried to take a taxi to the city centre so she could stroll in the streets, but after much misunderstanding, she discovered that there was no city centre, and no streets, merely long leafy rows of houses which led to more of the same, like an enclosed city of the dead, the houses like small tombs. She tried to phone friends in Ireland, but each call had to go through reception; the people who worked there were not in the habit of dealing with international calls and mostly failed to connect her. They began to view her lurking in the lobby waiting for taxis, her coming and going, with something between hostility and suspicion.

She had seen America in the movies, but nothing here, a short plane ride from Hollywood, belonged to the images she had seen on the screen. The flatness, the deadness, the long waits for taxis, the tiredness of every object did not come from any Hollywood drama. Only once did she see a sight worthy of the movies. She had felt a craving for Chinese food, and had asked at reception for the name of the nearest Chinese restaurant. The receptionist seemed to have no idea what she meant. In the end, Lisa spoke directly to the taxi company, who dispatched a driver after forty-five minutes to take her to a nearby mall.

On the way there, as evening fell, she saw the beautiful graveyard, the headstones all low and uniform, the grass freshly cut. She noticed the slanting sunlight, as though the graveyard were in brave Technicolor and the rest of the world in black and white. On the way back to the motel, having picked at her food and eaten almost nothing, she asked the driver to stop and she walked among the graves, looking at the foreign names and the foreign places of birth and sensing in this community of the dead, resting in this twilit clearance, some warmth, something even close to hope, and for some seconds the dread lifted of what was in store when she arrived at the morgue.

She asked each time she returned to the motel if anyone had called, but there was no message. She had given the number to her father in case Matt rang. But there was nothing except the receptionist's irritation. She presumed that the people at the morgue would know the circumstances of Julie's death, whether anyone else had checked into the motel with her. Thinking about the questions she could ask distracted her.

THEY WHEELED Julie's body into a small, cold, narrow room. There was no sheet over her face so Lisa could instantly see her. Julie was smiling. It was not a dead or distant smile; no make-up artist could have painted it. It was a smile which belonged to Julie alone, it was how she often looked before she spoke, the smile impatient, it was how she smiled when she was ready to interrupt. It seemed astonishing that her face, being frozen and dead, could produce this smile. One of the orderlies who had wheeled the body in stood and waited as Lisa touched her sister's hand and forehead and spoke to her, whispering what words she could, telling her how much they had loved her, adding what their father had said. She thought of singing a verse of something, but the thought was enough to make her cry.

If only now, in this next half an hour, she had known what to ask, whom to ask for. She showed her passport and signed a form. There were, she remembered, three men in the room, but only one spoke and she had no idea who the other two were. She saw on the form that Julie had died of heart failure. She was so concerned that she could be allowed to see the body one more time that she requested nothing else. It was arranged that she could come back the next day.

She went back to her graveyard, sunlit now, leaving a bewildered taxi driver waiting for her. She believed that she would find an office or a priest attached to the cemetery where her sister's funeral could take place, but there was no chapel and the only people she met told her that this was an Armenian graveyard. Lisa found the most recent grave and looked at the unused plot beside it, and this was where she imagined her sister would lie in earth warmed by the sun, among these strangers in a place which was neither Ireland nor America. In these days, however, especially once she had slept for a while, she did not have the will or energy to organize it.

JULIE'S FACE had changed when she saw her for the second time. Her smile had fallen inwards. There was no life in her.

'She has gone,' Lisa said to an orderly who nodded to her kindly.

'She has gone,' she repeated.

She wondered if taking the body from the freezer the previous day might have caused this new deadness in her sister's face, or if Julie had been mysteriously waiting, holding on, until her sister came. In life she had great strength; maybe in death, too. But it was gone now whatever it was, and there was nothing left. She phoned her father one more time to make sure that he did not want Julie's body flown to Dublin. He assured her that he did not. Through the morgue, she found a funeral director and arranged to have her sister buried, after Mass, at the edge of the Catholic graveyard at the other side of town among the emigrant Irish.

OVER THE NEXT few years, as she worked as a photographer, she asked any musician she met who had been in the United States if they had ever seen Matt Hall, or even heard of him. Phil, when he came to Dublin, looked her up and remarked when they met how strange it was that Matt had disappeared. America was big but the music business was small. He must be in another business now, Phil said. Strangely, it was Shane, the member of the band who had been unhappiest with the music, who wanted the albums reissued when CDs became current, but by that time Lisa wanted to forget what had happened, and, to Shane's puzzlement, she refused.

She could not refuse Luke, however, since he was so proud of what he had done. She did not protest or announce that she would not listen. She kept a large camera close to her in case she would need to cover her face or distract herself.

Luke was all competence and pride as he set up the disc in the player.

'I put the best track first,' he said, 'and I had space at the end so I put it on a second time.'

She knew what it would be, and, as Julie's voice sang the opening verse of 'Famous Blue Raincoat' with no ornamentation or instrumental accompaniment, Lisa saw her face that day when she was dead, the features all filled with life, ready to start an argument, enjoying her own lovely authority. Soon, when the echo effect was added and the cello came in and Lisa's own voice appeared, she was glad she had spent the years not hearing this music. Of all the songs on the CD this was the only one which still seemed alive, the rest were relics, but the song which began and ended the disc gave her a hint, in case she needed one, of her own reduced self, like one of her negatives upstairs, all outline and shadow, and gave her a clear vision of her sister's face in the days when the recording was made. Now, as the CD came to an end, she hoped she would never have to listen to it again.

A Priest in the Family

SHE WATCHED the sky darken, threatening rain.

'There's no light at all these days,' she said. 'It's been the darkest winter. I hate the rain or the cold, but I don't mind it when there's no light.'

Father Greenwood sighed and glanced at the window.

'Most people hate the winter,' he said.

She could think of nothing more to say and hoped that he might go now. Instead, he reached down and pulled up one of his grey socks, then waited for a moment before he inspected the other and pulled that up too.

'Have you seen Frank lately?' he asked.

'Once or twice since Christmas,' she said. 'He has too much parish work to come and visit me very much, and maybe that's the way it should be. It would be terrible if it was the other way around, if he saw his mother more than his parishioners. He prays for me, I know that, and I would pray for him too if I believed in prayer, but I'm not sure I do. But we've talked about that, you know all that.'

'Your whole life's a prayer, Molly,' Father Greenwood said and smiled warmly.

She shook her head in disbelief.

'Years ago the old women spent their lives praying. Now, we get our hair done and play bridge and go to Dublin on the free travel, and we say what we like. But I've to be careful what I say in front of Frank, he's very holy. He got that from his father. It's nice having a son a priest who's very holy. He's one of the old school. But I can say what I like to you.'

'There are many ways of being holy,' Father Greenwood said.

'In my time there was only one,' she replied.

WHEN HE HAD gone she got the *RTE Guide* and opened it for the evening's television listings; she began to set the video to record *Glenroe*. She worked slowly, concentrating. In the morning, when the *Irish Times* had been read, she would put her feet up and watch this latest episode. Now in the hour she had to spare before she went out to play bridge, she sat at the dining-room table and flicked through the newspaper, examining headlines and photographs, but reading nothing, and not even thinking, letting the time pass easily.

It was only when she went to fetch her coat in the small room off the kitchen that she noticed Father Greenwood's car still in front of the house; as she peered out, she could see him sitting in the driver's seat.

Her first thought was that he was blocking her car and she would have to ask him to move. Later, that first thought would stay with her as a strange and innocent way of keeping all other thoughts at a distance; it was something which almost made her smile when she remembered it.

He opened the car door as soon as she appeared with her coat held distractedly over her arm.

'Is there something wrong? Is it one of the girls?' she asked.

'No,' he said, 'no, there's not.'

He moved towards her, preparing to make his way back into the house. She wished in the second they locked eyes that she could escape now to an evening of cards and company, get by him quickly and walk to the bridge club at the hotel, if she had to. Anything, she thought, to stop him saying whatever it was he had come to say.

'Oh, it's not the boys! Oh, don't say it's the boys have had an accident and you're afraid to tell me!' she said.

He shook his head with certainty.

'No, Molly, not at all, no accident.'

As he reached her he caught her hand as though she would need his support nonetheless.

'I know you have to go and play bridge,' he said.

She believed then that it could not be anything urgent or important. If she could still play bridge then clearly no one was dead or injured.

'I have a few minutes,' she said.

'Maybe I can come back another time. We can talk more,' he said.

'Are you in any trouble?' she asked.

He looked at her as though the question puzzled him.

'No,' he said.

She put her coat down on a chair in the hallway.

'No,' he said again, his voice quieter.

'Then we'll leave it for another time,' she said calmly and smiled as best she could. She watched him hesitate, and she became even more determined that she would go immediately. She picked up her coat and made sure the keys were in the pocket.

'If it can wait, then it can wait,' she said.

He turned away from her, walking out of the hallway towards his car.

'Right you be,' he said. 'Enjoy your night. I hope I didn't alarm you.'

She was already moving away from him, her car keys in her hand, having closed the front door firmly behind her.

THE NEXT DAY, when she had finished her lunch, she took her umbrella and her raincoat and walked to the library on the Back Road. It would be quiet, she knew, and Miriam the new girl would have time for her, she hoped. There was already a molly@hotmail.com, Miriam had told her on her last visit to learn how to use the library computer, so for her first email address she would need to add something to the word 'Molly' to make it original, like a number maybe, hers alone.

'Can I be Molly80?' she had asked.

'Are you eighty, Mrs O'Neill?'

'Not yet, but it won't be long.'

'Well, you don't look it.'

Her fingers had stiffened with age, but her typing was as accurate and fast as when she was twenty.

'If I could just type, I'd be fine,' she said now as Miriam moved an office chair close to the computer and sat beside her, 'but that mouse will be the end of me. It doesn't do what I want it to do at all. My grandsons can make it do whatever they want. I hate having to click. It was much simpler in my day. Just typing. No clicking.'

'Oh, when you're sending emails and getting them, you'll see the value of it,' Miriam said.

'Yes, I told them I was going to send them an email as soon as I could. I'll have to think of what to put into it.'

She turned her head when she heard voices and saw two women from the town returning books to the library. They were studying her with immense curiosity.

'Look at you, Molly. You've gone all modern,' one of them said.

'You have to keep up with what's going on,' she said.

'You never liked missing anything, Molly. You'll get all the news from that now.'

She faced the computer and began to practise opening her Hotmail account, as Miriam went to attend to the women, and she did not turn again when she heard them browsing among the stacks of books, speaking to one another in hushed voices.

Later, when she felt she had used enough of Miriam's patience, she walked towards the cathedral and down Main Street into Irish Street. She greeted people she met on the street by name, people she had known all of her life, the children of her contemporaries, many of them grown middle-aged themselves, and even their children, all familiar to her. There was no need to stop and talk to them. She knew all about them, she thought, and they about her. When news spread widely that she was learning how to use the computer in the library, one or two of them would ask her how it was going, but for the moment she would be allowed pass with a kind, brisk greeting.

Her sister-in-law sat in the front room of her house where the fire was lighting. Molly tapped on the window and then waited while Jane fumbled with the automatic system.

'Push now!' She could hear her voice through the intercom.

She pushed the door, which was stiff, and, having closed it behind her, let herself into Jane's sitting room.

'I look forward to Monday,' Jane said, 'when you come down. It's lovely to see you.'

'It's cold outside, Jane,' she said, 'but it's nice and warm in here, thank God.'

It would be easier, more relaxing somehow, she thought, if one of them made tea, but Jane was too frail to move very much and too proud to want her sister-in-law in her kitchen. They sat opposite each other as Jane tended the fire almost absent-mindedly. There was, she thought, nothing to say, and yet there would never be a moment's silence between them.

'How was the bridge?' Jane asked.

'I'm getting worse at it,' Molly replied, 'but I'm not as bad as some of them.'

'Oh, you were always a great card player,' Jane said.

'But for bridge you have to remember all the rules and the right bids and I'm too old, but I enjoy it, and then I enjoy when it's over.'

'It's a wonder the girls don't play,' Jane said.

'When you have young children, you've enough to think about. They never have a minute.'

Jane nodded distantly and looked into the fire.

'They're very good, the girls,' she said. 'I love it when they come down to see me.'

'You know, Jane,' Molly replied, 'I like seeing them and all that, but I wouldn't care if they didn't visit from one end of the week to the next. I'm one of those mothers who prefers her grandchildren to her children.'

'Oh, now,' Jane replied.

'It's true, Jane. I'd go mad if a week went by and my lovely grandsons didn't come down on a Wednesday for their tea, and I'm always raging when their mothers come to collect them. I always want to keep the boys.'

'They're nice when they're at that age,' Jane said. 'And it's so handy that they live so close together and they get on so well.'

'Has Frank been here?' Molly asked.

Jane glanced up at her, almost alarmed. For a moment a look of pain came on her face.

'Oh Lord no,' she said.

'I haven't seen him much since Christmas either,' Molly said, 'but you usually know more about him. You read the parish newsletter. He gave up sending it to me.'

Jane bowed her head, as though searching for something on the floor.

'I must tell him to call in to you,' Molly said. 'I don't mind him neglecting his mother, but neglecting his aunt, and she the holiest one in the family . . .'

'Oh, don't now!' Jane said.

'I will, Jane, I'll write him a note. There's no point in ringing him. You only get the machine. I hate talking into those machines.'

She studied Jane across the room, aware now that all the time her sister-in-law spent alone in this house was changing her face, making her responses slower, her jaw set. Her eyes had lost their kind glow.

'I keep telling you,' she said, as she stood up to go, 'that you should get a video machine. It would be great company. I could bring you down videos.'

She noticed Jane taking a rosary beads from a small purse and wondered if this were being done deliberately as a way of showing that she had more important things to consider.

'Think about it anyway,' she said.

'I will, Molly, I'll think about that,' Jane replied.

DARKNESS WAS falling as she approached her bungalow, but she could clearly make out Father Greenwood's car parked again in front of her car. She realized that he would have seen her in one of the mirrors just as soon as she saw him, so there would be no point in turning back. If I were not a widow, she thought, he would not do this to me. He would telephone first, minding his manners.

Father Greenwood got out of the car as she came close.

'Now, Father Greenwood, come in,' she said. 'I have the key here in my hand.' She brandished the key as though it were a foreign object.

She had put the heating system on a timer so the radiators were already warm. She touched the radiator in the hallway for a moment and thought of taking him into the sitting room, but felt then that the kitchen would be easier. She could stand up and make herself busy if she did not want to sit listening to him. In the sitting room, she would be trapped with him.

'Molly, you must think it strange my coming back like this,' Father Greenwood said. He sat down at the kitchen table.

She did not answer. She sat down opposite him and unbuttoned her coat. It struck her for a moment that it might be the anniversary of Maurice's death and that he had come to be with her in case she needed his support and sympathy, but she then remembered just as quickly that Maurice had died in the summer and that he had been dead for years and no one paid any attention to his anniversary. She could think of nothing else as she stood up and took her coat off and draped it over the armchair in the corner. Father Greenwood, she noticed, had his hands joined in front of him at the table as though ready for prayer. Whatever this was, she thought, she would make sure that he never came to her house unannounced again.

'Molly, Frank asked me—'

'Is there something wrong with Frank?' she interrupted.

Father Greenwood smiled at her weakly.

'He's in trouble,' he said.

Immediately she knew what that meant, and then thought no, her first reaction to everything else had been wrong, so maybe this too, maybe, she thought, maybe it was not what had automatically come into her mind.

'Is it . . . ?'

'There's going to be a court case, Molly.'

'Abuse?' She said the word which was daily in the newspapers and on the television, as pictures appeared of

159

priests with their anoraks over their heads, so that no one would recognize them, being led from court-houses in handcuffs.

'Abuse?' she asked again.

Father Greenwood's hands were shaking. He nodded.

'It's bad, Molly.'

'In the parish?' she asked.

'No,' he said, 'in the school. It was a good while ago. It was when he was teaching.'

Their eyes were locked in a sudden fierce hostility.

'Does anyone else know this?' she asked.

'I came down to tell you yesterday but I didn't have the heart.'

She held her breath for a moment and then decided she should stand up, push her chair back without caring whether it fell over, not moving her eyes from her visitor's face for one second.

'Does anyone else know this? Can you answer a straight question?'

'It's known about all right, Molly,' Father Greenwood said gently.

'Do the girls know?'

'They do, Molly.'

'Does Jane know?'

'The girls told her last week.'

'Does the whole town know?'

'It's being talked about all right,' Father Greenwood said. His tone was resigned, almost forgiving. 'Would you like me to make you a cup of tea?' he added.

'I would not, thank you.'

He sighed.

'There will be a court hearing before the end of the month. They tried to have it postponed, but it looks as if it will be Thursday week.'

'And where is Frank?'

'He's still in his parish, but he's not going out much, as you can imagine.'

'He abused young boys?' she asked.

'Teenagers,' he replied.

'And they're now grown up? Is that correct?' she asked.

'He'll need all——'

'Don't tell me what he'll need,' she interrupted.

'It's going to be very hard for you,' he said, 'and that's killing him.'

She held the side of the table with her hands.

'The whole town knows? Is that right? The only person who hasn't known is the old woman? You've all made a fool out of me!'

'It was not easy to tell you, Molly. The girls tried a while ago and I tried yesterday.'

'And them all whispering about me!' she said. 'And Jane with her rosary beads!'

'I'd say people will be very kind,' he said.

'Well, you don't know them, then,' she replied.

HE LEFT HER only when she insisted that he go. She checked the newspaper for the evening television and made her tea as though it were an ordinary Monday and she could take her ease. She put less milk than usual into the scalding tea and made herself drink it, proving to herself that she could do anything now, face anything. When a car pulled up outside, she knew that it would be the girls, her daughters. The priest would have alerted them and they would want to come now, when the news was raw, and they could arrive together so that neither of them would have to deal with her alone.

Normally, they walked around the side of the house and let themselves in the kitchen door, but she moved quickly along the short corridor towards the front door and turned on the light in the porch and opened the door. She stood watching them as they came towards her, her shoulders back.

'Come in,' she said, 'from the cold.'

In the hallway, they remained for a second uneasily, unsure which room they should go into.

'The kitchen,' she said drily and led the way, glad that she had left her glasses on top of the open newspaper on the table so that it would be clear to them that she had been occupied when they came.

'I was just going to do the crossword,' she said.

'Are you all right?' Eileen asked.

She stared at her daughter blankly.

'It's nice to see the two of you together,' she said. 'Are the boys well?'

'They're fine,' Eileen said.

'Tell them I'm nearly ready to take messages from them on an email,' she said. 'Miriam said one more lesson and I'll be away.'

'Was Father Greenwood not here?' Eileen asked.

Margaret had begun to cry and was fumbling in her handbag looking for tissues. Eileen handed her a tissue from her pocket.

'Oh yes, today and yesterday,' Molly said. 'So I have all the news.'

It struck her then that her grandsons would have to live with this too, their uncle on the television and in the newspapers, their uncle the paedophile priest. At least they had a different surname, and at least Frank's parish was miles away. Margaret went to the bathroom.

'Don't ask me if I want tea, I don't want tea,' Molly said.

'I don't know what to say,' Eileen replied. 'It's the worst thing.'

Eileen moved across the kitchen and sat in the armchair.

'Have you told the boys?' she asked.

'We had to tell them because we were afraid they'd hear in school.'

'And were you not afraid I'd hear?'

'No one would say it to you,' Eileen said.

'You didn't have the courage, either of you.'

'I still can't believe it. And he's going to be named and everything.'

'Of course he's going to be named,' Molly said.

'No, we hoped he wouldn't be. He's pleading guilty. So we thought he mightn't be named. But the victims are going to ask that he be named.'

'Is that right?' Molly asked.

Margaret came back into the room. Molly noticed her taking a colour brochure from her handbag. She put it on the kitchen table.

'We spoke to Nancy Brophy,' Eileen said, 'and she said that she would go with you if you wanted to go to the Canaries. The weather would be gorgeous. We looked at prices and everything. It would be cheap enough, and we'd pay the flight and the hotel and everything. We thought you'd like to go.'

Nancy Brophy was her best friend.

'Did you now?' Molly asked. 'Well, that's lovely, I'll look at that.'

'I mean when the case is on. It'll be all over the papers,' Eileen continued.

'It was good of you to think of it anyway. And Nancy too,' Molly said and smiled. 'You're all very thoughtful.'

'Would you like me to make you a cup of tea?' Margaret asked.

'No, Margaret, she wouldn't,' Eileen said.

'It's the boys you both should be worrying about,' Molly said.

'No, no,' Eileen replied. 'We asked them if anything had ever happened. I mean if Frank . . .'

'What?' Molly asked.

'Had interfered with them,' Margaret said. She had dried her eyes now and she looked at her mother bravely. 'Well, he hasn't.'

'Did you ask Frank as well?' Molly enquired.

'Yes, we did. It all happened twenty years ago. There was nothing since, he says,' Eileen said.

'But it wasn't just a single episode,' Margaret added. 'And I read that you can never tell.'

'Well, you'll have to look after the boys,' Molly said.

'Would you like Father Greenwood to come back and see you again?' Eileen asked.

'I would not!' Molly said.

'We were wondering . . .' Margaret began.

'Yes?'

'If you'd like to come and stay with one of us for a while,' Margaret continued.

'What would I do in your house, Margaret?' she asked. 'And sure Eileen has no room.'

'Or even if you wanted to go to Dublin,' Eileen said.

Molly went to the window and looked out at the night. They had left the parking lights on in the car.

'Girls, you've left the lights on and the battery'll be run down and one of your poor husbands will have to come and bail you out,' she said.

'I'll go out and turn them off,' Eileen said.

'I'm going out myself,' Molly said. 'So we can all go.'

'You're going out?' Eileen asked.

'I am, Eileen,' she said.

Her daughters looked at each other, puzzled.

'But you usually don't go out on a Monday night,' Eileen said.

'Well, I won't be able to go out until you move the car, because you're blocking the drive. So you'll have to go first. But it was nice to see you, and I'll enjoy looking at the brochure. I've never been in the Canaries.'

She saw them signalling to each other that they could go.

THE TOWN during the next week seemed almost new to her. Nothing was as familiar as she had once supposed. She was unsure what a glance or a greeting disguised, and she was careful, once she had left her own house, never to turn too sharply or look too closely in case she saw them whispering about her. A few times, when people stopped to talk to her, she was unsure if they knew about her son's disgrace, or if they too had become so skilled at the plain language of small talk that they could conceal every thought from her, every sign, as she could from them.

She made clear to her daughters that she did not wish to go on any holidays or change her routine. She played bridge on Tuesday night and Sunday night as usual. On Thursday she went to the gramophone society, and on Wednesday, after school, she was visited, as always, by her four grandsons, who watched videos with her, and ate fish fingers and chips and ice cream, and did part of their homework until one of their mothers came to collect them. On Saturday she saw friends, other widows in the town, calling on them in her car. Her time was full, and often, in the week after she had received the news of what was coming, she found that she had forgotten briefly what it was, but never for long.

Nancy Brophy asked her one day when she had called to Nancy's house if she was sure she did not want to go to the Canary Islands.

'No, I'm going on as normal,' Molly said.

'You'll have to talk about it, the girls say you'll have to talk about it.'

'Are they ringing you?'

'They are,' Nancy said.

'It's the children they should be worrying about,' Molly said.

'Well, everyone is worried about you.'

'I know. They look at me wondering how to get by me quickly enough in case I might bite them, or I don't know what. The only person who came up to me at the bridge club was Betty Farrell, who took my arm and asked me, with them all watching, to phone her or send word or call around to her if I needed anything. She looked as if she meant it.'

'Some people are very good,' Nancy said. 'The girls are very good, Eileen and Margaret. And you'll be glad now to have them so close.'

'Oh, they have their own lives now,' Molly said.

They sat for a while without speaking.

'Well, it's an awful shock the whole thing,' Nancy continued eventually. 'That's all I'll say. The whole town is shocked. Frank was the last person you would expect . . . You must be in a terrible state about it, Molly.'

'As long as it's the winter I can manage,' Molly said. 'I sleep late in the mornings and I'm kept busy. It's the summer I dread. I'm not like those people who suffer from that disorder when there's no light. I dread the long summer days when I wake with the dawn and think the blackest thoughts. Oh, the blackest thoughts! But I'll be all right until then.'

'Oh Lord, I must remember that,' Nancy said. 'I never knew that about you. Maybe we'll go away then.'

'Would you do something for me, Nancy?' Molly said, standing up, preparing to leave.

'I would, of course, Molly.'

'Would you ask people to talk to me about it, I mean people who know me? I mean, not to be afraid to mention it.'

'I will, Molly. I'll do that.'

As they parted, Molly noticed that Nancy was close to tears.

★

Two days before the trial, as she was walking back to her house with the morning newspaper, Frank's car drew alongside her and stopped. She noticed a pile of parish newsletters on the back seat. She got into the front passenger seat without looking at him.

'You're out early,' he said.

'I'm just up,' Molly replied. 'I go out and get the paper before I do anything. It's a bit of exercise.'

When they reached the house, he parked the car and they both walked into the kitchen.

'You've had your breakfast, I'd say,' she said.

'I have,' he replied. He was not wearing his priest's collar.

'Well, you can look at the paper now while I make toast and a cup of tea.'

He sat in the armchair in the corner and she could hear him fold and unfold the pages of the newspaper as she moved around the kitchen. When the toast and tea were ready, she set them out on the table, with a cup and saucer for each of them.

'Father Greenwood said he was down,' Frank said.

'He was,' she replied.

'He says you're a lesson to everyone of your age, out every night.'

'Well, as you know, I keep myself busy.'

'That's good.'

She realized that she had forgotten to put butter on the table. She went to the fridge to fetch some.

'The girls are in and out to see you?' he asked.

'If I need them, I know where they are,' she said.

He watched her spreading the butter on the toast.

'We thought you might go away for a bit of a holiday,' he said.

She reached over for the marmalade, which was already on the table, and said nothing.

'Do you know, it would spare you,' he added.

'So the girls said.'

She did not want the silence that began then to linger for too long, yet everything she thought of saying seemed unnecessary. She wished he would go.

'I'm sorry I didn't come in and tell you myself what was happening,' he said.

'Well, you're here now, and it's nice to see you,' she replied.

'I think it's going to be . . .' He didn't finish, merely lowered his head. She did not drink the tea or eat the toast.

'There might be a lot of detail in the papers,' he said. 'I just wanted to warn you myself about that.'

'Don't worry about me at all, Frank,' she said.

She tried to smile in case he looked up.

'It's been bad,' he said and shook his head.

She wondered if they would let him say Mass when he was in prison, or have his vestments and his prayer books.

'We'll do the best we can for you, Frank,' she said.

'What do you mean?' he asked.

When he lifted his head and took her in with a glance, he had the face of a small boy.

'I mean, whatever we can do, we will do, and none of us will be going away. I'll be here.'

'Are you sure you don't want to go away?' he asked in a half-whisper.

'I am certain, Frank.'

He did not move. She put her hand on the cup; the tea was still hot. Frank smiled faintly and then stood up.

'I wanted to come in anyway and see you,' he said.

'I'm glad you did,' she said.

She did not stand up from her chair until she heard him starting the car in the drive. She went to the window and watched him reversing and turning the car, careful as always not to drive on her lawn. She stood at the window as he drove away; she stayed there until the sound of his car had died down in the distance.

A Journey

'MAMMY, how do people die?' he had asked, and Mary had explained how the soul left the body and then God . . . well, God . . . took your soul because he loves you.

'Will everyone die?'

'Yes, David.'

'Every single person?'

She was amused by his earnestness, but tried to treat him seriously and answer as well as she could. He must have been about four then, going through the stage, she remembered, of asking questions and wanting to know how everything worked and why.

He was their only child, born after almost twenty years of marriage when Seamus and she had long given up hope of ever having children. At first she could hardly believe it and then was frightened; she asked herself why it had happened then and not years before but she could find no explanation. She felt that perhaps they would be too old and set in their ways to bring up a child. They were used to being free. Yet David did not really make the great change in their lives that she expected. Mrs Redmond, who lived in a nearby cottage and whose husband died just after

David was born, came in every day to help her and babysat at night if they wanted to go out. Their house was just beside the small country national school where Seamus was principal. As David got bigger he began to spend more and more time with Mrs Redmond. Often, when Mary went down to the cottage to collect him, he did not want to come home. But then, once he was back in his own house, he would start to smile again and follow her around asking her questions or, when he was older, telling her what had happened to him at school.

IT WAS LATE and she was not used to driving long distances in the dark. She found it difficult to concentrate, and even though she knew the road very well, she had to drive slowly. It was March and a thin frost was beginning to settle. The road had been widened for stretches, and the car lights beamed on wooden fences instead of the old ditches. The road was no more the hidden, almost guilty thing it had been, huddled away from the land around. There were fewer accidents now, she supposed. She remembered the old narrow road, and her mind began to slip back until she found that she was trying once again to pinpoint the day it had started, the day she first noticed that David had grown beyond their reach and become sullen and withdrawn. Were they to blame, she and Seamus, and in what way, for the fact that their twenty-year-old son whom she was driving home from hospital had spent the last seven months there suffering from silence, as she called it; the doctors called it depression. David had refused to sit in the front seat beside her and would not talk to her. He sat in the back of the car and lit one cigarette after another from the packet he had asked her to stop in Bray and buy for him. She wondered if he had made a decision not to speak to her, or if this was natural for him, if the silence made him comfortable, as it made her uneasy and weary. She decided that she would have to speak.

'Your father's not well, David,' she said.

There was no answer. As a car came towards her, she dimmed her own lights, but the oncoming beams were too strong and she had to fix her eyes on the margin to avoid them.

'He had another stroke last week,' she said, but it sounded false and untrue, as if she had invented it merely to shock him into speaking to her. But he did not speak; she could hear him drawing hard on his cigarette.

The long main street of Arklow was deserted, and there was just Gorey, Camolin and Ferns and all the roads that stretched between them, and afterwards home. The car's headlights illuminated a short distance and there seemed always to be absolutely nothing beyond them. There was very little traffic. Mary found the dense cigarette smoke in the car almost sickening. The moon came into view for the first time.

She tried not to think, tried to keep her mind fixed on the road ahead, but random images of places in the past kept coming to her, and there was nothing she could do to stop them. The Mont Clare Hotel in Dublin where she had spent her honeymoon, she could picture the room they had and recall the strange street noises in the morning. She tried to conjure up the impression that the city, which she knew very slightly then, had made on her, but other scenes ran into that picture and made it blurred. The network of lanes around Cush where they used to go for the summer and the midges that used to circle at twilight and get into your hair. She saw the portrait of her mother hung after she died in the unused musty parlour over her father's shop in Ferns.

She pictured as well their first sighting of the old two-storey house beside the school that her father had bought for them when they got married. She remembered the atmosphere inside the house the day they went to look at it, all bare walls and the hollow sounds their feet made. Now Seamus was lying upstairs in that same house. The whole right side of his body was paralysed. That scene Mary could picture more sharply than anything. Even when she read the newspaper to him, Seamus did not seem interested.

David lit another cigarette in the back of the car.

'Would you like to sit in the front for a while?' she asked. There was silence for a few moments and then a muffled sound.

'No, thanks.'

She stopped the car suddenly and pulled into the side. She could not see him properly when she turned around so she flicked on the dim light over her head. David opened the window to let the smoke out. He had inherited her thick blonde hair but nothing of her large-boned face. In the faint light he reminded her of Seamus when she had known him first, but David's face was even thinner. His expression was strained. He made it clear in the way he turned that he did not wish to speak to her.

'What are you going to do now? Do you have any idea?'

she asked, and for a quick second she caught his eye. He looked away.

'I don't know. Just don't ask me anything, is that agreed? Just don't ask me anything.'

'You might stay at home for a while. Maybe you could get a job at home.'

'I don't know.'

He threw his half-smoked cigarette out of the window.

'I get very tired driving at night. I must be getting old.' She laughed and he gave her an edgy smile.

'Anyway, we'd better hurry up.'

She reached to turn off the light and then she re-started the engine.

'Your father will be expecting us.'

He will be lying with his eyes open, she thought, and he'll barely glance at me when I come in. She smiled at the idea that now she would have two of them for company. Nonetheless, she wanted David to stay at home, no matter how grim his silences, no matter how many days he spent in his bed with the curtains drawn. She dreamed now of going back to Cush with him, of a bright summer day and the light from the sea giving him back something long lost, an old vitality he seemed to have wilfully discarded. She thought if he could walk on the sand in his bare feet, it might lift his spirits, but she sighed as she realized that nothing would be as quick or simple. It was, she knew, an illness, but it did not seem like one. It seemed to her like something David would not give up, a special dark gift he had been offered. Something which comforted him and which he had accepted.

'What was it like, David, the hospital? I never could get any sense of it when we visited. I could never tell how you were.'

'No questions, Ma, I said no questions.'

'Just tell me.'

'It was lousy.' He sighed, and she could hear him blowing out smoke. 'All of it. It was lousy.'

'But it was the best thing at the time, wasn't it? I mean, there wasn't anything else we could have done.'

'Yeah.'

She knew that he had his pills, but she did not know what they were meant to do. The doctor to whom she had spoken had referred to David throughout as 'the patient' and said that he might benefit from a later admission. He did not seem ready to answer any direct questions so Mary had asked none. No one would employ David, she thought, and he was qualified for nothing. She imagined that when she was an old woman she would have him in the room upstairs. She wanted to ask him something else, but she stopped herself, she did not want to irritate him. The silence in the back of the car had become more alert, more hostile. She could almost feel that it was directed at her as she drove faster. She was eager to arrive.

The car headlights hit the modest square steeple of the Protestant cathedral in Ferns. Each Sunday before they had a car, Seamus and she used to ride on bicycles into the town and then get the train to Ferns where they used to spend the day with her father. In the months when he was dying, when he seemed so mild and good-humoured, Mary stayed on alone with him, and sat with him. It was, she thought, for both of them a happy time.

As the car lights flashed against the glass of the squat, modern Catholic church at the T-junction, she remembered they had been married from the old one and wondered what it was used for now. She still had her father's steel-rimmed glasses in a drawer somewhere. When he died, they had sold his shop and built an extension to their own house and bought a car. She dreamed for a second that they had not sold it and thought that working there every day might help David, and she would oversee him, make sure that it did not become too much for him. When she was a little girl she loved working in the shop.

'Is he in bed all the time?' David suddenly asked her.

'Most of the time,' she said. 'He was meant to go into hospital but he wouldn't go, so Mrs Redmond comes up every night. We have to lift him and he's very heavy. Mrs Redmond's getting very old. She'll be staying the night tonight.'

She pretended to herself, as she spoke, that she and David had been having a casual conversation for all of the journey.

'Do you know what I'd love?' she asked familiarly. 'I'd love a cigarette, haven't had one for ages. Your father hates me smoking. Would you ever light one and pass it into me?'

She could hear David flicking a lighter in the back of the car. He handed her a cigarette.

'Are you sure you wouldn't like to sit in the front seat?' she asked. 'We're nearly home.'

'No. I'm all right.'

They came into the town along the narrow road by the river that was overhung with trees. The moon appeared over the hill, and she could see the bare branches and the stars of frost on the road. She found that she could not finish the cigarette so she put it out in the ashtray. The street lights in the town were a dirty sinister yellow. As she drove past the post office and then towards the mill, David pulled the ashtray from its container in the back door of the car and emptied it out of the back window. She noticed the cold air coming into the car.

'We're just home now,' she said.

She turned off the road and up the tarmacadam drive to the house. There were lights on, and Mrs Redmond opened the front door to meet them. David took his bag from the back seat.

'How has he been?' Mary asked in a half whisper.

'He slept for a while earlier, but he's wide awake now. He's been very low all day,' Mrs Redmond said.

When they went inside, Mrs Redmond insisted that David come into the kitchen with her. He followed her, but he held the bag firmly in his hand as though he were on his way somewhere else. Mary stood and watched them from the bottom of the stairs before she turned and went up to the bedroom.

The curtains were drawn and there was a bowl of water beside the electric fire. The room was very warm.

'Is he here?' Seamus asked.

She did not answer but walked over and sat on a stool in front of the dressing-table mirror from where she could see him. She noticed how strange her well-kept blonde hair looked beside the wrinkles around her eyes and mouth. Her crocks, David used to call them. It was time, she thought, to let the grey appear. Seamus was staring at her from the bed and when their eyes caught she was struck for a moment by a glimpse of a future in which she would need to muster every ounce of selfishness she had. She shut her eyes before she turned around to face him.

'Is he back? Did you bring him?' he asked her again.

Three Friends

ON THE MONDAY, when the others had gone to the hotel for lunch, Fergus stayed alone with his mother's body in the funeral parlour. She would, he knew, have so far enjoyed her own funeral. The hush of conversation with old friends, the conjuring up of memories, the arrival of people she would not have seen for years, all of this would have put a gleam into her eyes. But she would not, he thought, have enjoyed being alone now in the shadowy candlelight with her son, all the life gone out of her. She was not enjoying herself now, he thought.

He was tempted to whisper to her some words of comfort, to say that she would be all right, that she was at peace. He stood up and looked at her. Her dead face had none of her live face's softness. He hoped some day he would be able to forget what she looked like as she lay inert in her coffin, with faint traces of an old distress behind the mask of stillness and peace and immobility. The undertakers or the nurses who had laid her out had made her chin seem firmer and more settled, almost pointed at the end with strange creases. If she spoke now, he knew, her old chin would come back, her old voice, her old smile. But that was all gone now; anyone seeing her for the first time would never know her. She was beyond knowing, he thought, and suddenly realized that he was going to cry.

When he heard the noise of feet outside, a man's heavy shoes against the concrete, he felt almost surprised that someone should come now to break his vigil with her. He had been sitting there as though the door were closed and he could not be disturbed.

The man who appeared was middle-aged and tall; he walked with a slight stoop. He had a mild, modest look; Fergus was sure that he had never seen him before. He paid no attention to Fergus as he moved towards the coffin with a stiff reverence, blessing himself, and then reaching down gently to touch the dead woman's forehead. He had the look of someone from the town, not a neighbour, Fergus felt, but someone she must have known years earlier. Being on display like this, being touched by anyone who came, would, he knew, have horrified his mother, but she had only a few more hours of it before the coffin would be closed and taken to the cathedral.

The man sat down beside him, still watching his mother's face, gazing at it as though waiting for it to do something in the flickering candlelight. Fergus almost smiled to himself at the idea of telling the man that there was no point in looking at her so intensely, she was dead. The man turned to him as he blessed himself again and offered his large hand and his open-faced sympathy.

'I'm very sorry for your trouble.'

'Thank you,' Fergus replied. 'It was very good of you to come.'

'She's very peaceful,' the man said.

'She is,' Fergus replied.

'She was a great lady,' the man said.

Fergus nodded. He knew that the man would now have to wait for at least ten minutes before he could decently go. He wished that he would introduce himself or give some clue about his identity. They sat in silence looking at the coffin.

As the time elapsed, it seemed odd to Fergus that no one else came. The others surely would have finished at the hotel; his mother's friends had come all morning, and some relatives. It made no sense that all of them had left this gap for Fergus and a stranger to sit so uneasily beside each other for so long. This stretch of time appeared to Fergus to belong to a dark dream which took them out of all familiar elements into a place of dim, shimmering lights, uncomfortable silence, the unending, dull and neutral realm of the dead. As the man cleared his throat, Fergus glanced at him and saw in his dry skin and his pale face further evidence that these minutes did not belong to ordinary time, that they both had been dragged away by his mother's spirit into a place of shadows.

'You were never a hurler,' the man said quietly. His tone was friendly.

'That's right,' Fergus said.

'Conor was the hurler of the family,' the man said.

'He was good in his day all right,' Fergus said.

'Are you the brainy one?'

'No,' Fergus smiled. 'That's Fiach. He's the youngest.'

'Your father,' the man began and hesitated. Fergus looked at him sharply. 'Your father taught me in school.'

'Is that right?'

'I was in the same class as George Mahon. Do you see that dove on the wall there? George drew that.'

He pointed to the back wall of the funeral parlour.

'He was to make a big painting when the place opened. That was just the drawing for it, a kind of preparation. He had to fill in the colours still.'

Fergus looked at the faint outlines in pencil on the wall behind the coffin, he could make out a dove, a few figures and perhaps a hill or a mountain in the distance.

'Why did he not finish it?' Fergus asked.

'Matt's wife,' the man said, 'died suddenly a few weeks before he was ready to open this place and he had to decide whether to coffin her himself or give her to the main competition. So he did it himself, even though this place wasn't finished. It was fine, there was no problem with it, but the painting hadn't been done. And once Matt's wife had been laid out here, George Mahon said he wouldn't come back. He'd be too frightened, he said. The space was all ruined. Or so he said. He couldn't work. You'd never know what'd come up behind you, he said, when you'd be painting here.'

The man spoke in a monotone, staring at the coffin all the time. When Fergus looked away from him, he tried to picture his face, but he could not; his features appeared to fade as soon as Fergus turned. He would, Fergus realized, be hard to describe; tall, but not especially so; thin, but not very thin; his hair brown or sandy-coloured; the face was unremarkable and the voice disembodied. In the silence of the funeral parlour when the man had stopped talking, if someone were to whisper that this man had come to take away his mother's spirit, it would not have seemed strange.

It was, for a few seconds, the most likely possibility that this visitor had suspended time to utter banalities and tell stories while he was working to take Fergus's mother away so that all that was left of her to be buried was her spent and useless body.

Soon, however, when the man had left and the others come back, and some neighbours called, the spell was broken and the man's visit seemed ordinary, what was to be expected in a small town, not worth describing to the others, even though it had left its mark.

THE NEXT DAY, as they followed the coffin down the centre aisle of the cathedral towards the waiting hearse, Fergus kept his head down. He listened to the music, the last hymn to be sung for his mother, and tried not to think of the people congregated on each side of the aisle, standing now, studying him and his sisters and brothers and his aunt as they walked slowly towards the main door. When he came to the last few rows, however, he looked around him and was surprised to see three friends from Dublin, from his life at the weekend and from a recent trip to Amsterdam, standing sombre-faced, as though they were ashamed of something, catching his eye now, but not smiling or even nodding at him in recognition. He had never seen them serious before; this must be how they had looked in school when they were in trouble, or during job interviews or when questioned at airports or stopped by the cops. He was tempted to whisper to them, ask laughingly if they had any drugs, but by the time he thought of this he was out in the open.

In the graveyard, his father's gravestone looked like history now, the carved dates already fading. The priest had set up a microphone and a stand at the other side of it. The early September sunshine made the day warm. There was no wind, but nonetheless the whole place seemed oddly windswept. He wondered why they did not grow trees in this graveyard, even evergreens. As the priest began to intone the prayers, Fergus noticed George Mahon the painter and decorator standing close to a gravestone in the distance. He was the only figure in the graveyard who did not come close, who did not huddle in the crowd standing close to the grave. He was over six feet tall and was resting his hands on the headstone. Fergus could feel the power of his gaze, and could sense that George Mahon had drawn an invisible line in the graveyard which he would not cross. He was, as the man who had come to the funeral parlour explained, afraid of the dead. He had known Fergus's mother all of his life so he could not have easily stayed away, but his not coming near the grave, his keen study of the scene around the priest and the hearse and the coffin, the fierce independence of his stance, made Fergus shiver as the coffin was moved towards the open grave.

Afterwards, Fergus stood and shook hands with anyone who came, thanking them and trying to smile. He noticed that one of his sisters was crying. At the end of the line, shyly, stood Mick, Alan and Conal.

'The three musketeers,' he said.

'I'm sorry for your trouble, Fergus,' Mick said and shook his hand. He was wearing a jacket and tie. The other two approached and embraced him softly.

'I'm really sorry,' Alan said.

Conal held his hand and shook his head sadly.

'Will you come to the hotel for a bite?' Fergus asked.

'We'd love to, but we have to go,' Mick smiled. 'When are you heading back to Dublin?'

'Thursday, I think,' Fergus said.

'Will you come around Thursday night, or give us a ring on the mobile?'

'OK, thanks, I'll do that.'

ON THE NIGHT after the funeral, he and his siblings and his brother-in-law drank until four in the morning. Most of them stayed over the next night, promising each other that they would go to bed early, but over dinner they began to drink wine and then went on to beer and whiskey until there was nothing left but more wine which Fergus and his sisters and brothers drank until the dawn had long appeared. He did not wake until the early afternoon. It was Thursday now and time to leave. He had planned all along to stop at the graveyard on the way out of the town and stand by his mother's grave and offer to her, or receive from her, some comfort, but he was tired and drained. All night they had laughed until there were no more funny stories left. He felt a gnawing guilt at her death as he drove past the graveyard, as though he were implicated in its cause. Rather than move closer to her, he needed to get away from her house, her grave, the days of her funeral. He drove directly to his house in Stoneybatter, dreaming that he would never go out again, but would sleep once darkness was down and do this night after night.

As he was preparing for bed, the phone rang. It was Mick.

'It doesn't matter about tonight,' he said. 'It matters about tomorrow night. We have something special for you. The lads are coming. It's a beach rave.'

'No,' Fergus said. 'I'm not coming.'

'You have to come,' Mick said.

'I'm too old for techno,' Fergus said. 'Actually, I take that back. Techno is too boring for me. And I hate beaches.'

'This is special. I said it was special. Bring two warm pullovers and a big towel.'

'No.'

'Nine o'clock at my place. I'm driving. If it's boring I'll leave with you. But please come.'

'Nine?' Fergus asked and laughed for a moment.

'Nine sharp,' Mick replied.

'And we can stay for half an hour?'

'It'll be nine in the morning and you won't want to leave,' Mick said.

THEY SET OUT from the city when night had fallen. It was warm as they drove north; they kept the windows open until Alan lit a joint and then they closed them so they could enjoy wallowing in the smoke. Already, in Mick's flat, they had each snorted a line of cocaine, which had made Fergus feel sharp and nervous, and oddly lucid. He pulled on the joint with all his energy, taking too much smoke in, and then concentrating on holding it, relishing the taste and the power as he closed his eyes; he felt almost faint. He put his head back as a thrill of weakness coursed through him. He was ready to sleep, but it was a readiness which came with darting thoughts which led nowhere. He tried to relax in the back of the car, taking pleasure in the battle going on between the golden lethargy which the dope brought and the sweet electric shock of the cocaine.

'You know something?' Alan said. 'I felt so bad after your old lady's funeral that I decided I was neglecting mine. So I bought her flowers and went out to see her.'

'A small step for mankind,' Conal said.

'I should have phoned her first,' Alan said, 'but she's no good on the phone, she treats it like it was a poisonous snake.'

'How long was it since you'd seen her?' Mick asked.

'June. And the time before that was February and she kept nagging at me about it and I said: "Well, I'm here now," as though that would make up for everything. And she nearly bit me. She kept saying: "That's all very well." She gets very narked very easily.'

'Is that where you get it from?' Mick asked.

'So I turn up with the flowers and there's no one there and Miss Bitch next door appears in her apron and shouts at me that I'm not getting the key. "And your mother's in Italy," she says. And on a beach, if you don't mind, one of the trendy places, with oul' Mrs Kingston, buying up property the two of them, or new earrings.'

'What did you do with the flowers?' Mick asked.

'I fucked them into the bin beside the bus stop.'

'Jesus,' Conal said. 'Maybe we shouldn't be talking like this in front of Fergus. Are you all right, Fergus?'

'I'm fine,' Fergus said. He had his head back and his eyes closed.

'There'll be more white powder when we get there,' Mick said. 'Don't worry.'

'I'm ready for bed,' Fergus said. 'When I was a kid I used to love staying in the car while the rest of them went down to the strand.'

'Well, you've grown up now,' Mick said.

Mick drove slowly, once he was off the main road. Fergus guessed that they were somewhere between Drogheda and Dundalk but heading directly towards the coast, or driving parallel to it. He noticed that Mick had difficulty seeing in front of him because of patches of thick fog which appeared at intervals. He stopped several times and switched on the dim overhead light so he could consult a page of elaborate directions.

'We're very near now, but I have instructions not to ask for directions from anyone or behave suspiciously,' Mick said. 'I'm looking for a second bungalow on the right and then I have to turn down a narrow, sandy lane.'

'Are you sure someone isn't making a complete eejit out of you?' Alan asked.

'Yeah, I am. It's the same crowd who did the last one. They're sound.'

He stopped at the second bungalow and got out of the car to check in the fog that there was a lane to the right.

'We're here,' he said. 'Down this lane and we're there.'

Briars and brambles hit against the body of the car as they drove along the narrow lane, so rutted that a few times something seemed to cut through the underbelly of the car and Mick was almost forced to stop. They were silent as though frightened as the car rocked from side to side more than it appeared to move forward. When the lane ended, Mick opened the window and they could hear the roar of the sea. He parked the car close to a number of others. Once they opened the doors and stood out in the night the sound of electronic music came clearly towards them from the distance. Fergus noticed that there was a mild, warm wind coming in from the sea, like a summer wind, even though the summer just ended had offered nothing but low skies and constant rain.

'We should have a snort here in the car so the wind won't blow it away,' Mick said.

They sat back into the car, closing the doors and the windows, and Mick laid out the lines neatly on the surface of a CD cover. Having waited his turn to snort the cocaine, using a fifty-euro note which Mick recommended, Fergus relished the sour taste of the powder as it made its way towards the back of his throat. He swallowed hard so that he could taste it better and then, since he was the last, he put his finger on the CD cover to absorb any stray grains of white powder and rubbed them into his gums.

In a holdall, they carried pullovers and towels, bottles of water and cans of beer, and a bottle of tequila. They stood watching as a set of headlights appeared and a car approached and parked and six or seven dazed figures emerged from it. Mick lit a joint and passed it around.

'We're not too early and we're not too late,' he said.

With the help of a torch, he guided them along a headland towards the music, which came from a sheltered cove, down a set of steep stone steps from a field which they had crossed.

'The music is boring,' Fergus whispered to Mick.

Mick handed him the joint again. He pulled on it twice and then handed it back.

'I want you to close your eyes and open your mouth,' Mick said. He shone the torch into Fergus's face as Alan and Conal stood by laughing. Fergus saw Mick biting a tablet in two; as he closed his eyes, Mick put one half on his tongue.

'Swallow that,' he said. 'It's what doctors recommend for boredom.'

THE ORGANIZERS must have been working all day, Fergus thought, as soon as he saw the lights and the generators and the powerful speakers and decks. They had set up an elaborate, instant disco in the cove, with throbbing lights and loud techno, but far away enough from the nearest house or road that if they were lucky they would remain undisturbed all through the night. It was still early, he knew, and even though the Ecstasy tablet had not begun to affect him, the cocaine, the dope and the fresh sea air made him feel exhilarated, ready for a night which would not end, as nights in the city invariably ended, with bouncers shouting and places closing too early and no taxis in the city centre and nowhere to go save home.

As they joined the crowd, leaving their belongings in a safe place in the darkness, about thirty people were dancing. Some of them looked like friends who had travelled together, or maybe they had just become friends, Fergus thought, as they coordinated their movements while also remaining tightly apart from each other.

He stood at the edge of the dancers sipping from a can of beer which Mick had handed him, aware that he was being watched by a tall, skinny, black-haired guy who was dancing to a beat of his own invention, pointing at the sky and then pointing at Fergus and smiling. He was glad that he had spent enough time among straight people to know that the dancer had taken Ecstasy; he was happy and was smiling to show this. It was not a come-on, even though it could seem like one; there was no sexual content in what he was doing. He was like a child. Fergus pointed his finger at him to the stark dull rhythm of the music and smiled back.

He noticed that his nose and chin were tingling with pins and needles as the Ecstasy made its way through his body with its message of support. He began to dance, with Mick and Alan and Conal dancing close by. He was pleased that they were beside him, but he felt no need to look at them or speak to them, or even smile at them. Whatever was happening now with the drugs and the night and the tinny piercing sounds as the tempo rose and the volume was turned up meant that he was wholly connected to them, a part of the group they had formed. He needed only to feel that connection and a rush of warmth would go through him and he hoped that he might stay like that until the dawn and maybe after the dawn into the next day.

When he and Mick had shared another tablet and drunk some water and smoked a joint together, the music, in all its apparent monotony, and then its almost imperceptible variations, began to interest Fergus, pull him towards it with a greater force than the faces or the bodies around him. He listened out for changes in tone and beat, following the track of the music with the cool energy which the night, as it wore on, offered him. He kept close to the others and they to him. They pushed against each other sometimes in mock aggression, dancing in strange and suddenly invented harmonies, smiling at each other, or touching each other in reassurance, before stepping easily away, each of them dancing alone in the surging crowd.

Mick was in control, deciding when joints would be lit, more pills taken, beer sipped, water swigged, or when all four of them should retreat from the crowd, lie on their towels on the sand smoking, laughing, barely talking, knowing that there would be much more time to dance, and that this was a small respite which Mick thought they would need from the shifting beauty of the music and the dancers.

ALL NIGHT they moved around each other, as though they were guarding something deeply playful and wonderful that would disappear if they ceased to remain close. Fergus could feel the sand in his hair and embedded in the sweat down his back and in his trainers. Sometimes he felt tired, and then it seemed that the tiredness itself was impelling him, allowing him to sway with the music, and smile and close his eyes and hope that time was passing slowly, that this cocoon of energy had been left alone for the moment and could enclose him and keep him safe against the night.

It seemed hours later when Mick took him aside and made him move away from the lights and showed him the first stirrings of the dawn in the horizon over the sea. It resembled grey and white smoke in the distance, no redness or real sign of the sun. It looked more like fading light than the break of day. They joined the dancers again for the last stretch under the frantically flickering lights.

As the first rays of sun hit the strand, the light remained grey and uneasy as though it were building up for a day of low clouds and rain. Shivering, they walked over to where they had left the pullovers and towels and began to swig from the tequila bottle. At first it tasted like poison.

'This is rich in toxic energy,' Fergus said. Alan fell down on the soft sand in laughter.

'You sound like God the father, or Einstein,' Conal said.

Mick was putting the towels into the holdall, and checking to make sure that they had left no litter.

'I've got bad news,' he said. 'We're going for a swim.'

'Ah, Jesus!' Alan said.

'I'm on for it,' Conal said, standing up and stretching. 'Come on, Alan, it'll make a man of you.'

He helped Alan to his feet.

'I've no togs,' Alan said.

'And no clean underpants either, I bet.'

Mick handed Fergus the bottle of tequila, which they drank from as they walked away from the last ravers to a point at the far end of the cove, where there was nobody. Mick left down the holdall, took out a towel which he left on the sand and began to undress. He handed an Ecstasy tablet to Alan and Conal.

'This will warm you up,' he said.

He bit on another and handed half of it to Fergus, who was suddenly aware of Mick's saliva on the jagged edge of the pill he put into his mouth, and sharply alert to the afterglow of the long hours when they had been sharing and touching and staying close. He stood on the strand watching Mick until he was fully undressed, realizing with a gasp that he was going naked into the water.

'Last in is Charlie Haughey,' Mick shouted as he neared the edge of the sea.

In the strange, inhospitable half-light, his body seemed oddly and powerfully awkward, his skin blotchy and white. Soon, Alan followed him, also naked, skinnier, shivering, dancing up and down to keep the cold at bay. Conal wore his underpants as he moved gingerly towards the water. Fergus slowly undressed, shivering too, watching as the others shrieked at the cold water, jumping to avoid each wave, until the look of them there began to interest him. Mick and Conal chose the same moment to dive under an incoming wave.

As soon as his feet touched the water, Fergus stepped back. He watched the other three cavorting further out, swimming with energy and abandon, letting themselves be pulled inwards by the waves, and then diving under as though the water itself were a refuge from the cold. This, he thought, as he wrapped his arms around his body to keep warm, and allowed his teeth to chatter, was going to be an ordeal, but he could not return to the strand and dress himself now; he would have to be brave and join the others, who showed no sign of coming back to dry land as they beckoned him not to be a baby.

He made himself think for a moment that he was nobody and nothing, that he had no feelings, that nothing could hurt him as he waded into the water. He crashed into a wave as it came towards him and then dived under it and did a breast stroke out towards his friends. His mother, he remembered, had always been so brave in the water, never hesitating at the edge for a single second, always marching determinedly into the cold sea. She would not have been proud of him now, he thought, as he battled with the idea that he had wet himself enough and could run back quickly to the strand and dry himself. He dismissed the thought, tried to stay under the water and move blindly, thrashing about as much as he could to keep warm. When he reached his friends, they laughed and put their arms around him and then began an elaborate horseplay in the water which made him forget about the cold.

When Alan and Conal waded in towards the shore, Mick stayed behind with Fergus, who was oblivious enough now to the cold that he could spread his arms out and float, staring up at the sky growing lighter. Mick did not venture far from him, but after a while urged him to swim out further to a sandbank where the waves made no difference and it was easy to float and stand and float again. As they swam out they kept close and hit against each other casually a few times, but when they found the bank Fergus felt Mick touching him deliberately, putting his hand on him and keeping it there. Fergus felt his own cock stiffen. When Mick moved away he floated on his back, too happy in the water to care if Mick saw his erection, being certain that Mick would swim back towards him before long.

He did not even open his eyes when Mick swam in between his legs and, surfacing, held his cock, putting the other hand under him. When he tried to stand, he realized that Mick was holding him, trying to enter him with the index finger of his right hand, pushing and probing until he was deep inside. Fergus winced and put his arms around Mick's neck, moving his mouth towards Mick's until Mick began to kiss him fiercely, biting his tongue and lips as he stood on the sandbank. When Fergus reached down, he could feel Mick's cock, hard and rubbery in the water. He smiled, almost laughed, at the thought of how difficult it would be to suck a cock under water.

'I have sort of wanted to do this,' Mick said, 'but just once. Is that all right?'

Fergus laughed and kissed him again. As Mick worked on his cock with his hand, he tried to ease a second finger into him and Fergus cried out but did not pull away. He spread his legs as wide as he could, letting the second finger into him slowly, breathing deeply so that he could open himself more. He held his two arms around Mick's neck and put his head back, closing his eyes against the pain and the thrill it gave. In the half-light of morning he began to touch Mick's face, feeling the bones, sensing the skull behind the skin and the flesh, the eye sockets, the cheek-bones, the jawbone, the forehead, the inert solidity of teeth, the tongue that would dry up and rot so easily, the dead hair.

Mick was not masturbating him now, but putting all his concentration into his two fingers, moving them in and out roughly. Fergus touched Mick's cock, his hips, his back, his balls; then he began to direct his energy, all of it, all of his drug-lined grief and pure excitement, into taking Mick's tongue in his mouth, holding it there, offering his tongue in return, tasting his friend's saliva, his breath, his feral self. He realized that neither of them wanted to ejaculate; it would, somehow, be a defeat, the end of something, but neither could they decide to stop, even though both of them were shivering with the cold. Fergus became slowly aware that Alan and Conal were standing on the strand watching them. When finally the water became too cold for them and they began to wade in towards the shore, the other two turned away nonchalantly.

BY THE TIME they were all dressed and ready to walk back towards the car, the day had dawned. They passed the organizers taking the machinery of the previous night asunder, working with speed and efficiency.

'How do they make their money?' Alan asked.

'They make it on other nights,' Mick said, 'but they do this out of love.'

Mick had to reverse the car without any passengers so that the wheels would not get stuck in the sand. When he had the car turned, Fergus sat in the front passenger seat and the two others in the back. They rocked silently along the lane, the brambles on each side laden with blackberries. Fergus remembered some road out of his town, empty of traffic with tall trees in the distance, and each of them, his brothers and sisters and his mother, with a colander or an old saucepan gathering blackberries from the bushes in the ditches, his mother the most assiduous, the busiest, filling colander after colander into the red bucket in the back seat of the old Morris Minor.

As they made their way from a side road towards the main Dublin road, Fergus realized that he could not face the day alone. He was not sleepy, although he was tired; he was, more than anything, restless and excited. The taste from Mick's mouth, the weight of him in the water, the feel of his skin, the sense of his excitement, had allied themselves now with the remnants of the drugs and the tequila to make him want Mick again, want him alone in a bedroom, with clean sheets and a closed door. He regretted that he had not come off in the sea, and was sorry too that he had not made Mick come off with him. Their sperm mingling with the salt water and the slime and the sand would have put an end to his yearnings, for a time at least. He knew that his house was the first stop as they entered the city; he wished he could turn to Mick, without the two in the back overhearing, and ask him to stay with him for a while.

When Alan asked Mick to stop the car, announcing that he was going to be sick, and Mick pulled in on the hard shoulder of the dual carriageway, they watched him without comment as he heaved and vomited, listening calmly to the retching sounds. Fergus thought then that it might be a good moment to mention to Mick that he could not go home alone.

'Conal, why don't you go and help him?' he asked.

'He always pukes,' Conal said. 'It's genetic, he says. There's nothing I can do for him. He's a wimp. His father and mother were wimps too. Or so he says, anyway.'

'Did they go to raves?' Mick asked.

'Whatever it was in their day,' Conal replied. 'Dances, I suppose, or hops.'

Alan, much chastened and very pale, got back into the car. Since there was no traffic, Fergus knew that he would be home in half an hour. He would have no chance now to tell Mick what he wanted. He could try later on the phone, but this would be a day when Mick might not answer the phone. His own desperate need might have abated by then in any case, become dull sadness and disappointment.

His small house, when he came in the door, seemed to have been hollowed out from something, the air inside it felt trapped, specially filtered to a sort of thinness. The sun was shining through the front window so he went immediately to close the curtains, creating the pretence that it was still the early morning. He thought of putting music on the CD player, but no music would please him now, just as alcohol would not help and sleep would not come. He felt then that he could walk a hundred miles if he had somewhere to go, some clear destination. He was afraid of nothing now save that this feeling would never fade. His heart was beating in immense dissatisfaction at how life was; the echo of the music in his ears and the aftershine of the flashing lights in his eyes were still with him. He felt as though he had been brushed by the wings of some sharp knowledge, some exquisite and mysterious emotion almost equal to the events of the past week. He lay on the sofa, dazed and beaten by his failure to grasp what had been offered to him, and fell into a stupor rather than a sleep.

He did not know how much time had passed when someone banged the knocker on the front door. His bones ached as he went automatically to answer it. He had forgotten what he had wanted so badly in the car, but as soon as he saw Mick, who looked as though he had gone home and showered and changed his clothes, he remembered. Mick had a bag of groceries in his hand.

'I'm not coming in unless you promise that you'll wash all that sand out of every orifice,' Mick said.

'I promise,' Fergus said.

'Immediately,' Mick insisted.

'OK.'

'I'll make breakfast,' Mick said.

Fergus deliberately turned the hot-water tap on too high to see if this could restore him to the state of excitement he had been in. He washed and shaved and found fresh clothes. Quickly, he changed the sheets and the duvet on his bed. When he came downstairs the table was set; there was steaming tea and scrambled eggs and toast and orange juice. They ate and drank ravenously, without speaking.

'I would have bought the morning papers,' Mick said, 'except I can barely see.'

Fergus wondered how quickly he could move Mick to the bedroom once breakfast was finished. He smiled at him and nodded in the direction of upstairs.

'Are you ready so?' he asked.

'I am, I suppose, but I haven't been converted or anything. Just once, OK?'

'You said that before.'

'I was drugged. I mean it this time.'

Mick took out a small plastic bag from his pocket and pushed back the tablecloth to the bare wood of the table. With his credit card he began to make two long orderly lines of cocaine. He took a fifty-euro note from his pocket.

'Which of us goes first?' he asked and grinned.

A Summer Job

SHE CAME DOWN from Williamstown, the old woman, when the baby was born, leaving a neighbouring girl in charge of the post office. She sat by Frances in the hospital, looking fondly at the child even when he was sleeping, and holding him tenderly when he was awake. She had not done this when any of her other grandchildren were born.

'He is lovely, Frances,' she said gravely.

The old woman was interested in politics and religion and fresh news. She loved meeting people who knew more than she did, and were better educated. She read biographies and theology. Her mother, Frances thought, was interested in most things, but not children, unless they were ill or had excelled in some subject, and certainly not babies. She had no idea why she stayed for four days.

Her mother, she knew, was careful with her own grown-up children, even Bill her youngest son, who still lived with her and ran the farm, asking them few questions, never interfering in their lives. Frances watched her now maintaining silence when the subject of a name for the baby arose, but she was aware that her mother was listening keenly, especially when Jim, Frances's husband, was in the room.

Frances waited until late at night when her mother had gone before she discussed the baby's name with Jim, who liked names that were ordinary and solid, like his own, names that would cause no comment now or in the future. Therefore, she was sure that when she suggested John as a name for the baby, Jim would agree.

Her mother was jubilant. Frances knew that her mother's father had been called John, but it did not occur to her that she would now think the new baby was to be christened in his honour. It had nothing to do with him. She asked her mother not to talk to Jim about the name of the baby, and hoped that the old woman might soon stop saying how proud she was that the name was being carried on in the family in a time when the fashion was all for new names, including the names of film stars and pop stars.

'The Irish names are the worst, Frances,' her mother said. 'You couldn't even pronounce them.'

John was cradled even more warmly by her mother now that he had a name. She seemed happy to sit for hours saying nothing, rocking him or soothing him. Frances was glad when she could go home, and happy when her mother suggested that she herself might return to Williamstown to her small post office, her books, her daily *Irish Times*, her specially selected television and radio programmes and a few kindred spirits with whom she exchanged views about current events.

ONCE JOHN was home, the old woman began to pay more attention to his siblings' birthdays, no longer merely sending a postal order and a birthday card, but, having arranged a lift, coming personally the forty miles from Williamstown, staying for tea, bringing the postal order in her handbag. No matter whose birthday it was, however, all of the children knew that their grandmother had come to see John. The old woman, Frances saw, made sure not to try to lift him or cuddle him or demand his attention when he was busy playing or sitting in front of the television. She waited until he was tired or wanted something and then she made clear to him that she was watching out for him, she was on his side. By the time he was four or five, he was often speaking to her on the telephone, and was looking forward to her visits, keeping close to her once she came, showing her his schoolwork and his drawings and asking his parents' leave to stay up late so he could fall asleep beside her on the sofa, his head in her lap.

Soon, once Bill was married and she was alone in the house, the old woman began to invite Frances and her family for Sunday lunch once a month. She made sure that her grandsons were not bored in the house, suggesting that Bill take them to hurling or football matches in the locality, or knowing what they and their sisters might want to watch on television. By the time John was seven or eight, his grandmother would send Bill down to collect him so that he could come on his own to stay on the Saturday night before the lunch. Within a short time, he had his own bedroom in his grandmother's house, his own boots and duffle coat, pyjamas, books and comics.

Frances was not sure what age he was when he began to go to Williamstown for a month in the summer, but by the age of twelve he would stay in his grandmother's house for the entire summer, helping Bill on the farm, working in the post office and sitting with her at night, reading, or talking to her, or, with his grandmother's full encouragement, going out with some local boys his own age.

'Everyone likes John,' her mother said to Frances. 'Everyone he meets, young and old. He always has something interesting to say to everyone and he's a great listener as well.'

FRANCES OBSERVED John move effortlessly through the world. There were never complaints about him, even from his sisters. He was quiet most of the time, he did his share of the housework and knew how to negotiate with his mother and father if he wanted money or permission to stay out late. He appeared to Frances self-contained, unlikely to make mistakes or misjudgements. He took most matters seriously. When, a few times, she tried to make light of his relationship with his grandmother and his special place in her house, he did not smile or acknowledge that she had spoken. Even when she made remarks about the more comic customers of his grandmother's post office, people who did not seem to have changed since she had worked there thirty years earlier, John did not share her amusement.

In those years as soon as spring began her mother would telephone to say that she was already looking forward to the arrival of John.

THAT SUMMER when Frances drove him to Williamstown, she went upstairs with him as soon as they had been met by her mother. His bedroom, she saw, had new wallpaper and there was a new bed. On the chest of drawer lay a stack of shirts, all freshly ironed, a few pairs of jeans, shaving cream, a new fancy razor and special shampoo.

'No wonder you come here,' she said. 'We don't treat you properly at home. Ironed shirts! Done by your special girlfriend!'

As she laughed she did not notice that her mother was waiting outside the door. She realized, as they went downstairs, that both John and her mother wanted her to leave, both were careful not to respond to anything she said. They were almost hostile, as though she had left a gate open in a field, or given too much change to a customer. Neither of them came to the car with her as she departed.

Soon, she learned that her mother, while making the farm over to Bill, had set aside a field and convinced Bill to construct goalposts at each end so that John could play hurling there. John rounded up enough locals to form a team and they found other teams to play against so that almost every evening there were games or practice sessions. Even spectators came, including Frances and Jim one evening, but the old woman herself was too frail to walk up the lane to see John playing.

Frances realized how deeply content she was that John had a large set of friends now and something to do in the evenings so that he would not, as she put it, get fed up listening to her.

FRANCES, while visiting her mother, watched one evening as John came in from a game. He was rushing to go back out again, with just time for a shower and a change of clothes. He barely looked at his grandmother.

'John, sit down and talk to us,' Frances said.

'I have to go, Mammy, the others are waiting.'

He brusquely nodded to his grandmother as he left the room. When Frances looked across at her, she saw that the old woman was smiling.

'He'll be back later,' she said. 'I'll be fast asleep when he comes in.'

She purred, as though the thought gave her great satisfaction.

BY THE TIME he returned home in late August, John had grown taller and fitter. He began to play hurling with his school team, where the talents he had developed over the summer as a midfielder were quickly recognized.

Frances had dutifully gone to watch her other children playing sport, anxiously waiting for the event to be over so she could go home. None of them ever excelled, or cared very much, but John that winter and spring trained every evening and played whenever he could with a view to making the county minor team.

John stood out on the pitch because he appeared never to run or tackle, but instead waited, remained apart. His father, who became excited about very little, could not be contained when John, unmarked, would find the ball coming his way and make a solo run to score a point, brushing off tackles with real bravery and skill, or, judging distances accurately, would lob the ball in a deliberate arc towards the mouth of the goal. It was clear to Frances that the spectators around her noticed him as much as his parents did. Although he was not selected for the minor team that season, he was told that he was being watched with keen interest by the selectors.

IN MAY, as the school year was coming to an end, John remarked casually that he, along with several of his friends, had filled in an application form for a job in the strawberry factory in the town for the summer months. However, Frances had put no further thought into it until he asked her one day for a lift into the town for an interview.

'How long will the job last?' she asked.

'All summer,' he said. 'Or at least until August.'

'What's your grandmother going to do?' Frances asked. 'Only yesterday she was on the phone saying how much she was looking forward to June and your coming to stay. We were there two weeks ago and you heard her yourself.'

'Why don't we wait and see if I get the job?'

'Why do you want to do the interview if you know you can't take the job?'

'Who says I can't take the job?'

'She's old, John, she's not going to last. Just do one more summer with her and I'll make sure that you won't have to do another if you don't want to.'

'Who says I don't want to?'

She sighed.

'God help the woman who marries you.'

★

JOHN ARRANGED for one of his friends to take him into the town for the interview, and a week later a note came from the manager of the factory saying that he could start in the second week of June. John left the letter on the breakfast table for them all to read. When Frances looked at it, she did not speak. She waited until he came back from school.

'You can't go to her every summer and then when she's old and weak, decide you have better things to do.'

'I haven't decided that.'

'I have decided you are going and that's it. As soon as you get your holidays you are going to Williamstown, so you can start getting ready.'

'What am I going to tell the team?'

'That you'll be back in September.'

'If I stayed, I could get on the minor team.'

'You can hurl all summer in the field your grandmother set aside for you. And keep in mind that it might be her last summer and she has been very good to you. So you can pack your bags now.'

For the next few days he did not speak to her, and thus she knew that he had accepted his fate and would go to Williamstown. Over the previous few months Frances had conspired with her mother to get John a provisional driving licence, finding his birth certificate and a photograph and forging his signature and then keeping the arrival of the licence a secret. John's grandmother had paid Bill for the old car when he was buying a new one. She was going to give it to John for the summer and allow him and his siblings to use it thereafter.

John's mood in the car was so downcast and sullen that Frances was tempted to tell him what was in store, but she resisted. He would never be as silent and withdrawn as this with anyone else, but she did not mind. Her job was to deposit him at Williamstown. She would be happy when she drove away, leaving him there for the summer.

HER MOTHER, she saw when she arrived, was walking with the help of a stick. Although she had had her hair done and was wearing a colourful dress, it was clear to Frances that she was ill. Her mother noticed Frances watching her and looked back defiantly, as though daring her to mention her health. All her energy was being used to surprise John, first with the driving licence and then with the keys of the car.

'Bill says you can drive perfectly,' she said. 'So you can go all over the county now in this. It's old, but it flies along.'

John said nothing, eyeing Frances and then his grand-mother gravely.

'Did you know about this?' he asked Frances.

'I'm the one who forged the signature,' she said.

'But I paid for it,' his grandmother interrupted. 'Make sure he knows that.'

By something in her voice and her face Frances could tell that she was in pain. She stood out of the way as John started the car and drove down the hill away from his grandmother's house and turned and approached them again.

'Oh, he's a great driver,' his grandmother said.

John took his bags from his mother's car. As Frances left them, they were both still looking at John's new acquisition. Frances loved John for not giving his grandmother the slightest hint of his unwillingness to stay with her all summer, but as she waved at him before she drove away, he gave her a look which suggested that he would not forgive her for a long time.

OVER THE next month she heard various reports about John's driving, including his travelling the forty miles to the town for a hurling match and not calling to see his family. Despite his consistent play, she was told, he had still not been selected for the minor team. She was glad that he had turned up for the match and played, thus his failure to make the team could not be blamed on her.

It was a beautiful summer. Each year, she and a group of women from the golf club took one day out to go to Rosslare Strand for a long and leisurely lunch at Kelly's Hotel after a morning's golf. If the weather were good enough, they spent the afternoon on the beach.

They had finished the first course before she noticed John and her mother at a corner table in the hotel restaurant; they were sixty miles from home. John had his back to the room and Frances realized that her mother's sight was too poor for her to be able to see them. Since none of her friends knew her mother, she decided not to mention their presence, to continue her own lunch without interrupting her son and his grandmother. Nonetheless, she could not, as the meal went on, help noticing that her mother's voice was louder than any other in the restaurant. John's voice was loud too, raised so that the old woman could hear him.

Her mother began to laugh as one or two of Frances's

party turned and looked at her. Frances watched as John stood up and, taking his white linen napkin in his hand, began playfully and lightly to brush against the old woman's head with it, as though he were assaulting her, making her laugh until she began to cough loudly, unable seemingly to catch her breath. By the time John returned to his seat, her gasping for breath had made the whole restaurant pay attention and caused comment among Frances's group.

On their way out John and his grandmother saw her, and as they approached she explained to her friends that, although she had seen them all along, she had decided to leave her party in peace for the meal. She noticed that a number of them seemed embarrassed at the comments they had made.

'You were making so much noise,' she said to them, 'that I pretended I wasn't related to you at all.'

'We're out on a spree, Frances,' her mother said, and then greeted each person at the table as she was introduced to them. John nodded politely, but stood back and said nothing.

'And so far from home,' Frances said. 'Are you thinking of getting the ferry?'

'We'd be well able to,' his mother said. 'And why wouldn't we be? He's the best driver in Ireland.'

Frances took in her mother's summer dress, all white with a pattern of roses, and her light pink cardigan. Her mother, she saw, was wearing make-up, but there was something strained about her appearance, emphasized now by her cheerfulness, manifested in the way her mouth hung open when she was not speaking and a sort of deadness in her eyes. There was a moment's silence between them when her mother seemed aware that Frances was examining her face.

'Well, it was a great surprise to see you,' Frances said, quickly filling the silence.

'We've been all over the country,' her mother said. 'And we're going over to Kilmore Quay now. And with the help of God we'll meet no one else we know. Isn't that right, John? We were planning to have a day out to ourselves. But it's nice to see you all the same, Frances.'

John glanced at his mother uncomfortably. It was clear that he wished his grandmother would stop talking. As she was turning to go, leaning heavily on her walking stick, the old woman addressed the table.

'I hope now you are all as lucky as I am, having a grandson as handsome and helpful in your old age.'

Frances saw several of her friends looking at John, whose head was now bowed.

'It must be the sea air has you in such good form,' Frances said.

'That's right, Frances.' Her mother turned back towards the table. 'It's the sea air. And a good driver. But don't say anything else now, you're only detaining us.'

She reached for John's arm as she said a final goodbye to them; she leaned on him and on her stick as the two of them slowly left the hotel restaurant.

THE OLD WOMAN died in the winter, barely surviving Christmas and lingering into the New Year, trying bravely to eat and drink what she could before she sank too low to touch food. In the two or three weeks when it was known that she would not live long, her children, now in their fifties, came and went, and a local nurse, home from England, spent much of the day in the house.

Frances brought John to see her a few times in the company of one or other of his siblings. She thought as the days passed that he might like to spend time alone with his grandmother, but she did not want to spell this out in case he thought she was putting pressure on him. Instead, she tried to ensure that he could have time with her if he wanted. She was certain every time she came that the old woman was looking out for John, waiting for him, but she noticed too that John always waited until someone else was going into the sick room and that he held back as his grandmother's eyes lit on him.

Her mother during those weeks was afraid. Despite her years of praying and her reading of theology, despite her age, she struggled now to add these extra days to her life. In her last week, she was alert and restless. She was never for one moment left alone.

She died late on a Friday evening, her breath coming in great gasps followed by unearthly silence until the gasping ended and the silence held. Those in the room were afraid to move, afraid to meet one another's eyes. None of them wanted to break the spell. Frances watched quietly as her mother lay still, all the life gone out of her.

When she was washed and laid out, they discussed who among them was the least tired, who would be most able to keep vigil through the night with the old woman's body, which would not be put into a coffin and brought to the church until Sunday.

On Saturday morning, Frances and her sisters and

brothers decided that the grandchildren, some of whom were already arriving for the funeral, would sit with the body in the candlelit room for all of Saturday night and then on Sunday morning.

When John came to the house wearing a suit and tie, Frances went upstairs with him; she remained by the door as he blessed himself and knelt by his grandmother's bed, touching her cold hands and her forehead as he stood up. Frances waited for him on the landing.

'We're all wrecked, John,' she said. 'We're going to ask the children to sit with her tonight. I thought you'd like to do it as a way of saying goodbye to her.'

'What about the others?' John asked.

'Some of them will sit with her too, but none of them was as close to her as you were.'

He said nothing for a moment. They began to walk down the stairs together.

'Sit with her?' he asked.

'It's only one night, John.'

'Have I not done enough?' he asked as they reached the hallway.

Frances thought he was going to cry.

'You were very close,' she said.

'Have I not done enough?' he asked again. 'Will you answer me that?'

He turned and walked out onto the road. Frances thought, as she watched him through the window, that he was about to burst into tears and wished to be away from her and from the people who were calling to express their condolences. But when she was able to see his face clearly as he stood outside, she noticed a new toughness in him, a look of pure determination. She decided that she would not argue with him or approach him again until the funeral was over.

She remained at the window observing him as he shook hands with one of the neighbours; the expression on his face was serious and formal like an adult's. She had no idea what he was thinking or feeling. Upstairs, the old woman who had wanted him so badly from the day he was born lay dead. Frances did not know whether her going was the lifting of a burden for John or a loss which he could not contemplate. The more she looked at him the more she realized that at this moment she did not herself know the difference. Suddenly John glanced at the window and saw her watching him. He shrugged as if to say that he would give nothing away, she could look at him as long as she liked.

A Long Winter

1

EVEN AS the days grew darker, the wind was mild. Miquel watched from the bedroom window as his father and Jordi walked along the lane which ran from the lower fields up to the barn. They were both in shirtsleeves as though it were a summer's day.

'We'll have no winter this year,' his father had said over dinner the previous evening, 'the priests have announced it as our reward for constant prayer and kindness to our neighbours.'

Miquel had managed a laugh to please his father, a role normally played by Jordi. But Jordi and their mother had remained silent. Jordi seldom spoke now and responded with hardly even a gesture if anyone said a word to him. On Saturday he would be taken to La Seu for a special haircut and be gone by Tuesday to do his military service. He would be away for two years.

A week earlier, when the final summons arrived, Jordi had asked Miquel what it was like, travelling by lorry to Lérida, being handed a uniform, spending the night in a barracks like a prisoner, eating their food, and travelling by train to Zaragoza or Madrid or Valladolid, wherever they decided to billet you.

'You've just described it,' Miquel said.

'Yes, but what's it like?' Jordi asked.

Miquel shrugged and held Jordi's gaze; there was nothing to be said about it. It was not worth remembering or commenting on. Without realizing, he had let his mind wander over certain details from his own two years in uniform, but he stopped himself suddenly when he saw that Jordi had become frightened.

Jordi, who seemed to spend most of his last days at home petting his dog Clua or playing with him, had not spoken to Miquel since then but he did not seem angry with him or in a sulk with him; rather, he understood that since they could not speak easily about the ordeal ahead of him, then they had better not speak at all. Even in the bedroom they shared, as they undressed or prepared to turn off the light, neither of them said a word. Miquel was deeply aware that the other single bed in the small room would soon be empty. He supposed that his mother would strip the sheets from it and leave the mattress bare during his brother's absence.

More than with fear or hunger or constant discomfort, he associated his years of military service with dreams of home. In the early months, as he received useless training under the punishing sun, he wondered why he had never viewed his life with his family in the village as precious and fragile. He dreamed of cold dawns, being woken by his father to get up and come with him in the jeep to the uplands where the flocks of sheep were summering. He dreamed about Jordi, who loved his sleep, deciding whether or not he would come with them. He dreamed about his own bed, the familiar room, the sounds of night and morning, the scops owl near the window in summer, the creaking of the floorboards as his mother moved in the night, the bringing of the flocks down to the barns in the winter, the narrow street of the village full of their cries.

Every day he had planned his return, longed for it in detail, lived in the ordinary future where the smallest domestic detail – the sound of a jeep starting up, a chainsaw, a hunter's gun or a dog's bark – would signify that he had returned, that he had survived. He had imagined this homecoming in all its satisfying comfort and freedom so closely that he had put no thought into how soon Jordi's turn would come, how soon his brother would have to submit himself to the humiliation of the haircut and the standing in the cold waiting for the lorry to take him to Lérida. Miquel knew how bad it would be for his brother, and it was as though some more vulnerable and innocent part of him were going to have the haircut, leaving an empty bed behind.

For the past week their mother had not been able to stay still. At times, it seemed to Miquel as if she were searching for something, moving around the kitchen and the long dining room and the storeroom. The great sporadic restlessness of hers had begun, he knew, as soon as he came back from the mili; he noticed it not long after his return. He did not think it had happened while he was away as Jordi had not mentioned it to him, and seemed too preoccupied to notice it now.

Her inability to settle came and went as though governed by the weather. In these last days, as Jordi prepared to go, the jittery, nervous movements had intensified, she seemed to Miquel like a strange, hungry animal who was living with them, barely able to cook or set the table, barely able to feed her hens and rabbits and geese. He wondered why she was so upset about Jordi's going; she had not behaved like this in the time before he left.

Now, however, as they had breakfast before the journey down to La Seu, she sat still at the table, wearing her good clothes, nervous and not speaking, but more composed than she had been for some weeks.

He had been so charged with happiness at coming home, he thought, that he had not bargained for this, the sitting into the back seat of the jeep with Jordi beside him and his mother and father in front as though they were transporting Jordi to be sold and slaughtered. But once the jeep got going, moving through familiar territory, there were moments when he fooled himself in thinking that this was an ordinary visit to La Seu on a market day with baskets of eggs to sell and a list of things to buy, then the dull fact of Jordi's departure would hit him again and the old dread would return.

His father was to accompany Jordi to the barber's, its owner a man known for his solemnity, and understood to be a communist, having served years in prison after the war. Thus he could be guaranteed to make no jokes or gleeful, mocking comments as he cut Jordi's hair according to army regulation. He would maintain his mournful tone and preserve, as much as he could, Jordi's dignity.

That day they had no eggs or poultry to sell, but groceries to buy. They would even have to purchase vegetables since their own garden had yielded hardly anything in the past weeks. Miquel and his mother, carrying two shopping baskets each, did not stop at the barber's, arranging instead to meet Jordi and his father in the body of the market in an hour's time.

Once they were alone with each other, his mother's step was lighter, she seemed almost happy as she faced into the market, greeting a number of stall-holders warmly, familiarly, announcing proudly to one of them that she had nothing to sell today, she was here only to buy, and laughing when the woman retorted that if more people did the same then all the stall-holders would become rich.

Then she left him, telling him to wait for her, there was something she needed to buy. It would not take long, she said. Her parting was abrupt, as though she felt that he would argue with her if she stayed a moment longer. He watched her slipping between two stalls, still carrying the baskets.

He wished she had given him something to do. He could easily have gone and bought the oil, or ordered the bottled gas so that it would be ready when they drove by at the end of the day. He watched the flower-sellers, alone among the stall-holders in not having a queue to buy their wares, the two women contented-looking. He wondered who would have the spare money to buy flowers.

Slowly, as he waited, he grew tired and bored. He supposed that his mother had gone to the butcher's or the poultry shop where there could be long queues, or even to buy something quite private at the pharmacy. After a while, he made his way, as his mother had done, between two of the stalls to the line of shops on the other side of them where he thought he could find her, believing that he could wait with her. If he saw that she was in the pharmacy, he would stay outside. The thought of standing beside her in a line of people, carrying the bags for her, pleased him. She had a way with people – strangers, or shopkeepers – a sort of charm which drew people towards her, and made him enjoy being with her in those moments when she smiled at someone or made a passing remark; it almost made him proud.

She was not in the queue at the butcher's, which was long. He had decided to walk up the street towards the poultry shop when he suddenly saw her with her back to the plate-glass window of a bar he had never noticed before. He was about to knock on the window, expecting her to turn and smile at him, but the expression on the face of the bar owner made him stop for a moment. Miquel watched as the owner counted out some coins and moved to a row of bottles at the back of the bar. He filled a large glass, the sort normally used for water, with a thin yellow liquid, like pale tea or light sherry, and brought it back to Miquel's mother. It was, he guessed, a fino, or a cheap wine, or a muscatel. He saw her grip the glass and finish it in two gulps; and, before he turned away, he noticed two empty glasses beside her on the counter, the same type of tumbler that she had just drunk from. He quickly went back to the spot where she had left him earlier, where she soon found him, her face flushed, her eyes bright, and they began the day's shopping.

He knew what he had seen; he understood now why she had gone alone, leaving him waiting; it was clear to him why she was so happy, almost carefree, as she made her first purchases. He also realized that he had known this vaguely for some time – the smells from her breath, the mood swings, the restlessness, were evidence enough to suggest something – but he had not allowed himself to put a name to it. She had downed the tumbler of wine the way a thirsty person would drain a glass of water. She must have done the same to the other two. There was no other explanation. He wondered if this would be enough for her, how long she could keep going on these tumblers of wine or sherry or whatever it was, if she would need more soon, or something stronger. He wondered if his father knew about this, or if Jordi knew. He supposed that their father must know, since he shared a bed with her every night, knew all her moods and movements. He was not sure, however, of the extent of his mother's drinking; maybe it merely happened in the early part of market day in La Seu, but he did not think so. And even if it were bad and went back a long time, it would be typical of his father not to mention it, or make anything of it, to store it up instead as another amusing aspect of the world.

When they had bought all the vegetables and were walking out of the bread shop, his mother spoke to him, moving her head carefully away, he noticed, so that he would not smell her breath.

'When you went to the mili,' she said, 'I thought you would never come back, but the time was actually short. It won't seem long at all before Jordi is back too.'

They stood in the queue at the butcher's, where he had imagined finding her before. It was all different now, even though only fifteen minutes had passed. He listened to her voice and watched her move with a new suspicion. Maybe, he thought, he had drawn conclusions too quickly. Maybe these were her only few glasses of the week, and she was, he thought, entitled to look forward to them, living in a village where there was no bar, no shop, nothing except hostile neighbours and a long winter.

His mother knew the butcher's wife, having often sold her rabbits. When she informed her now about Jordi going to the mili, the owner's wife and the women all around commiserated with her and, on noticing Miquel, smiled and said that she was lucky to have this one, so tall and handsome. She would be lucky if he were not married soon, the owner's wife said. One of the women joined the conversation to say that she had a daughter of the same age and they would make a great match. Miquel smiled and said he had no time for things like that, he would have too much work to do now that Jordi was going.

Jordi was wearing a cap when they met him. He grinned at Miquel and put his arm around him. They walked with their parents past the stalls which sold cheese and olives towards a small bar near the bus station where they ordered bocadillos and soft drinks.

'You'll have to take off your cap eventually,' Miquel said.

'I'm going to wait until the very last minute,' Jordi replied.

They ate quietly, the silence interrupted only by their father's views, spoken almost to himself, on the clientele, or the delays in the service, or the price of things, including communist haircuts. Miquel saw no reason to respond, and was surprised to see Jordi following suit. When he was away, he thought, his father's comments on all matters was one thing he did not miss, but Jordi was softer, more willing to create harmony, and he would, Miquel knew, miss everything as soon as he left them. He watched his mother gazing happily around her, sipping a glass of water.

Later, they separated, their mother going alone to purchase household goods and the men going to get bottled gas and to look at a saw their father had noticed in a shop window. Miquel was sure that his father did not need a new saw, but, perhaps more than any of them now, he needed something with which to distract himself. Miquel studied him as, suggesting affluence and serious intent, he sought and received the shop assistant's full attention, and then had the saw removed from the window. He watched his father demand a block of wood so that the saw could be tested; his father stood impatiently, with the air of a master woodcutter, until it was brought. When it came, he knelt and applied the saw, frowning regularly at the assistant and his two sons, ignoring the small audience which had built up around him as he set out to prove, Miquel realized, that the saw's blade was as good as blunt. Having done so to his own satisfaction, he stood up and wiped the sawdust from his hands.

When they drove to collect their mother, Miquel and Jordi descended to fetch her packages. She told them that the oil was not ready. It would, she said, have to be delivered during the week. When their father suggested that they go to another shop, she said no, they had already paid for it. It was, she said, the best oil and the best price, and the shopkeeper had promised faithfully that it would be delivered in a few days. Miquel noticed that she came close to losing her self-possession as she spoke, explaining what would happen with the oil in too much detail. Their father, already driving out of the town, said that a grocery shop without oil was like a winter without snow, it was not natural. Not natural at all, he laughed to himself.

Jordi would have two more days with them. That night, when they went to their bedroom and in casual silence prepared for bed, Miquel took in everything so that he might remember it in all its detail – the closing of the door so that they were in the room alone together, the creaking of the floorboards, the parcelling out of the small space so that they did not get in one another's way as they undressed, their soft shadows on the wall. Jordi was slower in his movements than he was, Miquel noted as though for the first time, but tidier also, he loved folding things. He kept his pyjamas folded neatly under his pillow. In the mili, in the long dormitories in a vast barracks somewhere, such habits could be easily mocked.

He watched Jordi who had his back to him quietly taking off his pullover and leaving it on top of the chest of drawers for the morning. Miquel was usually in bed before his brother. He was careful not to look directly at Jordi as he changed into his pyjamas; instead, he put his hands behind his head and studied the ceiling, making comments on things, much as his father did, sometimes doing imitations of his father's harmless daily grumblings, to Jordi's shocked delight.

This familiar life was now ending. Jordi would come back eventually, but he would soon have to leave soon afterwards to find work, begin his own life. The house and the land would be left to Miquel, as his father, in turn, had been left the house and farm by his father. Nights like this would not come again. There must be people, he realized, who relished this change, who longed for the first night of a marriage, all the newness and separation, the moving to a new house, the making of large decisions. His mother must have lain at night in her village over the mountain, knowing it would be her last night there. His father must have seen his own brothers go, one by one. Miquel understood that he himself had no interest in change; he wanted things to remain as they were. By the time he had thought this through and begun to puzzle over its implications, Jordi had fallen asleep. Miquel could imagine his innocent white face and his black hair, cut down to the scalp; he could hear his peaceful breathing. He almost wanted to touch him, move towards him and put his hand tenderly for one moment on his face.

Their mother was busy in the kitchen all the following day as she prepared a supper for the four of them, making a terrine with marinated rabbit and carrots and onions that Jordi loved, and roasting a stuffed goose for the main course. As Miquel came in and out of the kitchen, passing her as she worked, he looked for signs of a bottle near the work table or a glass of wine or brandy close to her, but he could see nothing.

That evening, she put a white tablecloth on the good old table, and set it as though her brother and sister-in-law were making a visit from Pallosa over the mountain, or one of her husband's brothers had come from Lérida. In the late afternoon, Miquel had noticed a bottle of white wine already opened; he supposed she needed it for the cooking, but now when he looked again he saw that it was gone.

Their mother brushed her hair and put on fresh clothes; their father wore his suit and a white shirt. It would have been easier, Miquel thought, if one or two of the neighbours

bours had called, or were invited to eat with them, but too much had happened in the village over the years for that. While all the neighbours would know the date of Jordi's departure, it would not be mentioned, it would remain part of the heavy silence which had gathered since the row about the water. They would eat alone.

On nights like this he saw his parents young, his father attentive, full of sweetness in the way he lit the candles and passed food and poured wine; his mother would be free now to talk about her own mother and the food she made for different occasions and what was said about her, and the parties in the old village, the good neighbours they had there. She would do this carefully, not implying any criticism of the life she lived here, which they were celebrating more than any past life.

2

ONE MORNING after Jordi had left, Miquel surprised his mother by coming silently into the kitchen as she was gulping from a glass. She put it down hurriedly. He tried to get close to her to see what he could smell from her breath, but she seemed to keep away from him deliberately, moving quickly out to the rabbit house and the hen house. As soon as she left, however, he found the glass. It was empty, but the residual smell was of strong wine; to his nostrils that morning the smell was pungent, almost rotten. He left the glass back where he had found it in case she came suddenly back into the room.

His mother had left Jordi's bed untouched for the first few days. Only the folded pyjamas under the pillow were missing. It was when she took the sheets and blankets from the bed, leaving a bare pillow and a bare mattress, that Miquel dreaded going up to his bedroom at night. A few times in the first days he managed to forget that Jordi was gone; he thought he heard him breathing in the night, and on one of the mornings, when the first sounds could be heard, he found himself looking over at his brother's bed to see if Jordi was awake yet.

Since the days remained dry and the sun was warm, his father expressed the view that they should keep busy, repair a wall of the barn, work they might never do, he said, but always plan to do until their barns were rubble and the sheep were shivering with the cold out in the fields all night. He mentioned Castellet, one of his neighbours, whose laziness was a constant source of interest. If we don't repair the barns, we'll end like Castellet. Saying the name alone appeared to give his father pleasure, made him smile in the calm, amused way to which Miquel had become so accustomed.

The work was tough, with heavy stones to remove and replace and beams to shore up and slates to take down. His father, who had worked as a stone cutter, repointed the stones and cut new ones which he had bought from the owner of a ruined barn in a nearby village and painstakingly transported to his own holding. He gradually made clear that he planned to dismantle one whole side of the barn, using cheap bricks on the inside and facing it with stone. Miquel was doing all the lifting and carrying, his father having found a place in the sun where he could chisel and shape and flatten. Each time Miquel passed him with a loaded wheelbarrow, or presented him with a new pile of stones, he had remarks to make, on the habits of the neighbours, or the poorness of the brick, or the durability of the stone, or the shortness of the lambing season, or the lunch which might be waiting for them, or where Jordi might be now and when they might hear from him.

When it went beyond two in the afternoon, and the sun disappeared behind the hills, it would grow bitterly cold, letting them know that, despite the bright days, they were

in the depths of winter. Miquel tried to convince his father
that they should not work after lunch, except the usual
work with the animals and their feed, but his father insisted
that another hour each day would make all the difference.
Once they started, however, they seldom stayed long, his
father nodding and smiling when Miquel stood in front of
him announcing that he had carried his last stone of the
day.

On one of those days when Miquel returned to the
house in the afternoon earlier than expected he found his
mother sitting at the kitchen table. She did not look up
when he came in. Normally, she sat down in the morning
to have a cup of chocolate but otherwise, he knew, she
disliked sitting down until after supper. She preferred moving around all day, cooking, washing clothes and looking
after her hens, rabbits and geese. He pretended at first not
to notice her, filling a glass of water from the tap, but when
he turned he saw that she was sitting with her arms wrapped
around herself and was rocking back and forth. When he
asked her if she was all right, she did not look at him.

'Get your father,' she said.

When Miquel came back with his father, she was still
rocking, as though this were her only way of keeping the
pain, whatever it was, from overwhelming her. She did not
look up.

'What is it?' his father asked.

'You know what it is,' she said calmly, and recoiled
when his father made to touch her.

'Was it both of you, or just you?' she asked.

'Just me,' his father said.

'What did you do?' Miquel asked.

'Dumped the containers of wine just delivered, emptied them,' she said.

'I didn't see any wine,' Miquel said.

'You could barely call it wine,' his father said. 'Acid. You didn't see it because she hid it. I watched the whole adventure from the top floor of the low barn with those binoculars you brought back from the mili. They were delivering the oil, but it was just an excuse.'

'Spying on me,' his mother said.

'And what did you do?' Miquel asked his father.

'I went down,' his father said, 'when they had gone and I emptied it, all of it. And I put the containers back where they were, but they were empty now of their poison.'

'You know all about poison,' she said.

Miquel was surprised by the suddenness of her anger, her sharpness.

'I'm the one has to sleep with you,' his father said. 'And the smell of that stuff rotting you as you sleep.'

His mother continued to rock back and forth, as though they were not there. They stood close to her, Miquel noticing a look on his father's face, both sorry and nervous – concerned, it seemed to Miquel, that he had said too much and ready now to be softer with her.

'I am sorry,' his mother said quietly, 'that I ever knew any of you.' Her tone was definite, decisive.

Miquel's father looked at her puzzled.

'Any of us?'

'That's what I said. Did you not hear me?'

'Who do you mean?'

'I mean the people in this house.'

'Who? Let us know who you mean.'

'I mean everyone, but especially you.' She spoke quietly again. 'That's who I mean.'

'Well, there's no point in speaking to you, then, is there?' he asked.

'Are you going to replace what you threw out?' she asked.

'I am not.'

'Well, that's the end, then,' she said and began to cry.

As his father left the house, Miquel was unsure if he should remain. He watched his father from the window walking down towards the barn they were repairing. Miquel listened as his mother's crying grew louder, more uncontrolled. He moved closer to her and put his hand on her shoulder. Slowly, she moved her hand towards his, caught one of his fingers and caressed it and then took his whole hand in hers and held it. Her crying now stopped but she was still rocking gently back and forth.

3

His mother did not move and would eat nothing. When Miquel had lit the fire, and put extra kindling on it until it was blazing, he suggested that she sit near it. She allowed him to lead her there and put her sitting as though she were blind or had no will of her own. She insisted that she was not hungry. Asking her if she wanted something to drink would sound like a bitter joke at her expense so he did not ask her.

Miquel and his father sat at the table and had the soup left over from the previous day, and then ate some ham and tomatoes and bread. It was not the dinner they normally had, but they did not mention it or complain. When he was about to go to bed and he met his father on the upstairs landing, Miquel spoke quietly to him, proposing that they should go to La Seu in the morning and buy her some wine, better wine than the stuff the grocer had delivered, and tell her now that she could come with them if she wanted. His father put his arm around him before he replied.

'No, it's better like this. We did that when you were away. She has to stop altogether. That's what the doctor told us a few months ago, the only way to stop was to stop. Now, since she has no drink, she will stop. It's the best thing. She'll be fine in a few days.'

'How long has she been drinking?' Miquel asked.

'A few years.'

'How is it we never noticed?'

'We all noticed,' his father said.

'Jordi didn't,' Miquel replied.

'He did, son, he did,' his father said.

When he went back downstairs, his father followed him; they found his mother still sitting in front of the fire. She was shaking as though with the cold. Miquel left them and went to bed.

As he lay in bed with the light out, while hearing vague stirrings from the floor below him, he remembered how different Jordi was with him at first when they were alone in the bedroom after he came back from the mili. Before this Jordi and he had been natural and relaxed about undressing in front of each other, but Jordi would now cover himself if Miquel came in, or would sit awkwardly on the side of the bed taking off his shorts and putting on his pyjama-bottoms as modestly as if there were a woman in the room. Jordi and his father took time to get used to his homecoming, disguising the fact that they had managed without him, Jordi loath to hand over some of the jobs which naturally belonged to his older brother. Thus they did not tell him that his mother, while he was away, had become a hopeless drinker. In keeping the secret, they had treated him like a stranger.

In the night he heard their voices in the room below; his father's was calm but his mother's was high and whimpering. Eventually, they came to bed and there was silence for some time until he heard the floorboards creaking and one of them going downstairs again. Soon the other followed and the voices started again. He knew that he would not sleep. It was hard anyway since Jordi was absent from the other bed; it was the no sound coming from there kept him awake, the no snoring or rhythm of breathing, the no turning over which seemed to disturb him more than the wind, which appeared now to have changed direction, blowing fiercely from the north in the few hours before the dawn, rattling the window.

In the morning he found his father in the kitchen. His mother, he presumed, was in bed. His father began to shave, using the small mirror over the kitchen sink, working with slow concentration.

'Should we not go to La Seu and get her what she wants?' Miquel asked.

His father did not reply.

'Replace what was thrown out.' He raised his voice.

'No,' his father said, catching Miquel's eye in the mirror. 'She has to stop some day. The best day for everything is always today. Anyway, she's asleep now.'

He continued shaving even more slowly and carefully, as though this were a more pressing concern of his than any matter his son might care to raise. Miquel found some bread and rubbed some oil and tomato and salt into it, finding also a lump of cheese and cutting off a slice. He ate quickly, hungrily, before going outside to collect the eggs from the hen house, passing his father who did not speak to him.

Once in the shade, he noticed how intensely cold it had become; the water in the fenced-off piece of ground in front of the hen house was completely frozen. The sky was blue, but it was not the still, calm blue of earlier days, it was more that the clouds had been blown back by the wind, making the blue of the sky seemed exposed and raw. When he looked down towards the barns he saw that his father had found a sheltered spot in the sunlight. Miquel joined him and they spent the morning slowly facing the new brick of the barn with stone.

Before lunch they went to inspect the sheep, bringing down feed from the upper floor of the barn. They were not sure of the time, but, once they were finished with the sheep, Miquel was surprised that his mother had not called them in to eat. Then he remembered what had happened and wondered if she were still in bed or too distressed to cook for them.

When they came into the house, he knew that she had not been in the kitchen. Nothing had been touched or cleared away. Clua, he saw, had not been fed. His father went upstairs and then came down and said that she was not in their bedroom. By the time they had finished their first search of the house and the grounds around the barns and outhouses, Miquel knew that she had gone. Their leaving her all morning, not once going into the house, even to get a glass of water, or check her state of mind, seemed now like an invitation for her to go. As they searched once more, and this search too became futile, Miquel began to consider where she might have gone and how she might have travelled. She could not have taken refuge with any of their neighbours; nobody in the village would have known what to do were she to arrive on their doorstep, she had not been inside any of their houses for some years. There was no transport available out of the village, no bus until the main road ten or eleven kilometres away, and that service was irregular. Nobody would stop and collect her were she to walk towards La Seu, unless a stranger were to be in the area, which was unlikely.

She had, in any case, left them. When his father suggested searching the inside of the barns, Miquel shook his head. His mother would have had to walk right past them to get to the barns except for the short time they went to inspect the sheep, and even then they would have seen her. Her coat was gone and her good scarf and her boots. His father, even when Miquel had twice shown him the space where the missing coat had hung and the space where the missing boots had lain, went upstairs again and again in search of her, to the top loft, to the store, to the barn directly below them. Miquel sat down at the table, letting his father search for as long as he pleased, knowing that eventually he would have to sit down too and talk about what should be done now.

There were still ten or twelve houses inhabited in the village; nothing happened that was not noticed, the old people sat by windows watching, the few young men were in the fields or by the barns, the women did their housework checking regularly on the weather. There were no children in any of the houses; most of the young had fled to the cities or bigger towns. Miquel and Jordi were the two youngest left in the place. They had been brought up to depend on no one around them, but it was only in recent years that the hostility between their father and the rest of the village had grown so intense that there was almost no contact with the neighbours. Their father had denounced three families for diverting water in the summer months. He had gone to Tremp and given evidence against them, while the other families, despite having water stolen from them, had spoken in their defence. The judge imposed fines. The feelings about the willingness of Miquel's father to betray them were sharp and fresh in the households that had to pay the fines. Their father took pleasure, if he could make one of his sons listen, in calling his neighbours liars and thieves. The neighbours, in turn, passed him every day without speaking.

Now, he and Miquel would have to go from house to house, their search for his mother an admission that all was not well in their home. They could not be sure, Miquel realized, that the neighbours would even tell them what they had seen. But it was the only thing they could do. So once his father had ceased his searching, they put their coats on and set out, being careful to begin with the closest neighbour so that no one would think they had any special friends or favoured household in the village.

Mateu at the Casa Raúl came to the door slowly, his fat belly in front of him. He was one of the men who had to pay the fine. He screwed his eyes up in distaste as soon as Miquel's father opened his mouth, giving no sign that he understood a word spoken. Instead, he studied their faces, taking his time to consider what he saw. Miquel believed at first that whether Mateu had seen his mother or not he would be no use to them. The problem would be how quickly they could move away from his door. Miquel nudged his father and nodded his head in the direction of the next house, but his father stood there, resting himself against the doorframe, waiting for something, neither

repeating the question nor saying anything else as Mateu
cleared his throat. Mateu's house was the closest to theirs;
Mateu, Miquel imagined, had probably not left the house
all day, he had good views from his windows and would
have seen her easily no matter in what direction she had
gone.

As they stood in the doorway, the sky darkened suddenly, blue-black clouds appeared over them gathering in a
low dense mass. The light became a dark purple and there
was no wind. Miquel shivered. He knew that it meant
snow; it would be the first of the year, late in coming, and
all the more severe on a day as cold as this.

'I saw her going all right,' Mateu said, 'but there was no
sign of her coming back.'

'Which direction?' Miquel's father asked.

'She took the road towards Coll del So.'

'But that leads nowhere,' his father said.

Mateu nodded.

It struck Miquel immediately that it led towards Pallosa,
where his mother's brother still lived in the old family
house; it could be reached in four or five hours.

'How long ago did you see her?' his father asked.

'She's gone a few hours,' Mateu said.

'What? Three or four?'

'Yes, three or four, or somewhere in between.'

The snow came down gently as the air darkened even
further. The flakes were thick, they did not melt immediately on the back of Miquel's hand which he held out to
test them. The jeep, he knew, could make its way along the
narrow road which led to the small church at Santa Magdalena, and perhaps even further along the military road to

Coll del So, but after that, he thought, his mother would make her way down to Pallosa along old tracks and pathways which no jeep could follow and no outsider could find. In three or four hours walking she could be still on the military road, but it was unlikely. More probably, she would have reached Coll del So and then she might even have started along the steeper tracks, and he knew that they must race to the jeep and drive as fast as they could along the winding road to these uplands where they kept their sheep in the summer, territory which remained unvisited in the winter.

'You won't get far now,' Mateu said to them as they moved away from his door.

'Are you certain she went that way?' Miquel called back to him.

'Ask the others, we all saw her.'

They walked back quickly to the house. As his father turned the jeep, Miquel ran into the house to fetch his binoculars.

'What are you doing with those?' his father asked.

Miquel looked down at them resting in his lap.

'I don't know . . . I thought . . .'

'We don't have time for thinking,' his father said.

They drove along the narrow road out of the village; the windscreen wipers were on full, but still the snow impaired their vision and the jeep's headlights caught sheets of whiteness. Had she been on the road coming towards them, even with her arms outstretched, they would not have seen her. It must have been clear to his father, Miquel knew, that there was little purpose in their journey. The only hope, Miquel thought, was that she had left later than Mateu had said. He considered that for a moment and then the possibility that she had walked slowly, or had turned back at some point, and then he let his mind linger over another possibility – that she had walked quickly and left even earlier than Mateu had said and was within reach of Pallosa, that she was clambering down the old paths as best she could. Moving slowly and carefully, watching each step. It was territory she knew; she was, Miquel thought, unlikely to make mistakes. But he was not sure. Perhaps the paths down the slopes would be all hidden now and every step treacherous.

His father worked hard to manage the jeep as it began to sway and slide. Even when the snow was not blown hard against the windscreen, they could see it falling in dense waves and building up on the road in front of them so that after a while they were driving on a thick blanket of snow, which was gathering in strength as they moved forward. Soon it was obvious that their way would eventually be impeded, their way back made impossible.

Miquel knew that it would make sense for him to suggest they stop and turn, that their moving ahead was perhaps pointless and maybe even dangerous, but he knew also that if they turned and went home they would be facing into sheer emptiness, with no idea where his mother was and the long night ahead of them.

When there was a small clearing, his father, without saying anything, tried to turn the jeep, believing, it seemed to Miquel, that the snow covered a level surface. But it merely covered a sharp dip between the road and the verge into which one of the front wheels now sank. His father cursed as Miquel got out of the jeep to see if he could ease the vehicle back onto the road. He watched the wheel revolve frantically, like a spider caught in water. In the end, they had to find stones wherever they could and a short plank from the back of the jeep and settle these under the wheel; they were blinded by the snow as they scampered about the jeep. When he turned to avoid the driving snow, he found that it was blowing and swirling in all directions as though the four winds were competing with each other. They began to push the jeep once the wheel had been stabilized, trying to lift it back onto the road, but the wheels were stuck in the snow and would not easily move. They were, Miquel guessed, half an hour's walk from the village, maybe more in the snow, and he imagined, as his father revved the engine in one more large effort to move the jeep, that his mother, having avoided the worst of the weather, was now knocking gently on the door of her brother's house, the house where she was born. They loved her in that house and they would welcome her and in the morning they would find a way of sending a message to say that she was safe.

He heaved one more time as his father put sudden pressure on the accelerator. The jeep slid sideways; its four wheels were now on the road, still facing away from the village. His father shouted to him to get back in, he was going to try to turn the jeep again. He put it in neutral and let it inch forward as far as it could safely go and then he pulled up the handbrake and put it into reverse. He let the handbrake down and slowly accelerated. At first it did not move, and then the back wheels began to revolve in the snow until his father gave the accelerator fierce pressure and they moved back at speed, sliding on the road. But they were almost facing the village now; they could go back, cutting with difficulty through the settling snow on the ground and the gusts of thick snowflakes gathering on the windscreen as fast as the wipers could remove them.

Once home, they went through all the possibilities, how quickly she could walk, at what time she had left, how long it took along the road until you had to find the old paths which led down to Pallosa. Even in summer there were tough stretches, parts you had to scramble down rather than walk. She could, Miquel said, have turned back when the snow came. She knew how dangerous a snowstorm like this could be. Even if she were closer to Pallosa when it started, she might have thought that it was safer on the level track than on the slopes moving downwards, and even though it would take her hours, trudging through the snow, it might have been the wisest thing to do.

'If we went to La Seu,' Miquel said, 'we could ask the police there to find out if she arrived in Pallosa. We could report her as missing.'

His father sighed.

'I know she's alive somewhere,' he said.

Miquel did not answer him.

When a knock came to the door, he believed in the first instant that their troubles were over, she had come back. Then, however, he realized that she would not knock the door of her own house. Whoever had knocked remained outside. Perhaps they had found her or knew where she was. When his father went into the hallway and opened the door, Miquel saw that it was Josep Bernat and his wife. They had not come to this house, he knew, since the court case.

'We saw her going,' Josep said. 'We thought it was a strange time to be setting off. She had a bag with her.'

'A shopping bag,' his wife added.

'We noticed it because it was the wrong direction for shops.'

'She was going back to Pallosa, I suppose,' Miquel's father said.

'Could you not have driven her there?' Josep asked.

As his father sighed again, Miquel moved towards the window where he could see dense whirling snow still falling outside. The visitors remained standing; they had not been asked to take their coats off, nor offered any refreshment. Miquel could sense that Josep now regretted his last question. He smiled hesitantly at their neighbour as his father turned away.

'We could report her missing to the police in La Seu,' Miquel said.

'The road is probably impassable now and the phone lines from there might be down,' Josep replied. 'It'll be worse later because it's starting to freeze as well. They'll open the road in the morning, I hope.'

'Do you remember what time she left at?' Miquel asked.

'She didn't leave in time to get to Pallosa before the snow,' Josep replied.

'She could have turned back when it started,' Miquel said.

'It would be hard in that blizzard to have any sense of direction,' Josep said.

'Don't say anything more!' Miquel's father said.

'We were going to say that the men will all search for

her when the light comes,' Josep's wife said. 'The minute there's light. But they can't search for her now. The snow has not done its worst yet. They cannot go out in the blizzard.'

'She's gone, then,' Miquel's father said, sitting down and sighing. 'No one could last the night in the open. She'll die of the cold.'

'You never can tell,' Josep said.

'We'll talk in the morning, then,' Miquel's father said. 'We can ask the police to check if she ever arrived in Pallosa.'

When Josep Bernat and his wife left the house, Miquel stood with his father watching them as they trudged through the snow. Then Miquel went outside to make sure that there was enough feed in the hen house, collecting eggs at the same time, and then feeding the rabbits and closing their shed for the night. At the doorway, he gave Clua, who seemed ravenous, some scraps. As his father sat silently at the table, he fried six eggs in oil, letting the oil splutter onto the tiles around the cooker, as his mother would never do. He cut some stale bread and brought some salt and oil and the one half-tomato that was left to the table. He put three fried eggs on a plate for his father and three for himself. As they ate in silence, Miquel thought over and over of the possibility that this was not really happening, it was a long dream he would soon wake from, or a scene which would change without warning as another knock came to the door or a jeep pulled up outside, or her face, smiling and nervous, appeared at the window as they both stood up to greet her, their food half eaten.

In the morning he woke to the sound of boots on the

stairs, boots on the floorboards below and men's voices. He quickly dressed in the freezing bedroom before opening the shutters to a world of pure glaring whiteness. He went downstairs. Five or six men from the village were there, one of them had brought a pot of coffee and some brandy. His father, he noticed, looked shrunken and cowed beside these other men. He realized that in all his life he had seldom seen other men in this kitchen, his uncle a few times and the postman, or men coming to sell or repair something, but they were always somehow in the shadows. These men, up at dawn and ready for the search, held the centre of the room; they were confident, brusque and sharp-eyed.

Outside on the steps of the house their dogs waited. It was bitterly cold and the snow was still falling; in the night it had settled knee-deep on the ground. It would, he thought, be hard to make any progress under these conditions. His mother, the neighbours agreed, had been gone for more than three hours when the snow came. If she had fallen or found shelter, it was not likely to be close by. The snow would have covered any tracks she had made and the air was probably too cold for the dogs to be able to trace any scent. Their only hope was that she had moved quickly or found company on the road and made her way with assistance to her brother's house before real darkness fell and the thick snow began to settle.

The men moved slowly, with determination. It seemed to Miquel that they knew as well as he did that this quest was pointless, that even a body would not be found under the relentless covering of snow, and that under these conditions, even reaching Coll del So would be impossible.

They were doing it, he knew, because they could not do nothing, despite their dislike for his father. They would not wish it to be known that they had idled in their houses, or done easy winter work, when a woman of the village had disappeared in the snow. And so all morning they moved carefully along the road which his mother must have travelled. They stopped only when a flask of brandy and some bread and cold sausage were passed around. They did not speak much to each other but they did not speak to Miquel or his father at all.

It was well past midday, with the snow falling still, and they had not yet reached the church of Santa Magdalena where the narrow military road began. Miquel watched them consulting with each other while his father stood apart. He knew that they wished to abandon the search for the day; it would take them three hours to get back to the village. This meant that they could go forward for another hour or more and still be back before dusk, but it was clear that they were already tired, each step in the heavy snow took its toll on their energy; they would be exhausted by the time they reached home.

It was easier to dream than do anything else, to imagine his uncle driving his mother home from Pallosa after her night of rest, and his uncle's jeep appearing in the village at the same time as they all arrived back. As they turned, it struck Miquel forcefully that they all knew that his mother had not survived, that the men from the village had taken him and his father out on this vain search as a way of distracting them from the cold fact that Miquel's mother was missing, she lay dead somewhere near or below the Coll del So, covered in a metre or more of snow, that she would not ever come back to their house, unless they brought her coffin there when they found her. Walking, then, was a way of getting them used to the new fact without their having to wait all day in an empty house, with nothing happening, and nothing to say.

When they came back into the village they saw a police jeep outside their house, with two uniformed members of the Guardia Civil inside. As soon as the group of villagers came fully into view, one policeman got out of the jeep, and then, when they were closer, the one who had been in the passenger seat emerged. He was very young, Miquel noticed, and seemed almost shy. He kept his hat on as he glanced at the men coming towards him and then looked away. His companion, the driver, was middle-aged, stocky, hatless. Miquel watched him singling out his father and himself as the two men he would need to speak to and wondered how the police had been alerted. As they approached the jeep, Miquel checked the back seat in case they had found her and had her body. But there was nothing except an old rug.

His father explained, as soon as they were inside, that his wife could easily be safe, could easily have arrived in Pallosa and be in her brother's house. The older policeman took note of the brother's name and said in a heavy southern accent that if the single telephone line to Pallosa, which was in the police station there, were back up he would call as soon as he returned to La Seu, and if the road were open would go to Pallosa. In the meantime, he needed a description of her.

As Miquel's father spoke and the policeman took notes, the younger policeman leaned against the wall, just inside the door of the kitchen, pushed his hat back on his head so Miquel was able to see his clear, unwrinkled forehead and his large dark eyes. As these eyes examined the room, seeming to concentrate briefly on the scene between the two older men, they locked with Miquel's eyes. Miquel was aware that he had been staring at the younger man since he came into the room and it would be better now if he looked away, let whatever had happened dissolve into a moment of unconcealed curiosity and nothing more. But he did not look away. He took in the young policeman's face in the shadowy light of the kitchen, the full redness of his lips, the square, hard stubbornness of his jaw and chin and then the softness of his eyes, the eyelashes like a girl's. The young policeman, in turn, watched only Miquel's eyes, his gaze cold, expressionless, as though he were sullenly blaming him for something. When Miquel looked down at the policeman's crotch, he too glanced down at himself and he briefly smiled, opening his lips, before resuming his former expression, but more intense now, almost feral, staking out an object within his grasp.

As his colleague finished taking his notes and appeared ready to depart, the younger policeman took off his hat. Miquel, across the room, quietly acknowledged the gesture. Then the young policeman, who had not spoken once, turned and opened the door, allowing his colleague to leave first, gesturing to Miquel's father to follow, trying, it seemed to Miquel, to engineer a moment when the two older men would be outside and the two younger ones at the door, or inside the hall. But Miquel's father held back, insisting, out of politeness, that the younger policeman should go out before him. Miquel watched the younger policeman carefully as his companion reversed the jeep and turned and slowed for a second before driving away.

As Miquel busied himself doing his mother's tasks, his father went outside and began to chop wood, striking frantic blows with the hatchet, splitting blocks of wood they could have easily burned in one piece. Miquel dreaded the night, when they would have nothing left to do but wait for news of her, knowing that it might not come soon.

He remembered a game he had begun to play with her as soon as he could walk. He did not know how it had started, but, with her in the room, he used to hide under the table, or under the bed, or behind a chair, and she then would pretend that she could not find him, and they would both let it continue until the moment before he became scared. Then he would appear and she would feign surprise and shock and delight, and lift him up in the air. He had no memory of ever doing this while his father was present and, once Jordi could understand things, he would grow frightened by the disappearance and the mock search and was made jealous by his mother's and his brother's shouts of recognition and sudden greeting. As Miquel moved around the house now, he was acutely alert to the shadowy places, becoming darker in the twilight, the places where you could hide and then appear, as though his mother might mysteriously arrive and position herself where she could not be instantly found.

That evening they ate in silence some more fried eggs and stale bread and cold sausage until Miquel asked their father what they should do about Jordi. Even though they had no address for him, no idea where he was, they could ask the police in La Seu to make contact with him.

'And say what?' his father asked.

Miquel did not answer him.

'He has enough to worry about,' his father said.

'He might hear it from someone.'

'He's well out of earshot.'

'You can meet people from home,' Miquel said. 'You never know who you are going to meet, and they could have heard the news.'

'For the moment,' his father said, 'we'll tell him nothing, we'll leave him in peace.'

When they had eaten, Foix, who had made himself the leader of the search all that day, called to the door but refused to come in, even though it was snowing hard outside. The phone lines, he said, were still down. His brother-in-law, he added, had made it through to the village and left behind two dogs who were trained to follow a scent. He had worked with them before, he said, and they were the best. So they would set out with the dogs at first light, all the men who had been with them would come again, even though the terrain might be more difficult because there could be a bigger fall of snow during the night.

Before they went to bed, his father told him that he was going to try to drive the jeep to La Seu the next day and then across the paved road to Sort and then, if he could, to Pallosa. Miquel said that he would go with the men, but when he went to the window and looked out and saw the snow coming down even thicker than before, he realized that neither his father nor the men would go very far the next day, and the village could, if the snow continued to fall as it was falling now, be cut off on both sides.

His father and himself, Miquel realized, were sleeping alone in rooms where the stark absences were palpable; it was hard to remember that both his mother and Jordi were gone, and that should Jordi return and she should not, then her absence would seem even greater. He lay on Jordi's bed for a while until the cold made him undress and seek refuge under his own blankets. He wished it were two weeks earlier, before Jordi had left; he wished it were three years earlier, when he had just come home; he wished it were any time but now.

In the morning again he was woken by feet on the floorboards in the room below; he had slept deeply, and he longed for more time in the oblivion from which he had just been snatched. Instantly, he knew he would have to rise and spend the day searching for his mother in the freezing air, the snow getting into his boots; his toes, like his fingers, would be utterly frozen. He looked at Jordi's bed and wondered if he concentrated hard enough could he get in touch with him to reassure him that they were all well, despite the winter, and that he had no news to tell, nothing had happened since Jordi left.

Foix, when Miquel appeared in the kitchen, took him aside and said that the two dogs, waiting outside, would need a scent to work from, and the better the scent the better the chance of finding her. Thus he would, he said, need something that belonged to her, something she wore. He began to whisper as he told Miquel that her clothes, if they had been washed since she had last worn them, would not be of much use; the closer to her body the garment had been worn the more useful it would be. He looked at Miquel as though they were both conspirators against not only everyone in the room, but against the snow-covered world outside as well.

Miquel's father, sure now that he would not get his jeep up the steep hill beyond the curve out of the village on the road to La Seu, was sitting alone at the table as more men came and more dogs yelped in the freezing morning. The snow had stopped in the night; before the dawn the temperature had dropped which meant they had to watch for patches of ice as well as deep snow. His father seemed forlorn, exhausted, distant from what was happening around him. Miquel decided not to trouble him about Foix's request, to go upstairs alone and try to find something of his mother's which had preserved her scent.

He had forgotten how well he knew the chest of drawers under the window of his parents' bedroom. He had not been near it for years, but when he was a small boy his favourite pastime, under his mother's supervision, was opening each drawer and taking out the contents and then folding them and replacing them exactly as he had found them. In the top drawer she kept documents and bills and receipts on one side and handkerchiefs and scarves on the other. The middle drawer was where she kept her blouses and cardigans, and in the two bottom drawers she kept her underwear. When she opened these drawers the smell was not of her, but of lavender and perfume. He did not touch anything; nothing here would be any use to Foix and his dogs.

In a corner of the room was the old basket, the same size as the one in his own room, where dirty clothes were thrown. It was only half-full; on the top were shirts his father had worn with some socks and shorts and vests, and at the very bottom were the last things his mother had worn in this house and left here, as well as the blouse she had worn on the night of Jordi's dinner which, he imagined, she was keeping so she could wash it and dry it in some special way. Below this was some of her underwear which he took and held, and then, checking that no one was behind him, he lifted to his nose. He buried his face in the intimate smell of her, which was clear despite the days that had passed since she had worn this underwear. It carried a sharp hint of her into this cold room and, for a moment, he imagined the dogs moving blindly through the landscape, living only with this smell, seeking its loving source under the snow or in the undergrowth. He would walk behind them. He dropped all of the undergarments except one back into the basket, tucking them under his father's clothes, and carried the one he had selected downstairs and gave it to Foix, who was waiting with the dogs outside the door.

The day was much colder than the one before and progress was much harder as the two new dogs followed phantom scents which led them off the road and high into the hills while the men had to wait for them below. Miquel's father followed them far behind most of the time, giving no impression that he was searching for her or looking for clues as to where she might be. Miquel noticed Foix and Castellet and some of the other men glancing back at him, clearly irritated. He noticed also that their neighbours, on this second day's searching, were more animated, seemed to enjoy shouting at the dogs, had more life in them the more time went on. Their very excitement caused his father to appear uninterested, almost bored as he trudged behind them as though his only aim were not to wet his feet.

The two dogs, Miquel thought, had more energy than intelligence, and he wondered why Foix did not realize, as he did now, that anything buried under a mound of freezing snow would be unlikely to yield a scent. But he knew that there was nothing else he could do except move forward in what was, with the exception of fox and wild-boar tracks, a flat, virgin whiteness, seeming innocent, almost beautiful, utterly harmless, its treacherous nature lying in layers under its blank surface.

By early afternoon they could go no further; the snow was too deep, and it was becoming hard to tell where the road ahead began to dip and rise and where the margin was and how steep the fall. The dogs, who had not been fed since early morning, were increasingly difficult; two of them from the village began a vicious fight, snarling and yelping as they tore at each other, having to be held by their owners, and then kicked into surly submission. Miquel noticed that all the men took part in separating them and holding them and shouting at them except himself and his father, who stood back watching, and he felt that this, too, annoyed the men. Thus he was glad when they gave up the search, having to wait for the two new dogs to come back from whatever vain quest they had been on, and began to make their way back. Miquel was careful to walk with the other men, stay between two of them, or close to one. His father lagged so far behind that several times when he turned his head he could not see him.

That night his father insisted that there would be no more futile outings, that these men hated him and had spent two days uselessly walking the road merely as a way of torturing him and humiliating him. He would have no more of them, he said. In the morning, he said, they would go to La Seu, where it would be market day, whether the road was open or not; they would drive to the point where it was closed and wait there, or wade through whatever snow was blocking the road.

Miquel, without consulting his father, left the house and called on Foix, who, when he came to the door, asked him almost aggressively what he wanted. Miquel told him that they would not be searching the next day, but going to La Seu, where they might meet people from Pallosa. They could also speak to the police. He added that he wished to thank Foix for all his help.

'And your father?' Foix asked. 'We all know he has a tongue. Has he lost the use of it?'

Miquel held his gaze calmly.

'He is very upset.'

Foix closed the door without speaking. When Miquel went home, he did not tell his father where he had been.

The road to La Seu was open, but icy in stretches, dangerously so in the early morning. Miquel had slept a dreamless sleep and for the first few minutes of the day had believed that this would be another normal day in his life. The night had erased all memory of the days just passed. But his father, he saw when he went downstairs, had not slept at all, seemed worn out, stopping halfway through every sentence, having forgotten what it was he had wanted to say. His father's sleepless state appeared to make him drive more cautiously, keep his speed down on bends and slopes. There was almost no traffic on the road. Even the main road, when they reached it, was quiet and this was unusual for a market day.

Two weeks before this he had walked here with his mother, stood in the queue with her, noticed her snatching time from him to down three drinks, and now he and his father moved through the early hours of the market, as the stalls were barely set up, in search of someone from Pallosa or Burch or Tirvia, or any of the other villages around, who might have news of her. Miquel knew it was most likely that, because of the bad roads and the broken phone lines, no one would know anything about her, and they would have to be told, as though it were a guilty secret, what had happened, and then news would begin to spread. He thought of suggesting to his father that, instead of walking all morning through the ghostly market, they should find out if the road to Pallosa were open and go there now, consult his uncle before his uncle heard it as a rumour or a half-digested piece of news from someone else.

They had a bocadillo in a bar. Both of them were ravenously hungry; Miquel was tempted when he was finished to say that he wanted another. He was determined to buy some food as they had been living on the eggs collected from the hens and little else for three days now. But, since his father wanted to go to the police station, he thought he would wait, have a coffee now, and eat more later, perhaps even a proper lunch. They walked past the stalls in the direction of the police station, careful to look at none of the vendors and greet none of them, since they did not wish stall-holders, who might have heard about the missing woman, to ask them about her. But they were still watching for people from the villages around Pallosa.

As they turned into one of the side streets, having passed
the bread shop, they saw Francesc, Miquel's uncle, his
mother's brother from Pallosa, coming towards them, with
his wife and a neighbouring woman. Miquel stopped
immediately and let his father go forward to meet them. He
stood in a doorway as he watched his father greeting them.
He could see his uncle's and aunt's faces but he could not
tell, at first, anything by their expressions. His uncle merely
nodded, his aunt and the neighbour listened intently.
Slowly, however, he noticed his uncle's face darkening; it
was a small change, he did not wrinkle his brow or move
his mouth, but it was enough for Miquel. He knew even
before his uncle spoke and shook his head and his aunt put
her hand over her mouth and the other woman moved to
console her, he knew that his mother had not arrived safely
in Pallosa, and, from the way his uncle now seemed to
question his father, he knew that his uncle and aunt had not
been aware of his mother's disappearance. He moved out of
the shadows and made his way towards them.

The road to Pallosa had been cut off for two days, his
uncle said, and the single telephone line had been down. As
Miquel watched him, his uncle appeared to be having
trouble breathing, he was taking heavy breaths between his
words, staring at the ground, his brow all wrinkled now.

'And that day, the snow came down,' he said, 'faster
than anyone can remember. We were up to our necks in
it.'

Miquel could see his uncle holding back a fundamental
question as he discovered what time she had left at, who
had seen her, how long she had been walking before the
snow came. His uncle, it was obvious, wished to know why

she had left, how they did not notice her leaving, how they did not know at what time she had taken off on such a dangerous journey, and why she was walking when there was, if she needed to go to Pallosa, a jeep outside the door. As his uncle searched their eyes, Miquel became aware of his slow realization that she had left in distress, or after an argument, and, he thought, the more his uncle seemed quietly to make a judgement, the more guilty his father and he must have appeared.

They decided that they should walk to the police station together and declare her officially a missing person. His uncle believed that the police would then be obliged to look for her, using all their resources. His uncle, he knew, had a reputation for kindness and intelligence and, as Miquel watched him taking control, he remembered his mother's lamenting that there was no one like Francesc in their village, to whom you could go if you had a problem.

Close to the police station, out of the corner of his eye and then very clearly, Miquel saw Foix and Castellet standing behind a jeep in the company of two policemen. His uncle saw them too, but Miquel realized that he did not recognize them; his father looked only at the ground and Miquel did not draw his attention to the presence of the villagers in La Seu.

The policeman at the desk appeared to know about the case and told them that they would have to wait. There were only two chairs in the narrow hallway. All five of them, in turn, refused to sit down and they made an awkward grouping as policemen passed in and out, forcing them to move out of the way and stand aside. Eventually,

Miquel's aunt and her companion said they would go back
to the market and meet later at the cafe beside the bread
shop. Miquel said that he would go with them; he needed
to buy supplies in the market. It might be easier, he thought,
for his father to tell his uncle what had really happened if
he were not listening. He noticed before he left how
handsome his uncle was and how bright and alert he seemed
as he waited in the hall. Beside him, his father looked like a
poor man from a poor village, humble and uneasy in the
official building in the big town.

They walked towards the market. He knew by the way
his aunt was speaking to her neighbour, arranging to separate from her briefly, that she wanted to be alone with him,
and he presumed that she wanted to know what had
happened. She did not have her husband's patient ability to
fathom something in full without having to be furnished
with all the details. Miquel could see, her friend having
departed, that she was angling now for a complete account
of his mother's last hours in the house. He decided, without
knowing why, that he would not tell her.

When she asked him if he would come with her to the
butcher's, he realized that she meant to go to the one his
mother frequented, and he was not ready for the idea that
they would remember him, the young man whose brother
was going to the mili, and ask about his mother. He would
have no idea what to say. The dream in which he was
now partaking, a world of queues and shoppers and market
stalls, seemed by its very vividness to preclude the possibility that the darkness of the previous few days could have
any meaning, could even be mentioned. He told his aunt
that he did not want to go into the butcher's shop with

her, but would meet her later as arranged with his father and uncle.

'What happened?' she asked as they stood outside the shop.

'We don't know,' he said. 'She walked out of the village towards Pallosa.'

His aunt sighed in exasperation.

'Is that all that happened?' Her gaze was sharp and accusatory. 'She just walked out for no reason on a freezing winter's day?'

He nodded.

'Well, she didn't arrive,' his aunt said.

'I don't know what we are going to do without her,' Miquel replied.

He knew that he had now cut off any further questions from his aunt, but saying it, allowing the note of sadness which he had struck merely as a strategy to prevent her from continuing, had had its own effect on him, and he found that he had begun to cry. He turned and walked away from her, his hand over his face so that no one could see his tears, and he did not look back.

Later, when he came to the cafe, his father and uncle had not arrived. His aunt greeted him coldly. He ordered a sandwich and had to concentrate hard, when it came, not to grab it and eat it in a few bites. When he had eaten it, he felt once more a desperate need to order another one.

When his aunt's friend appeared and sat down, she examined him curiously.

'I could not believe it when I saw you earlier,' she said. 'You look the image of your grandfather from Pallosa, it's more than that, every single thing about you is like him. I mean even the way you are looking at me now.'

'He was old when I knew him,' his aunt joined in, 'but I remember them all saying it. Even when you were small you did things that reminded your mother of him.'

'I never met him,' Miquel said.

'Well, it's like meeting a ghost,' the woman said.

'She never mentioned it,' Miquel said.

'I wish my husband was here,' the woman went on. 'He would be amazed by you, even the way you are looking away from me now, he'd be amazed.'

'I suppose we all look like people in our families,' his aunt said. 'I suppose it's natural.'

It was clear to Miquel when his father and his uncle finally arrived that they had walked from the police station in silence. Miquel sensed also that his father had been asked questions which had deeply unsettled him. He could look at none of them as he sat down.

His uncle then explained that the police would set in train a professional search, working from both villages, the one she walked out of and the one to which she was bound. They saw no reason why the family or the villagers should join them, it would be a nuisance, he said. It would begin in the morning at first light as, in his opinion, it should have begun two days earlier. But there was nothing could be done, he said, except hope that this search would yield results. Miquel almost smiled at the thought that his uncle was speaking like a policeman.

When he and his father got home after a slow journey on the icy roads, the jeep stalling and slipping on each slope, and sliding dangerously on a number of curves, night had almost fallen. At first he did not recognize the three jeeps parked in front of their house. Everything that was happening had such newness to it that three strange jeeps meant nothing, were hardly worthy of comment. Then he saw that they were police jeeps and that there were two policemen standing at the door watching their arrival closely, having recognized them, and having, he surmised, been waiting for their return. He had not seen either of these policemen before. They nodded in acknowledgement but did not speak as they approached them. They let them pass into the house. In the kitchen, the young policeman who had come the day after her disappearance was already sitting on a chair near the window. He did not change his blank expression when Miquel turned on the electric light in the room.

When the older policeman, who had been in their house before, came downstairs, he announced that the police were searching the house and the barns below. They could hear the sounds of heavy boots on the floorboards of the rooms upstairs. Miquel moved to go up, but the older one barred his way.

'No, no,' he said. 'Both of you please stay down here.'

'What do you think you are going to find up there?' his father asked.

'Both of you stay down here,' the policeman repeated and nodded in the direction of the younger policeman, who stood up as if to guard the way. Miquel noticed that his eyes were duller than the last time, his hair less shiny. He responded to Miquel's gaze with pure equanimity, gazing back without seeming to heed in the slightest way what he saw. He did not once look at Miquel's father, who had taken a chair and was sitting at the kitchen table.

As the older policeman left the house, they heard a noise coming from one of the barns; one of the big old doors, Miquel guessed, was being pulled back. He moved towards the window so that he could see what was happening, but quietly the young policeman motioned to him without speaking that he must stay where he was.

'Are we under arrest?' Miquel's father asked.

The policeman did not look at him and did not answer. He kept his eyes on Miquel and then on his father; his look had no hostility in it, it was powerful merely because it was relentlessly vacant. His face in its wilful immobility resembled a heavy white mask. He had not yet spoken to them; his voice, his accent, would tell them too much about him. Being prevented from going to the window did not worry Miquel; he knew they were not under arrest, that the search of the house and barns was a routine matter, encouraged perhaps by Foix and Castellet. The young policeman had kept him from moving, he believed, out of timidity, a fear of his superiors rather than any authority of his own. As the three of them remained there, his father slumped in his chair staring at the ground, Miquel and the policeman locked eyes and then looked away, glancing at each other again after a while, Miquel running his eyes over the young man's body. The policeman watched him doing this with something between acceptance and indifference until Miquel stood up and went again to the window. The policeman shrugged but did not move.

Miquel could see that the seven or eight policemen now gathered in front of the house had been joined by Foix and

Castellet. He could not tell, however, from what direction they had come, if they had been in the barns as well. Their everyday clothes did nothing to undermine the authority they seemed to have among the policemen, who were all outsiders. They were listening closely now as Foix spoke and made gestures. Miquel's father came to the window and watched them too, but since he had not noticed them in La Seu, Miquel realized that he would fail to grasp the significance of their standing with the police outside the door. Miquel wondered what they had said to place themselves in such a position of apparent trust. When the young policeman was finally called to join the others, he left the house without speaking, and the three jeeps drove away, leaving Foix and Castellet to walk slowly up the village in the snow.

He and his father were alone now. Miquel did not think that any of their neighbours would come near them; they would not be needed in the search of the mountain which the police would conduct. Again, he thought that they should write to Jordi, but the letter would now have to say what he and his father had failed even to say to each other. He knew that Jordi, if he received such a letter, would have to come home, whether he got permission or not. But even if he did get permission, it would only be for a few days. Miquel imagined him arriving to find nothing, an emptiness in the house, his father reduced to silence, with nothing to do, no grave to visit, no body to touch, no coffin to carry, no words of consolation from those around. Instead, a frozen landscape and the dreaded days with no thaw.

Miquel could not visualize Jordi's response to a letter, he

tried to picture him reading it and then moving fast from wherever he was towards them. All his life, from the time he was a small child, an injured cat or a limping dog or any sort of hungry animal would cause Jordi to panic. All through his childhood they had to prevent him from befriending stray dogs or neighbours' cats. He had to be kept indoors when the hunters were in the forest shooting the wild boars and then dragging them bloody through the village. Away, he would miss Clua, whom Miquel and his father hardly tolerated, as much as he missed any of them. The idea that his mother might be missing or in danger would be unbearable to him; the fact that she was gone, buried deep in snow somewhere in the distance, could not be conveyed to him now. And yet Miquel also understood that not telling him, leaving him to live as though this event had not occurred, was a real piece of treachery.

As they were eating, a knock came to the door which made them look up at one another in fright. When Miquel answered, he saw Josep Bernat with a parcel in his hand. Bernat had come on the two days' search, but he had remained in the background so that he was hardly noticed. He said he would not come in, but his wife had made bread and there were some other things from her larder in the bag that he hoped they would find useful. He bowed to them and departed as soon as Miquel had thanked him.

Bernat began to call in the evenings, often bringing a can of milk or some fresh produce with him, almost as an excuse to visit. Since Miquel had started to go out alone, sometimes beyond Santa Magdalena to venture along the military road where the snow had hardened in the freezing temperatures and each step had to be taken with care, Bernat was full of advice and ideas about where he should look. He seemed to know about every death in the area since the Civil War, especially suicides and accidental deaths. La Senyora Fluvia, whose husband was still alive, who had fallen in the snow a dozen years back, was a favourite subject of Bernat's. Her family, he said, had passed where she was lying every day for two months but she was covered in a patch of ice on which the sun never shone and thus she lay there until there was a general thaw. Or that man who was married to the Englishwoman, who was a painter – and he drove his jeep off the road near Pallosa and killed a child as well.

'It's a pity,' he said one night, 'that you did not get through with the jeep that first day, you might have found her.'

Miquel's father nodded.

Miquel was interested in Bernat's real opinion about where his mother was and when or how she might be found, but he could never get direct answers. On the nights when Bernat came to the house, Miquel listened to his stories and then tried to turn the conversation to the possibility of a sudden thaw being the most dangerous for her, because her body would still not be easily found, but she would be open to birds and animals before they could get to her. Bernat agreed and thought for a while and waited until Miquel's father had left the room and told him that, since the police had not found her and they had looked closely, then in his opinion her body would not be located until the spring thaw, until there was no snow or ice at all on that stretch of land. And then they would have to watch the sky all day, he said, and if they saw vultures they would have to get into the jeep and race towards whatever it was the vultures were circling. And that is, he said, how you will find her.

4

NEITHER OF THEM could cook. His father refused to try but did not stop complaining about the monotony of the food. Too many eggs, he said. Too much cold ham. Miquel tried to cook rice but it came out grainy and hard, he did not know if had put in too little water or too much. The potatoes he boiled seemed to dissolve in the water. They depended on Bernat for bread. He did not know how his mother had found the meat for stews and could offer a variety of dishes with no shop or supplier in the village. When he tried to cook lentils, his father tipped the plate, full of hot food, into the bucket where food for the hens was kept.

Slowly, the hens began to lay fewer eggs, and gradually the rabbits began to die. Miquel knew that he had neglected them in the early days of his mother's disappearance, but, even though he had quickly established a routine of feeding both the hens and the rabbits, they did not thrive. He spent a day cleaning out the hen house, presuming that the accumulated dirt had caused them to lay fewer eggs, but when he found egg shells everywhere among the dirt, it caused him to wonder if the hens were not, in fact, eating the very eggs they laid. He wished there were someone in the village whom he could approach and ask, but he knew his father would object even if he were to mention his difficulty to Bernat.

As the rabbits died, he thought it strange how contented the other rabbits seemed, how normally they behaved, even though one of them lay dead in their cage, its body all stiff and useless, its eyes staring at some vague distant point. It was good for nothing now, he quietly buried it behind the barn. He did not want his father to know that he was having any domestic problems beyond the ones which were obvious.

After a time, only the big brown rabbits were still alive; they seemed to grow fatter and healthier the more white rabbits died. Miquel kept their cages clean while his father paid them no attention. In these days in the hen house he was lucky if he found even one egg in the morning. His father, he thought, must have presumed that he was not served eggs because he was tired of them. Nothing his father ate pleased him. He took to eating cured ham and bread softened with tomato and oil, and doing so not at mealtimes but when he felt hungry. He did not eat the crusts of the bread but left them on the table for Miquel to give to Clua.

One day he came into the kitchen as Miquel was eating a sausage with beans, which Bernat's wife had left him.

'I'm going to La Seu tomorrow,' he said. 'I thought I'd take a few rabbits to sell and some eggs.'

Miquel glanced up at him nervously.

'The rabbits are dying. I don't know how to keep them alive. The hens have stopped laying.'

'What did you do to them?' his father asked.

'I'm not a woman. I don't know anything about them.'

'You're no housekeeper,' his father said and laughed faintly to himself. 'Do you know that?'

'Why don't you look after them yourself?' Miquel asked.

'No, I won't be doing that,' his father replied. 'Dead rabbits! Does anyone in the village know?'

'No.'

'That's good. And we have no eggs?'

'There's one in the bowl on the shelf.'

'We should keep it as a souvenir.'

Miquel did not go to La Seu with his father; the sky had cleared two days in a row, which meant that some of the snow had melted. He took his binoculars and set out early with the intention of reaching Santa Magdalena well before noon and then seeing how far he could make it along the military road, some of which he knew was still deep in snow. Once he was in the sun, he was warm, at times too warm so that he had to remove his coat. For an hour or so he trudged along the narrow road. Knowing that he was free of his father's company and the empty shadowy bareness of the house, which bore the marks of his mother's absence in every corner and on every surface, made him almost happy. The only dread was having to turn back eventually, finding the limits which the banked-up snow had created. The road as far as Santa Magdalena was, he discovered, much clearer than anyone in the village had said. In some places the thaw had been complete and he scanned it with the binoculars in case there was any sign. It struck him how unlucky his mother had been in the hour she chose to make her desperate flight from them, and the day on which she had gone. Had she left an hour earlier, she would, he thought, have reached Pallosa safely, and had she departed an hour later, she would have got no farther than here, and known to turn back. She was caught, he believed, in the very wrong hour and she lay somewhere beneath a mound of snow in the slopes below the military road which he scanned as well, seeing nothing beyond the whiteness except stumps of trees.

It was strange, he thought, that hardly any melting of snow had happened on the military road. Much of it received the same sunlight as the road on which he had just walked. But the military road was open to the wind, was cut sharply into the mountain with no trees or undergrowth on either side. If the wind blew snow from most directions, it would bank up on the road, which was a groove made by outsiders quickly into the earth without any thought for the terrain or knowledge of what would happen in the winter. Soon he found that the snow was up to his knees and that each step required an effort and then a further effort to extricate himself.

He turned back and trudged through the slush for miles until he came to the village. He wished his father would learn to do something in the house, even learn how to light the fire. He would come back from La Seu, Miquel knew, with too many provisions or too few, with kilos of meat they could not keep fresh, or enough sausages for just one meal.

His father was not home, which was surprising as he had left early in the morning and had nothing much to do there. Perhaps he went and saw the police again but, as far as Miquel could see, there was no point in that. There was no bread; he fried some potatoes and the egg his father wished to keep as a souvenir and he lit a fire. In these days when he thought about his mother, the feelings were sharpened by guilt, a gnawing presence in his chest which he could obliterate only by deliberately thinking about something else but which could easily and stealthily return. He regretted now that he had never, in recent years, come in like this to her kitchen on an ordinary day and watched her cooking or lighting the fire and offered to help her, or keep her company while she worked. He also knew that he should have been braver the day before she disappeared, he should have gone to her and told her that he himself would replace what his father had thrown out. He should, he thought, have forced his father not to leave her alone in a room craving alcohol. He knew that if he had been brave, he could have prevented her from leaving.

It was late when he heard the jeep pulling up in front of the house. He had spent the evening looking into the fire, dreaming half the time of leaving there, going as suddenly as his mother did, but towards La Seu and then towards Lérida or Barcelona, or even further away, and never appearing again. Not ever seeing his brother, would, he thought, be a high price to pay for the new freedom he would win, but maybe they could meet elsewhere, maybe Jordi would leave too. And the rest of the time he entertained all the guilt that wished to call, carried in by the wind through the darkness, to enter his spirit as he pondered over and over his own responsibility for her disappearance and her death.

He heard voices outside and thought it odd that his father had given a lift to someone from the village. Perhaps Bernat, with whom his father seemed on better terms each day, had travelled back from La Seu with him or had been collected from some other place. As he heard footsteps cutting into the brittle sheet of ice on the path outside the house, he did not move. If his father needed help to carry goods from the jeep, he could come and ask him. His father, when he walked into the kitchen, smiled at him benevolently, warmly. He was carrying bags. Behind him appeared a pale young man, smaller in height than Miquel, but strong-looking and not yet twenty, he thought. He, too, was carrying bags. Miquel was sure that he had never seen him before. He glanced towards Miquel but did not smile. Miquel turned his attention to the fire as though he were alone, taking two blocks of wood from the basket and placing them strategically in the grate.

'We're hungry,' his father said. 'We haven't eaten. Manolo here will make the supper.'

Manolo turned towards Miquel, who stoked the fire casually and said nothing.

'I had my supper,' Miquel said, 'but I could do with some more.'

Manolo's eyes were dark, his hair jet black. He began to open cupboards, checking the contents and then storing any packages from the bags they had carried from the jeep.

As they ate a supper of sausages, beans and fresh bread, it emerged that Miquel's father had met neighbours of his brother-in-law from Pallosa to whom he had explained his plight. He needed someone to keep house for them, he said, but he did not think anyone could be found as they had no room for a girl or woman to sleep in, and there was no neighbouring woman available. The people from Pallosa had told him that Manolo, who was an orphan, was free;

he worked for local farms in the spring and summer and lived with them, but in the winter there was less to do. Not only would he welcome housework, they said, which he could do very well, but the people with whom he was now lodged would welcome a mouth less to feed. Miquel's father had decided, he said, to drive to Pallosa there and then and find Manolo and his employer, who had agreed to release him immediately.

'And so I bundled him into the jeep,' his father said. 'He says he can cook and we'll soon find out.'

His father smiled conspiratorially at Manolo, who did not respond but gazed gravely at Miquel, to whom it was clear that that his father's account of finding Manolo was like a story of buying an animal or a sack of rice. Manolo, it seemed to Miquel, realized this too, and became openly downcast the more his father, full of good humour, spoke.

As they were sitting at the table eating, Miquel realized that he himself had not spoken much and wondered if his silence was further disheartening the new arrival.

'My father is a monster,' he said. 'You've made a big mistake coming with him.'

He and his father began to laugh, but the boy remained silent, appearing to become even sadder the more they laughed. As soon as they had finished eating, he began to clear off the table; he put a pan of water on to boil and started to stack dishes, which had been left for days, to wash. Miquel moved back to his position by the fire while his father stayed at the table.

'Are there bedclothes anywhere?' his father asked.

Miquel shrugged. They had not changed the sheets since his mother left. He did not know if the sheets stored in the cupboard would need to be aired by the fire before they were used.

'Anyway,' his father said, 'the mattress on Jordi's bed will be well aired.'

'Why don't we move it down to the store room?' Miquel asked.

'The window is broken there,' his father said. 'He'll freeze.'

'I don't want him in my room,' Miquel said.

Manolo, who had his back to them, stopped moving. He made no effort to pretend that he was not listening.

'We'll put him there tonight,' his father said. 'And I'll show him where the sheets and blankets are, so he can make his own bed.'

Miquel sighed and stared into the fire. When he looked up again, Manolo had resumed his work at the stove and the sink. When he moved across the room to clean the table he did not look at Miquel. By the time Miquel went to his bedroom, his father had already shown Manolo the way, and helped him carry sheets and blankets and a pillow to the room, which seemed almost cramped when Miquel entered it. Manolo was studiously unfolding each blanket and then spreading it meticulously across the bed. He did not turn when Miquel came in, only when the door was closed. He did not greet him, but continued to work as Miquel stood and watched him, waiting until he was finished before getting undressed.

Manolo rummaged in a small suitcase as Miquel lay in bed. This was, as far as he could make out, the only bag Manolo had brought with him. It had barely space for a change of clothes. When Manolo took off his pullover,

Miquel saw that his shirt was torn at the back and frayed at the cuffs and collar. Downstairs, he had noticed a smell, like something rotting, which became more intense when Manolo took off his shoes. It was only when Manolo had removed his trousers and was putting them over a chair that Miquel realized the smell came from the boy's socks, which he now began to remove. He put them on the floor under his bed and looked at Miquel for permission to turn off the light.

'Can you leave your shoes and socks outside the door?' Miquel asked.

Manolo nodded, showing no sign that he had any objection to doing this. As he bent to collect his socks and then moved across the room to pick up his shoes, Miquel realized that he had brought no pyjamas with him and that he was not wearing any shorts. He was going to sleep wearing his old shirt. When he had put the shoes and socks outside, and closed the door, he turned off the light and crossed the room. Neither of them spoke as they lay in the dark. Miquel guessed that Manolo fell quickly asleep.

He imagined writing to Jordi now with the news. Our mother has disappeared, she is dead, lying encased in ice, we will have to watch the sky for vultures when the thaw comes so that we can find her before they do. Your bed is being slept in by a dark, silent, sad-looking boy who has arrived without many clothes and seems willing to do a woman's work. He has moved in beside me, I can hear his breathing, which is light and regular. In the morning, I will try and find another place for him to sleep.

5

He walked each day as far as he could; the snow was starting to melt along the military road and some stretches of the road to Santa Magdalena were dry. He walked each day at a different time, depending on the work he had to do, but he could often leave his father and Manolo to manage. His father, by this time, had begun to work cutting stones for Josep Bernat and spent some time away from his own house. Manolo worked hard, cooking and washing and cleaning and helping with the animals if he were needed.

As the thaw continued, Miquel's uncle came from Pallosa, and drove his jeep along the road out of the village as far as Santa Magdalena and then walked with Miquel along the military road, most of which now was clear, even though the land around it was deep in snow. He got out of the jeep several times and surveyed the landscape with Miquel's binoculars. When Miquel told him what Bernat had said about the vultures, he agreed. They would have to wait, he said, and watch for them, and hope to find her as soon as the temperature rose. He did not think, he said, that any vultures had appeared over Pallosa yet, nor anywhere higher than Sort. If he saw them hovering, then he would know that the real spring had begun.

When he came face to face with Manolo in the house, Francesc embraced him and greeted him warmly. Miquel stood back as Manolo smiled and asked about people and events in Pallosa; he was more animated than he had been since he came to their house.

Outside, before he left, his uncle told him that Manolo's father had been taken into custody and shot at the end of the war when his mother was still pregnant. His mother had lived only for another year, dying of tuberculosis, but dying too, he thought, because of the loss. Manolo was brought up by his father's cousins until he could work and then moved to various houses around Pallosa, some of whom treated him badly. It was a very sad story, his uncle said, because Manolo's father had been hardly involved in the war at all, he was just unlucky. He hoped Manolo would be happier here than he had been in some other quarters. Miquel knew by the way his uncle spoke that it was obvious that he and Manolo had not become friends. That evening, Manolo seemed grateful and surprised when he was given some of Jordi's clothes by Miquel, some shirts and shorts and a pair of old boots. He promised that he would look after them carefully.

The weather grew worse; fresh snow fell and there were two days and nights of wind which blew the surface snow into the air and whirled it about as though it were dust. Miquel's father disappeared to Bernat's barn as soon as he and Miquel had taken care of the animals. He returned for lunch and then left again. His new work seemed to make him happy; he was full of jokes and good cheer as soon as he sat down at the table.

In the days when Miquel could not work outside because of the weather, he remained in the kitchen, and tried to talk to Manolo about where he had learned to cook, and how he was feeding the hens, but the replies were merely polite and restrained. It was clear that Manolo did not want to talk. He worked quietly, moving about the house, his expression solemn, dutiful. Slowly, under his care, they began to have eggs from the hens again and the rabbits began to thrive. Despite their invitation, he did not eat with them, but ate standing at the stove, usually beginning when they had finished. And despite Miquel's telling him that he did not need to do so, he placed his shoes and socks outside the bedroom door each night before he turned off the light. He made sure that Clua was fed, but several times Miquel noticed him stopping the dog following him or jumping up on him affectionately.

Miquel's father joked with Manolo that he would make a great wife for a man; all Manolo would need was a skirt, his father said, and he could travel to all the festas in the summer and by the autumn he would be walking down the aisle. Manolo never smiled when this, or one of the many varieties of it, was said, but continued whatever he was doing. Slowly, it became one of Miquel's father's constant themes.

'Oh, we'll have to get a skirt for you,' he would say. 'You're the best housewife in the whole country. Better than any young girl of your age. You know, I think they might have sent us a girl. Maybe you're only pretending to be a boy.'

One day, when these comments had been made more than once in the course of a meal and had begun to sound like taunts, Manolo approached the table and stood in front of Miquel's father.

'If you say that again, I will leave.'

His father pushed his chair back and gazed up at Manolo, who had grown much paler than usual.

'I didn't mean . . .' his father began.

'I know what you meant,' Manolo said. 'And if you say it again, I will leave.'

'I didn't mean to offend you.'

'Don't say it again, then.'

'You've become very cheeky, haven't you?' Miquel's father said.

Manolo returned to the stove and kept his back to them. Miquel watched his father battling with his own face, trying to find a way to make a joke of this, and realizing, it seemed to Miquel, that Manolo had left him no opening.

'Are you not happy here?' his father asked Manolo, who did not turn or speak.

'I'm asking you a question,' his father said.

'Stop saying I'm a girl,' Manolo said without turning.

'I never actually said you were a girl. When did I say you were a girl? When did I actually say that?' his father said.

Manolo did not respond.

'Are you deaf?' his father asked. 'When did I say you were a girl?'

Miquel could see Manolo's shoulders hunching as though he were going to cry. His own feeling of powerlessness, his not finding a way to intervene, brought back to him the scene on the day before his mother had left. As his father stood up, he realized that he could not allow this cruel version of the earlier event to continue.

'Leave him alone,' he said to his father, 'and sit down!'

His father, he knew, would have no idea how to behave now. Miquel had been on the point of adding that his father had already caused enough trouble in the house, but was happy that he had restrained himself. His father stood with his eyes on the floor as Manolo crossed the room and gathered plates as though nothing had happened. Miquel did not move and made sure that his father could not even hear his breathing. He tried to do nothing. In the end, having heaved a long sigh, his father left the kitchen and returned to his work at Bernat's. Miquel smiled at Manolo when he returned to the table. The smile Manolo managed in return was all the more powerful for being half-hidden and quick to disappear.

For the first time that night Manolo spoke to Miquel in the bedroom. Having left his shoes and socks outside the door, he turned off the light and crossed the room and got into bed.

'The winds won't keep up like this,' he said.

'It's getting worse every day,' Miquel replied.

'You often cry in the night,' Manolo said. 'It's not loud or anything, but I hear you sometimes.'

'I didn't know I did that,' Miquel said.

'Do you have bad dreams?' Manolo asked him.

'Not really. I often dream that my brother is here and we are much younger.'

'You don't shout, but you cry, never for long,' Manolo said.

'I will try to keep quiet.'

'Don't worry.'

They began to talk about Miquel's mother's disappearance and how she might be found. Manolo kept his voice low and seemed to consider everything very carefully. Miquel told him that Jordi did not know anything about her disappearance. They had received a letter from him, saying he was in Valladolid, to which his father had replied saying there was no news. When Manolo did not respond to this, Miquel knew that he was not asleep but weighing up what he had just been told.

'Your father is wrong,' he said eventually.

'I know,' Miquel said, 'but I can't write to Jordi myself telling him. It's not my job. How could I tell him in a letter what has happened?'

Manolo said nothing; by the quality of his silence Miquel could see that he had made a clear judgement. They lay there saying nothing until Miquel knew that Manolo had fallen asleep.

He himself slept for a while, and then was woken by the wind. It felt, in its fierce whistling menace, that it was preparing to lift the house from its foundations or blow the roof off, or cut through the windows and swirl frantically into each room, dragging sleepers from their beds in its wake. He listened to its howling and the flat rhythm of Manolo's breathing and knew that he would not sleep. Soon, one of the barn doors began to bang; he knew from the sound which one it was, and he knew that he should have put stones against it earlier to secure it in place. He found his clothes in the dark and went downstairs to dress so that he would not disturb Manolo. His boots were in the hall.

It was snowing again, the flakes were being whipped in

every direction by the wind. He held his hand over his eyes to stop the wind blinding him. His torch was useless. He made his way down slowly, moving over the packed ice on which a covering of fresh snow had formed. The door was still banging. He found the stones he had used before and put them in place, holding the door firmly shut, and then he made his way back to the house.

6

THE SUN SHONE during the days that followed, but the wind still blew. Miquel resumed his old route, to Santa Magdalena without any difficulty, and then trying to walk along the military road where snow was banked up in all its new contours. On one of those days as he went back towards the village, with about half an hour left to go, he saw Manolo coming towards him, he had brought him some bread and ham and some biscuits. Miquel was surprised at how changed he was for the rest of the journey, how light he was, and happy that Manolo had thought of meeting him. The next day, as he was setting off, he asked Manolo if he would come again to meet him and Manolo said he would. He was already planning to do so, he said. Miquel found that this picture of Manolo standing by the stove saying these words stayed with him more as he walked than any thoughts about his father or Jordi, or where his mother's body might be discovered.

His father was making money from his work with Bernat and all the talk now was of expanding the stone-cutting business. He began to pay Manolo a small sum of money every week and this seemed to make him more cheerful during the time he spent in the kitchen while making no obvious difference to Manolo. On a Saturday night, when Manolo had been a month in the house, Miquel's father announced that it was bath night. His family, he told Manolo, differed from every other family in the village, as indeed from the beasts in the fields, because they regularly took a bath, usually once every two weeks, but because of what had occurred in the house, they had neglected performing their proper ablutions, a matter he now wished to rectify.

His father showed Manolo where the bright tin bath with the long back was kept, and together they carried it into the kitchen. He explained that Manolo's job was to fill the large pot and two of the saucepans with water and bring them to the boil, and mix this water with cold water. That would be enough for his bath. Then Manolo was to put more water on to boil, he said, and when the first bath had been taken, some of the water could be removed and replaced by more clean hot water for Miquel and later for Manolo. Then finally, his father explained, amusing himself, it seemed, greatly as he spoke, the water could be thrown out for the dog to drink. And each of them would also need clean clothes and underclothes, he added, to change into once the bathing was over.

Miquel was surprised that his father saw fit to include Manolo in the bath. Before, he and Jordi had boiled the water and changed the water, while their mother had remained out of the room. Finally, they had boiled water for her and filled a new bath for her, leaving her special soap and sponge on the chair, and a special towel, before they and their father had gone upstairs to offer her full privacy.

Manolo put three towels on a frame in front of the roaring fire; he closed the shutters, and, as the water in the saucepans began to boil, he poured the water into the bath and then refilled the saucepans. As the big pot boiled and his father began to undress, Miquel left the room. This was what he had always done, allowing his father as much privacy as he could. It was strange, he thought, leaving Manolo in there with his naked father, ministering to him, but Manolo, he knew, had a way of managing everything, of making sure that nothing he did was ever the cause of complaint.

When he came back to the kitchen, his father told him that he was almost finished and presently stood up in the bath waiting for Manolo to bring him the towel. Miquel had never watched his father like this before, his long legs, much stronger-looking than he had imagined, his fleshy penis and the pouch underneath larger and more real. His father stood in the firelight drying himself as though he were on display, as Manolo fussed around him, putting a mat under his feet, putting some dry thin wood on the fire and beginning to prepare Miquel's bath.

When his father left the room, Miquel stripped to his shorts, tested the temperature of the water, and then he slipped off his shorts and sat into the hot bath, half clean water and half the water used by his father. Before Jordi left they had a joke together, that their father had pissed in the water, and that Miquel was going to piss too, or had just done so, and Jordi would be thus left to soak in copious quantities of the family's urine. Jordi used to cringe, demanding a full bath of clean hot water, being told by Miquel that, since he was the youngest, that would be impossible.

Miquel did not think that Manolo would find this funny. He washed himself as Manolo began to boil more water for his own bath. He had observed Manolo looking at him as he lowered himself into the water. Manolo hovered close to the bath as Miquel washed himself. They could hear Miquel's father moving around in the room above. Miquel knew that he would not come back into the room until the bathing was finished.

As he stood up in the water, Manolo came towards him with the warm towel. Miquel stood shivering facing the fire as Manolo dried his back and his neck and torso, rubbing hard and then handing him the towel so Miquel could finish drying himself.

Manolo's own water was hot now; he cleared out some of the old water and then poured more from the saucepans and the big pot into the bath. As Miquel sat and dressed himself, he watched Manolo strip with his back to him, not facing him until he was naked. His shoulders were much broader than Miquel had ever noticed in the bedroom, the muscles on his shoulders and back more developed, his torso and buttocks completely hairless, but his thick, short legs covered in dark hair. He moved slowly, almost gracefully, towards the bath, seeming to be utterly alert to Miquel's eyes watching him.

7

SINCE HIS FATHER was now travelling every day with Josep Bernat, Miquel told Manolo that he could come earlier to meet him if he wanted, if he had time, and thus Miquel would not have to walk back all the distance on his own. He also told him to take food for himself and a bottle of water so they could both find a place in the sun and eat together. At night now, he looked forward to going to the bedroom and being alone with Manolo, talking to him for a while before they went asleep.

On one of these days as they were walking back, examining how the snow lay in ridges and banks, they heard shots being fired from the trees up above Santa Magdalena. The shots, which came in quick succession, echoed against the far hills so that it was impossible to be sure precisely where they had come from. Miquel remembered that a jeepload of men, including Foix and Castellet, had passed him earlier on the road and he had seen their empty jeep with a trailer parked at the hermitage at Santa Magdalena itself.

The shots seemed to disturb everything, the bird life scattered; every living thing, he knew, would have sought